KATE A. BOORMAN

AMULET BOOKS   NEW YORK

Library of Congress Cataloging-in-Publication Data

Boorman, Kate A.
Darkthaw : a Winterkill novel / by Kate A. Boorman.
pages cm
Summary: "Emmeline, kept so long behind walls, finally achieves her deepest desire: to leave the isolated world of the settlement and explore the wilderness that has long called to her. The subsequent journey, with First Peoples guide Matisa at her side, soon proves far more dangerous than anticipated"— Provided by publisher.
ISBN 978-1-4197-1663-8 (hardback)
[1. Fantasy. 2. Survival—Fiction. 3. Love—Fiction.] I. Title.
PZ7.B64618Dar 2015
[Fic]—dc23
2015008785

Amulet Books are available at special discounts when purchased in quantity for premiums and promotions as well as fundraising or educational use. Special editions can also be created to specification. For details, contact specialsales@abramsbooks.com or the address below.

ABRAMS
THE ART OF BOOKS SINCE 1949
115 West 18th Street
New York, NY 10011
www.abramsbooks.com

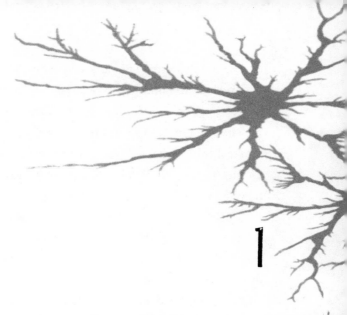

1

THE RIVER IS SWOLLEN AND VIOLENT.

The dead lie beneath.

I fix my eyes where the banks close to a narrow gap and the river rushes through in a torrent. Where the trees bud out with soft green tips, bending in the springtime breeze. Where they sent my pa to his peace.

They did it quick, that very day he died to save me, before *La Prise* howled in and blinded us, before the world went dark. Wrapped in cloth tied at each end, his body was thrown to the deadly chunks of whirling ice. I had the memory of those waters deep in my bones, the hollow scream of the river loud in my ears, and I went with him, swirling down that giant hole of black.

Then Kane put his hand to the nape of my neck and pulled me, gentle, to his chest, his woodsmoke warmth. I heard the winter winds whistling through the trees, Kane's heart beating loud in my ear. Matisa put her unfamiliar, familiar hand in mine.

We took shelter. The dark rushed in. The river froze.

And our dreams began. Matisa's of death: river on fire, shattering bone, deafening sound. A war destroying the people she and I love. Mine of life: tall peaks of rock, snowcapped trees, shining waters. A valley where warm winds drift across an impossible lake: blue like a robin's egg yet green like the newest poplar buds. And all of it, calling out to me.

Matisa says we're the dreamers of her legend—two dreamers from "different times" who were meant to find each other. Last fall, I dreamt about Matisa every night. I dreamt she was out in the woods beyond our fortification, and the pull, the desire to find her, was so strong, I risked my own life to do it. She was dreaming of me, too. She left her home and searched these woods, a forbidden place among her people, to find me. All winterkill long, my dreams have been about life—my new life, out there. A small part of me wants to cling to that idea, wants to believe that this alone is the reason she came.

But I know different. The disaster Matisa dreams: she believes we will prevent it if we stay together. And even if I don't rightly know how, I plan to try. I'll leave this place and journey to her home, that strange and beautiful place in my dreams. Find out how our dreams connect, how they can prevent death.

I fiddle the balsamroot in my hand. It grows much closer to the fortification, but I can't help but come out here to pick it. I bend low to pull some more from the bank, shifting my weight to my good foot before I remember it won't hurt to lean on my other, thanks to Matisa's tincture. She says I'll forget the habit soon enough.

The voices that used to whisper at me from the trees are silent. My Lost People, the ghosts of the First Peoples who once lived on this land, are here now. They have been found; we have been found.

But I hear new voices murmuring beneath the rush of river. Way down in those cold depths. Clamoring under the surface.

And they don't speak of life.

I close my ears to the murmuring and breathe the soft wind that sighs through the willows. The sun shines on the spot where they cast my pa. My pa's body, so still. I push the memory away and let my eyes fill up with the silver light gleaming off the waters. That once solid ribbon of frozen river is now a glimmering rush, feeding the thirsty willows and cattails, helping the trees burst into all shades of green.

With the Thaw comes promise.

I put that idea in my secret heart and hold it there. I cling to the truth that this river's melt brings new life, new beginnings.

I try to push away a different truth that creeps cold fingers across my chest: once ice thaws, what is hidden in its depths can resurface.

My world is changing. I have to believe it's changing to the good.

"Em!" A child's voice comes from far off, behind me.

I turn. Kane and his little brother Daniel are making their way from the fortification. The morning sun bathes them in a warm glow, but the walls loom dark behind them.

Kane's head is bare, and his shirt is open at the neck, like always. He walks casual; hands in his pockets, like he has all the time in the world to get to me. I know better; I know neither of us can get near the other fast enough.

Stolen moments from this past winterkill wash over me in a heat: desperate kisses and fumbling hands in the dark woodshed. Kane's breath on my skin, his woodsmoke scent all over me.

Nothing about those secret meetings was slow. And they were always far too short . . . heartbeats in time, only.

Tom's ma, my self-appointed guardian, would look on me hard when I stamped back into the common area, shaking snow from my winter cloak, hoping my cheeks looked flushed from the biting cold.

I watch Kane approach now, cabbage moths fluttering around in my belly.

Daniel breaks away from Kane and races toward me, his five-year-old legs pumping furious. "I got to feed them today!" he calls.

I pull my gaze from Kane and notice Daniel's bright eyes. "Feed them?"

He skids to a stop before me, dark hair all mussed. "The horses!"

Of course. Daniel plain loves those beasts. None of us had ever seen horses before Matisa and her cousin, Isi, and brother, Nishwa, showed up on them in the fall; such animals were taken by the sickness when our ancestors arrived. Matisa's horses are like something from a fairy-tale picture book: all long lines and sleek muscles.

I reach out my hand to smooth Daniel's hair. "You been wrestling with Nico?" Kane's other brother, Nicolas, is eight, but Daniel is the sort to bite off more than he can chew.

Daniel shakes his head but looks at the ground, a mischievous smile on his face.

"Why are you so messy?" I prompt.

Kane strolls up. "He lets Dottie snuffle his hair," he answers for him.

"Dottie?"

Daniel looks up, pleased. "Matisa's horse!" he says. "I named her."

"Did you now." I'm distracted, with Kane so close. His sleeves are rolled up, and the tilt of his head, his dark eyes on me . . .

"Yep. Dottie. Because of her spots. And she thinks my hair is grass!" Daniel giggles and grabs at my hand. "Come on, I'll show you!"

"Hang on, Daniel." Kane puts a hand on his shoulder. "Remember I told you Em and me had some things to speak on?"

Daniel drops my hand, his face crumpling in disappointment. "But—"

"That was the deal, right? You could come out to the river so long as you let me and Em talk?"

Daniel nods, reluctant.

"I'll come soon as we're done," I reassure him, smoothing his hair again.

"You pull some feed for her," Kane suggests, pointing to the pockets of new grass growing on the banks. "She'll love that."

Daniel's off and pulling grass in a heartbeat. I feel a pang. He's going to be so disappointed when we take those beasts away. Never mind his older brother.

Kane's dark eyes are studying me. I turn toward him, passing the balsamroot one hand to the other, keeping my fingers busy so they don't wander where they'd rather be—up near the open collar of his shirt.

"You've been out here a while," he says. They're nothing words—idle talk. But his voice is softer, huskier. The cabbage moths in my belly are furious.

"Just getting some things for my medicines," I say. I shrug like I'm at ease. "Mayhap I lingered a bit."

That funny half smile pulls at the corner of his mouth. "You and these trees," he says. "You've always loved them best."

"Not best. Just prefer them to being inside." I glance at him from under my eyelashes. "I love other things best."

His eyebrows arch. "That so?"

"Sure." I put the herb into my satchel and make my eyes go wide. "Spring strawberries, for instance."

He frowns to hide a smile. "Strawberries."

"Delicious," I say. "Better than trees."

"Ah," he says. "Well, I hear the ones out there"—he tips his head at the woods—"are the very best."

I smile, a fluttering starting in my chest. *Out there.* It's all so near. "Matisa says we'll leave this week," I say.

"She can tell?" Kane asks.

I nod, but guilt stabs me. "She says Soeur Manon will go soon." Soeur Manon, the healer woman who was teaching me her craft, the only one besides my pa who ever cared for me, is lying in her bed in the Healing House. Dying. I promised myself I'd stay to see her out. "She's barely opened her eyes in days," I say. "Don't think she even knows I'm there."

Kane's eyes search my face. "She'd be happy to know we're leaving," he says, gentle. "She'd want you to." His brow creases. He rubs a hand across the back of his neck. "Wish everyone were so inclined."

"You talked to your ma again," I guess.

He nods.

"And?" I cross my arms, like it'll shield me from the answer I don't want.

He shakes his head: it didn't go well.

"She's not worried about the *malmaci*, is she?" Before Matisa and the boys discovered our settlement, before this past winterkill, most people believed we were alone—mayhap even the last people left alive anywhere—living under the threat of the *malmaci*, an evil spirit, in the outlying forest. It attacked those who explored too far, turning them into rivers of blood, ravaging them from the inside out. It snatched people who wandered out beyond our borders. We know now it was lore, superstition only. We know now it was a sickness, one that Matisa's people had suffered with and fled from long ago. And that the Takings—the disappearances—were started by Brother Stockham's pa to protect his position as leader of the settlement. People shouldn't fear it anymore, but there's a sliver of doubt left in some.

"No. It's the fact of me going at all."

I sigh, though I don't rightly know what I was expecting. Did I really think she'd send him off with her blessing? His pa died years ago, and he has two little brothers; she counts on him for all manner of help. But . . .

She can only expect that so long.

I look over his shoulder at the tall wooden walls of the fortification, my gaze tracing up to the empty watchtower. Used to be a Watcher in there at all times, day and night, surveying the woods outside the fortification, ready to report any sign of danger, any sign of Waywardness. Things are different now. We can make our own decisions.

"You're . . ." I have to force myself to meet his eyes. "You're sure you still want to come?"

"Em." He reaches out and grasps my forearm. The way he says my name—my breath gets fast. His touch is fire.

"I'll go anywhere with you."

His hand slides down my arm, and I lace my fingers in his, drowning in his gaze—the gaze that sees straight into me, sees all of me. Our fingers tighten, and it pulls us closer. I throw a quick look at Daniel, but he's busy, his head bent to the grasses. Kane reaches for me with the other hand, and I let him draw me toward the heat of his body. I place my hand on his chest, my fingers grasping at the open laces of his collar. His mouth is so close. I could kiss him here, in the fresh air of the Thaw. It would be right . . .

Over his shoulder I see a figure emerge from the fortification gates. It's Tom, and his blond head is lifted like he wants to speak as he hurries toward us. Kane follows my gaze and turns, pulling away.

I miss the feel of Kane straightaway, but I'm distracted by the way Tom is moving, crossing the distance in long, loping strides.

For days he's been busy tending to his pa, who took ill at the end of *La Prise*. We'd been talking about the Thaw for months, talking about my dreams, about Matisa's people, but with his pa unwell, there's a chance he won't be seeing any of it. More likely, we'll be leaving without him.

My heart clenches tight at the thought. He should be coming; there's nothing for him here. It's not just that he's curious about what's beyond, it's what lies out there for him. Here, he'll be expected to find a life mate and produce children. But Tom is *ginup*, and his heart would only ever belong to another boy. Matisa has told me that such a thing isn't strange to her people and surely not persecuted. He should come with me, find a new life out there, one that doesn't have to be a secret.

But he would never leave with his pa sickly the way he is. And that thought washes me in a muddled wave of sadness, anger, and pride.

As Tom pulls up, I see his cheeks are flushed and his blue eyes are serious.

My stomach knots. Is the tea I've been giving his pa not working well? I start rifling my brain for my medicines knowledge, wondering what Matisa and I might be able to come up with in its place—

"It's Soeur Manon," he tells me. "Matisa says you need to come."

The Healing House is silence and shadow.

Isi and Nishwa stand on either side of the door. Nishwa offers me a soft smile as we approach, Isi inclines his head, his eyes unblinking. It's always the same these days: Nishwa with the easy look, Isi with the look that makes me feel tested— tested and found wanting. He's been pricklier ever since the Thaw began. Ever since I insisted we wait on Soeur Manon.

9

I ignore his weighty gaze. Heavy clouds are gathering above us, blocking out the morning sun. Surely that's what sets the tingle on my skin. I cross between the boys and push the door open.

Matisa sits beside the bed, her hand resting near Soeur Manon's snowy hair. The rest of the healing woman is covered by a mound of wool blankets—our futile attempt to chase away her chill. Futile, because it's not a chill that comes with cold.

Matisa beckons me close, her calm presence spilling out like much-needed light in the dingy hut. I feel Tom and Kane linger in the doorway.

"It's all right," I say over my shoulder. "I'll come get you . . . after."

Tom touches my elbow—a gesture of brother-like love— and leaves. Kane's parting look washes me in a different sort of love: fierce and protective.

The door shuts, sealing out the crisp air, the beam of sunlight. In the candlelit space, the room feels smaller. I cross to the bed, pulling a chair from the corner of the room with me, and sit.

Soeur Manon's wrinkled face is dwarfed by the bed and blankets; her eyes are shut, her breathing shallow, irregular. She's been this way for days. I search for some sign that she is near her end but find nothing different.

I look to Matisa. "How do you know?" I ask under my breath. Doesn't seem proper to be speaking on a person's death in their earshot.

"I have seen many people go," Matisa replies. "I know when it is time."

I study Matisa in the flickering light. Her dark-brown braid shines against the blue of her shirt. Her face is open, reassuring. Course she's seen people come into this world and leave it; she's a healer, like Soeur Manon. Like I was training to be. She and Soeur Manon spent months sharing what they knew with each other, taught me what they could. I turn my eyes back on Soeur Manon, reach out, and place my hand on the blankets that cover her shoulder. Matisa places her hand on my arm, rubbing her thumb back and forth in a soothing rhythm I'm glad for. It helps steady my racing heart.

Soeur Manon was always kind to me; she understood me in a way I didn't realize until it was near too late.

"Did anyone else stop by?" I ask. I wonder if everyone understands who—and what—we're losing. All of her knowledge, her methods, her cures.

Course, they probably assume I'll be here to take her place.

"Frère Andre," Matisa says. "He brought another blanket. It was covered in embroidered flowers. It was Soeur Bette's, I think. I didn't tell him that she is beyond all of that."

I think of the old Watcher with his wiry beard and failing eyes, offering the blanket that once warmed Soeur Bette—the life mate he lost not two months back. He's another who was kind to me, helped me see that I was worth being kind to. He was the one who opened the sealed fortification gates for me even though *La Prise*—the deadly winter storm—was howling down upon the settlement. Even though I was supposed to be dead. He told his Watchers not to be afraid, and he locked the weapons away so they couldn't do something foolish when Matisa arrived. If not for him, my Lost People wouldn't be here; Matisa wouldn't be here.

As if recalling that memory, the wind picks up outside. A soft patter of rain starts on the thatched roof above us.

"Rain is good," I say. "Greens everything up."

Matisa nods, her hand still tracing a soothing pattern on my arm.

"It'll be real pretty out there," I say. "Don't you think?" Don't know why I'm babbling like this. Feel a need to fill the silence. Fill these last moments. I pat the old woman's shoulder and clear my throat, forcing down a lump. "She'll be glad we're on our way. Last week she opened her eyes long enough to look straight at me. You know what she said? *Emmeline: allez-vous-en!* Go already!" I force a laugh, but it's cut short by the sob building in my chest.

"She always knew what was truly in your heart." Matisa's voice is gentle. Her hand is warm.

I blink back tears and nod. "She knows my new life lies beyond."

Matisa's hand stills.

I look at the old woman's snowy head. I keep the rest of what Soeur Manon told me to myself. About freedom bringing choices—*les choix que vous ne voulez pas*: choices I don't want.

Can't see how that can be. After years of being eyeballed, years of having no choices at all, the freedom waiting out in those trees has to be good.

"Em," Matisa's voice breaks my thoughts. "I want you to know something."

The winds pick up, gusting against the little shack.

I look at her.

"Our dreams led us to each other," she says.

I nod.

"You know that I believe we should stay together," she says. "But"—she clasps her hands together—"I will not ask it of you."

I study her face, trying to figure where this is coming from. Matisa knows I want to see what lies beyond. She knows I've always planned to leave this place with her. She saved my life last fall, risked her own to pull me from the river, but this is about more than repaying a debt to her: it's about starting a new life. It's about choosing a new life.

But she wants me to recognize it *is* a choice.

I look at Soeur Manon, my thoughts whirling around her last words to me.

She's still as ice.

I watch for the rise of her chest, listen for a rattling breath. Nothing.

Matisa puts her hand on my arm once more. "She's gone," she says, soft.

And, like they're answering my heart, the heavens open and the rain thunders down on the roof above, washing the Healing House in sorrow.

The soil shifts beneath my dream fingers as I dig. The river sings with the voices of the dead. I'm beneath the dogwood, a place I know so well, a place I've been dozens of times to dig roots for Soeur Manon.

But why?

We sent Soeur Manon to her peace. I glance up, across the Watch flats to the fortification. It's silent. Everyone has gone.

Suddenly Matisa is on the ground before me. Her eyes are closed tight, her skin is mottled an angry red and swollen with purple bruising. A trickle of blood streams from her nose.

I am digging, fast and furious, grabbing huge handfuls of soil.

And then, a rush of hoofbeats is tearing down upon me. Gunfire. Horses. Screaming.

The dead in the river sing out, telling me to hurry, hurry, hurry.

I wake in a sweat, the dream bleeding out into the chill morning air. Sitting up, I scrub my hands over my face and shiver. The screaming echoes in my mind. Shrill. Constant.

No. Not screaming. The Watchtower bell is ringing.

The Watchtower bell?

I leap from my bed, pushing off the wool blanket, my bare feet slapping against the cold wood floor. The sound of the bell doesn't send the same spike of fear through me it once did. We haven't abandoned Watch fully—there are still a few Watchers up on the walls each night, but they're not watching for an attack from some spirit monster from the forest. The alarm bell is kept as a way to get the settlement's attention in the case of something else urgent: a fire, a coming storm, a wild animal.

I dress quick, my pulse racing. As I pass my pa's old room, I notice Matisa is already up and gone, like always. I grab my cloak from a hook beside the door and push outside. There are people rushing toward me, headed for the east gate. At the wall, a crowd is gathering. I push through the people who are assembling in a silent semicircle. I notice a few weapons clenched tight in weathered hands, but no one seems to notice me jostling them aside. Everyone's craning their necks at something but hanging back, like they're reluctant to get too close.

When I get to the front of the crowd, I pull up short.

A man stands outside the east gates.

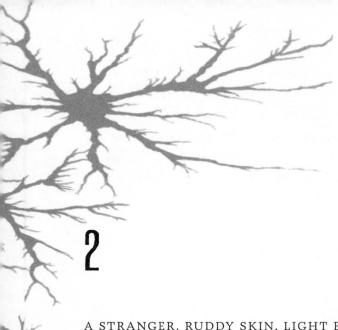

2

A STRANGER. RUDDY SKIN, LIGHT EYES. AT LEAST a week's worth of beard frames cheeks that have seen too much sun. His brown hair is plastered to his forehead, and one chapped hand worries a dingy, brimmed hat. In the other hand he holds the lead rope of a stocky chestnut horse laden with saddle-packs. His clothes are strange: boots with thick soles and, buttoned to his neck, a heavy coat with three bright stripes along the hem. He has a pack on his back.

The bell has long gone quiet—the boy who rang it stands on the wall above us, looking on with wide eyes. A Watcher stands a stride away from the stranger, rifle in his right hand ready, but not trained on the man.

The stranger stares at us, at the walls of the fortification behind us, and at us again. "You folks been here a while?" he asks, his eyes wide. His accent is strange.

I can't tear my gaze from this man, can feel everyone around me staring the same.

"As in a few . . . decades?"

Silence.

His brow furrows. "Do you speak English?"

Someone in the crowd clears their throat. "Yes."

His face relaxes. "That's a relief," he says. "Wasn't too sure . . ." He looks at the Watcher beside him, at the rifle in the man's hands. "Well, then, introductions first." He turns back to us and gestures to himself, speaking in a long-drawn-out kind of way. "Henderson. Robert Henderson. Pleased to make your acquaintance." He inclines his head formal-like. "If you don't mind, I won't ask for everyone's name." He glances up, tapping the side of his head with his hat. "I'll never remember. Never forget a face, but names are a horse of a different color, you know? I'm more a details man, if you catch my meaning. Comes in handy in my line of work."

He looks at us like he expects something.

More silence.

"Not a real talkative bunch," he remarks. He throws a quick look at the Watcher again. "But that's never stopped me. Especially when it comes to imposing. Speaking of, I don't suppose you'd let me shelter the night? My mare could use a rest, and I'd be grateful for a real bed." He tries a smile. "Pine boughs are only comfortable three weeks running. The fourth week, it starts to wear a little thin."

At this, people pull their eyes away to look round at one another.

The Watcher speaks, gesturing to the man with his rifle. *"Je l'ai vu dans les bois."* He saw him in the woods.

A tall south-quarter man with a fish-gut-stained apron steps forward. "Where did you come from?" he demands.

The man's eyebrows rise, the humor fleeing his face. He points with his hat to the southeast.

A low buzz starts in the crowd.

A north-quarter woman points to the man's pack. *"C'est quoi ça?"* she asks.

"This?" The man reaches behind and touches the leather, protective-like. "My parchments, a compass, a sextant—my effects."

Compass . . . sextant . . .

"Robert P. Henderson, cartographer," he says, like it explains everything. His brow creases at our wide-eyed stares. "I'm a mapmaker," he says, "contracted by the Dominion to map the way west."

Inside the ceremonial hall, the man—Henderson—is relieved of his jacket and given a chair and a cup of cooled wild mint tea. At least a hundred people crowd into the space, straining to get a look at our strange visitor. A south-quarter woman stands a distance away with more tea. The Watcher who found him lingers close, eyeing the man's pack suspicious-like.

Tom and I press through the crowd, trying to get to the front, but I notice Matisa hangs back, her head down. I spot Isi and Nishwa in the shadows at the edge of the hall. The ceremonial hall has no windows, and the light from the few candles at the table is enough to light up only the first few rows of the crowd.

"That's some good brew," Henderson says, leaning back and peering into his already empty cup. He looks to the south-quarter woman, who hurries to fill it.

"Obliged," Henderson says, taking another long drink.

Tom's ma, Sister Ann, has made her way to the front. She presses forward out of the crowd of gawkers and puts herself before Henderson like she's in charge. And mayhap she is: with Council disbanded, her voice has become one of the loudest in the settlement. Edith, Tom's little sister, peeks out from behind her.

"You are welcome here for the night," Sister Ann announces. A murmur starts at this. Sister Ann glances around with a hard look, a challenge to anyone who might raise their voice in protest. No one does. "We will share what we can. You are welcome at our table."

"Again, obliged," he says, a wide smile on his face. This man is like no one I've ever met: he's relaxed to the point of seeming a mite addled.

"You've travelled from a place we have never seen," Sister Ann ventures. "Might you speak on it a bit more?" At this the crowd stills. I find Tom's hand next to mine, and he squeezes it gentle.

We learned about the east from Matisa. We learned there were people there, our kind—those who didn't risk the trek west years ago—living in organized groups under a leadership called the Dominion, but she was repeating stories from her people, admitting she'd never been there and didn't know too much. There were some in the settlement who were talking about heading east once the Thaw came—they wanted to see these people who were supposed to be "our kind." But I've noticed no one has made any plans, save us. Could be they're all still too afraid.

I share a glance with Kane, who stands beside his ma on

the far side of the crowd, but it's hard to tell if the alert look on his face is excited or wary.

Henderson chuckles. "Speak 'on' it? Sure." He sits back and looks around the ceremonial hall. "But this just beats all, I have to say." He gestures to his open pack. Its contents are spilling onto the floorboards: rolled sheets of parchment and mysterious leather-covered cases. "Never thought I'd be including a settlement old as this in my maps. You people are an anomaly, you know?"

Our blank faces tell him that we do not know.

"It's a miracle you even exist."

Sister Ann clears her throat. It's plain she doesn't like being at the disadvantage. "Many of our people were taken by a . . ." At this, she falters. There are a few in the settlement still clinging stubborn-like to the notion of the *malmaci*. But most people believe Matisa's tale about the sickness, even if they don't full understand it. Tom's ma is one. "A sickness when they arrived generations ago."

"You're damn straight they were." Henderson shakes his head. "It's all the old people talked about when I was a boy. The Bleed, they called it. Anyone trying to settle out here perished from it. Discouraged migration, I'll tell you what. We thought everyone was long dead." He looks around and clucks his tongue. "But here you are."

The Bleed. Yes, it's exactly the right word. The stories we were told about it—about people turning into rivers of blood overnight, swelling, cracking, choking on their blackened tongues.

Bleed it: our curse when things go wrong, an old saying I never full understood. Is this why we say it? I glance at

Tom, but he doesn't look at me; he's hanging on Henderson's every word.

"We lost many people," Sister Ann says. She looks relieved she wasn't wrong. "Those of us who survived were . . . fortunate." It's as close to an explanation as we've got. When I asked Matisa why some of my people survived the sickness generations ago, she said it was because we moved out of the woods, away from it. For years we thought the virtues—Honesty, Bravery, Discovery—kept us safe, but now that we know the monster wasn't real, most people understand it was just luck.

Henderson shrugs. "Whatever you say. Something was working in your favor."

Murmurs wind through the crowd.

"But all that's over with."

"Our luck?" Sister Ann asks.

"Nah," Henderson laughs. "The Bleed. Word from the occasional traveller crazy enough to venture out this way is there are tribes of First Peoples living out here. Surviving just fine."

First Peoples. Matisa's people. They call themselves *osanaskisiwak*—a word that seems to describe them having joined together with other tribes—but Henderson wouldn't know any of that. I remember Matisa's dreams—about the Dominion bringing war to her people—and all at once I'm glad she's hidden in the throng behind me, that the boys are sticking to the shadows.

"First Peoples found our settlement in the fall," Sister Ann says. "They travelled months to find us."

Henderson tilts his head. "Where from?"

Again, Sister Ann looks at a loss. "The . . . west," she says. People shift in the crowd. Matisa isn't making any move to come forward, and I will the people near her not to force it. I don't want this man to ask her anything about her home.

"You don't sound very sure."

"It's not that," Sister Ann protests, her cheeks going pink. "We . . . we haven't ventured outside our borders for many, many years." She's distracted by appearing foolish in front of this stranger.

The man squints at her. "Could've guessed that, by the looks of you. No offense, of course."

Sister Ann clears her throat, trying to regain her composure. "So there is no one from the east—from the Dominion—living out here?"

Henderson raises an eyebrow. "Thought you might be able to tell me. This past year a few"—he searches for the word—"rogue types have started to press west."

"Rogue?"

"In the best sense of the word, rebels who carve their own path. In the worst, opportunistic thieves."

There are a few gasps.

Henderson grins. It's clear he's enjoying his audience. "See, the east is getting crowded, so the Dominion's been organizing groups to come out in a scheduled fashion. They wanted people to register their plans and whereabouts, but not everyone is so inclined. Some came out on their own accord." He leans back. "It's free land out here—no law. Some people find that attractive, if you catch my meaning." His gaze sweeps over us. "There's people around all right."

The crowd buzzes at this.

"How close?" Sister Ann asks.

"That's what I'm hired to find out. Closest Dominion outpost is at least two weeks away, over the river. It's a small military camp, houses only about a dozen of the Dominion's men. It's due east of the crossing, which is a week to the south." He notices our blank stares. "Look," he says, bending and pulling out a roll of parchment from his knapsack. He stands and unrolls it with a flourish. He gazes around at us, expectant—like he's answered all our questions. Except I can't make heads or tails of it, and from the looks of the faces around me, no one else can, neither. It's all lines and symbols on the right half of the paper, but the left—the west—is mostly blank.

He sighs and taps a squiggled line at the center of the paper. "This is the large river, outside your gates. It runs north and south for miles but winds something awful as it goes. Takes forever if you're wandering along it. Here you are"— he points to an *X* at the top of the curving line—"and a week south"—he points to a horizontal line across the river— "is a crossing I found. This river valley gets rocky as you continue south. The river has worn through the rock here, making a natural bridge. With the river flooded like it is from the spring melt, it's the only place to cross safely for miles. I traversed along the river to the south for about a week but found nothing like that crossing." He sucks his teeth, looking pleased with himself. "Now, supposedly there's a new settlement to the west of that crossing—they registered with the Dominion before setting out—but I don't know for sure. Heading that way was impossible—the land there is real dangerous right now."

"Dangerous?" Sister Ann asks.

"Saw the soil turn to mush before my eyes in the heavy rain. Could drown a man. I went south as far as I could along the river before hitting land so dry and inhospitable there's no way people would settle there." He taps a mass of dots at the bottom of his map. "If the unregistered folks are anywhere, they're settled up this way."

Up this way. Matisa said it would take us a week's ride to reach her people—that we'd head southwest. Are any of these people between Matisa's home and mine?

He rolls up the map and regards us. "I wouldn't necessarily go visiting, though," he says. "Unless you want to take your chances."

"And what does that mean?" Sister Ann frowns.

"Word is, these unregistered sorts mean to cause trouble for the Dominion. Claims to the land, and all of that. The Dominion wants to know where these people are. The tribes, too. They need to know what they're up against."

"And they have sent . . . you?" Sister Ann's voice is laced with doubt.

Henderson sits up a mite straighter. "They'll send law soon as they've got the lay of the land." He brushes at his shirtsleeves. "But they'll need my maps to do it. Right now, I'm their eyes and ears."

Tom and I glance at each other.

"But these—these rogue types," calls a mousy-looking woman. "Are you saying it isn't safe out there?" I recognize her as an old follower of Brother Jameson—the Council leader who spoke on the virtues fanatic-like, who wanted to keep our borders sealed tight no matter what, the Council leader who shot my pa before Kane brought him down with his knife. There's no one in the settlement as powerful as Jameson anymore. His family—including my age mate, Charlie—was banished a day's journey from the Watch flats; being found any closer was punishable by death. But there are some who still let fear rule their thoughts.

The people around her begin to whisper. Soft, but it grows in volume. A sickness starts in the bottom of my stomach. They're getting agitated, fearful. Feels like when we thought the *malmaci* roamed the woods. When we'd send people to the Crossroads for being Wayward because we thought they put us in peril. We should be beyond that. Matisa showing up here in peace should have set everyone straight. At once I feel a flash of resentment toward this Henderson. Strolling in here, telling us to be afraid all over again.

Tom squeezes my hand again, as if to reassure me, and I notice some of the people around us look intrigued, not scared. But I catch sight of Matisa and see her face is ashen, her eyes troubled.

Henderson holds up his hands. "Don't get all bent out of shape," he says, again with that calm one could confuse with foolishness. "Could just be rumors. You know how word gets twisted as it spreads."

But if he knew what we've been living with, would he throw around these thoughts so careless? Telling us horrors in one breath, telling us not to overreact in the next?

"How many?" It's out of my mouth before I know I'm thinking it.

"Sorry?" he asks, squinting into the crowd. Takes me a moment to realize he's asking me to speak again.

I drop Tom's hand and push forward, stepping out of the semicircle. "How many people are out here?" I ask again.

He looks me over. "Hard to say. A couple hundred, maybe."

"A couple hundred are here? Or a couple hundred left their homes in the east?" I ask.

"Aren't you the quick one." His face splits into a grin. "Word is they're doing fine—no dying from sickness like the last time—which is both a blessing and a curse for the Dominion. Now they know for sure they can settle out here without risk of disease. Problem is, their law didn't get here first."

The crowd buzzes.

I look back to Matisa. She's retreating slow, backing out of the throng.

"How can we know that what you say is true?" a man shouts. The crowd quiets at this.

Henderson frowns. "Why would I make it up?"

The man narrows his eyes. "You talk like you aren't even one of them."

"I'm not." Henderson's grin returns. "Government—the Dominion—is for sheep. I'm an *entrepreneur*." He smiles wider. "More opportunistic than a rebel, less unlawful than a rogue." He laughs, but since none of us know what he's speaking on, he laughs alone. This doesn't seem to bother him. He looks around at us. "Now, you mentioned sharing some grub? Could do with another breakfast."

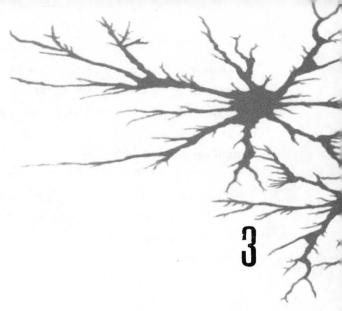

3

"MATISA!" I PUSH THROUGH THE DOORS OF THE
ceremonial hall and catch her disappearing around the side
of the weapons shack. When I round the corner, I near run
straight into her. She's huddled with Isi and Nishwa.

Her dark head snaps toward mine. "We need to go."

"Now?"

"As soon as we can get packed." She looks to her round-
faced brother, Nishwa. "Can you ready the horses?"

He nods.

She speaks in her own tongue to Isi, who claps Nishwa on
the shoulder. He seems relieved. They head off in opposite
directions. I look at Matisa, bewildered.

"Let's get our things," she says, beckoning to me as she
sets off for the east quarter.

"All right," I say, feeling like I'm not truly in the conver-
sation and not understanding why. I hurry after her. "But I
need to tell Kane."

"I've sent Isi to get him," Matisa says, pulling open the

door to our kitchen. She crosses the space and begins sorting through the dry goods we have stacked on the kitchen table.

"Kane said he can be ready in a heartbeat," I say, still feeling at a loss, and shoving down a niggle of unease at the thought of him telling his ma.

"Good." Her hands sort through packets of bulb flour and dried berries. She's rattled, and it's skittering me.

I grab her saddle-pack from the cloak hooks beside the door and bring it to the table. "This is about what that Henderson said," I venture.

She nods, stuffing the dry goods in the pack. Her eyes are elsewhere, like she's thinking hard.

"Matisa," I say, putting my hand on her busy arm. "He was enjoying the telling, but he might not be so sure on the knowing."

"Oh, I know that," she says. "He knows very little." She abandons the dry goods and heads for the sleeping quarters. I follow her into Pa's old bedroom, where she begins pushing clothes into a pack she grabs from under the bed.

"Then what—I mean, why are you . . . so skittered?"

She doesn't pause. "It is not what he knows; it is what he brings."

"And what is that?"

She stops.

"Matisa?"

She looks up, her eyes shifting to the door, back to me—they're troubled, like the rushing river. "I need to tell you something," she says. "It is about the sickness that took your people when they first arrived."

"All right," I say.

"I tell this to you alone," she cautions.

I frown. She's always spoken plain around us—Tom, Kane, her cousin and brother, me.

"Em?"

"Course," I answer.

She sinks to the edge of my mattress. "I told you that we left this area when the sickness came. I told you that our people dreamt more death was coming and that we knew this meant people. Newcomers."

I nod. Matisa's people moved into the mountains, away from the plains, after these dreams. They made peace with other groups of First Peoples to the south so they might be a unified front against an oncoming threat: settlers. Us.

"What I have not told you is that by the time we left this area, we had long been living with the sickness." She twists her hands together. "For years our people and the animals around us died in ways we could not explain. It was not like the sicknesses in the east we'd heard about. This sickness was not passed from one person to another, and it appeared and disappeared with no obvious cause." She hesitates. "Eventually we realized it was in the little waters."

"The little waters?"

"Creeks, small rivers. Your people survived all those years ago because they moved out of the woods, away from it."

I think about the remnants of those first settlements I found last fall; the crumbled cabins out in the woods, next to dried-up creek beds. Our stories tell us the settlers who survived banded together and built our fortification next to the big river, hiding away from the "evil in the woods" that had taken their kin. My eyes widen in understanding.

"For years, my ancestors studied this sickness. Boiling the water made it safe, but boiling was not something we could do forever, and it was impossible to know where the sickness was before it was too late. Over many years of watching certain animals survive, we discovered a remedy that keeps it away," she says. "It remains our most closely guarded secret."

I frown, trying to figure her words.

"Our protection from the sickness has always been our upper hand." She holds my gaze. "Do you understand?"

The Bleed, they called it, Henderson said. *Anyone who tried to settle out here perished from it.*

"You mean you could survive when others—people from the east—couldn't."

She nods. "It has long been the reason we have lived in peace."

"But Henderson said it's no longer here."

"He does not know what he thinks he knows," Matisa says. "It is here, but it comes and goes, appearing without warning. The remedy ensures we are protected, regardless."

"And all of your people know it?"

She shakes her head. "Very few. Only an inner circle of healers. The remedy is prepared as a mix of many secret herbs and plants, but only one of these is any use against the sickness. The knowledge of which plant protects against the sickness remains within the circle alone. I"—again she hesitates—"I am a part of that circle."

I stare at her. "You keep it from your people?"

"Please try to understand, it is valuable. If the knowledge were placed in the wrong hands . . ."

"Settlers' hands," I state.

"It would be a disaster for us," she continues. "Not everyone would understand that keeping this secret prevents what happened in the east from happening here."

The east. I know the stories from Soeur Manon. When the Old World kingdoms arrived in the new land, the First Peoples—those already here—taught them how to survive. Then they were imprisoned, enslaved, and killed for their kindness. Matisa's people are right to worry.

"For years we have sent scouts, in secret, to bring us information from the east. We have learned the languages of the Dominion; we have studied their war weapons. We have done everything we can to know what we are up against. But the remedy is our true advantage." She searches my face.

What she says makes good sense, but unease flickers in my belly. This secret—keeping the truth from people for their own good—feels familiar. Honesty is one of our virtues, but lies kept our settlement in fear for so long. Brother Stockham's pa lied to secure his position as leader, and Stockham kept his secret because he didn't trust people to make good decisions for themselves. Just like I didn't trust my pa with what I'd found in the woods: the journal explaining the truth. If I had, maybe he wouldn't be—

I shove the thought down deep.

"When the Dominion comes, we can offer protection from the sickness—we can treat them with the remedy—in exchange for peace and freedom. This has always been our plan."

"But they are arriving already," I say.

She nods, her face anxious. "This Henderson is the first of many newcomers. I believe he signals the beginning of . . ."

She trails off, but I know what she doesn't say: *war*. She believes he brings the war she's been dreaming on.

I look at my hands, try to think. I know that finding a way to deal with the newcomers on her people's terms is their best chance. And the more people who must keep a secret, the greater the chance it won't be kept. This is different from the secrets Stockham was hiding, I decide. This is necessary.

"The strongest and fastest of my people will be leaving my home soon to hunt the great herds. This leaves us vulnerable. I want to bring this news so they will stay to defend us."

"When will they go?" I ask.

"When the season of rain has passed, they will set out."

I think about how much time this leaves us. The balsamroot I've been collecting is only small shoots yet; it flowers once the rains have passed. And other summer plants I collect have not yet begun to grow. The Thaw, the rains, will be over in a couple of weeks, perhaps a bit longer.

"You say it will take us a week to reach your home?"

She nods. "I believe so."

This makes me feel better. Still, I wonder. "When you found our settlement, you had been looking for us all summer."

"We did not know where to look," she says. "Our path was . . . circular. The journey home will be much more direct."

Direct. Those settlements to the west and south Henderson talked about.

"Henderson said those newcomers are doing fine. How can that be?"

She spreads her hands. "I do not know. I suspect they have not encountered the sickness yet. Perhaps luck is on their side."

"Like it was for us," I murmur, but my thoughts race on ahead. If Matisa's people can't be sure which waters harbor this sickness—the Bleed—can they be sure it still exists? Or, worse, suppose our luck runs out. Suppose the sickness finally does come to this river? Kane's family. Tom's. I can't leave, knowing they don't have the remedy. Knowing how close they might be to disaster.

Matisa notices my alarm. She puts a hand on my arm. "It was more than luck that your people survived," she says.

I frown in confusion.

She hesitates. "If I tell you how I know this, you must never forget how valuable this information is. It is not for everyone to know: I tell you this. Only you."

"But what about Kane?"

"It is better not to know. Not knowing means you cannot tell."

"But Kane would never—"

"Whether or not he would, you have to believe me when I say that it is safer this way." Her face is pained. It's costing her something to share this with me.

What would her people do if they knew? Is it fair to ask her to break her oath twice over? I take a deep breath. "If it will keep him safe, I can keep it to myself." But unbidden, an image of Brother Stockham swims before my eyes. *You have lifted the burden,* he said, before he put that shotgun in his mouth . . .

"This settlement has always had the remedy," she says.

I draw back in shock.

"Long ago we observed that animals who consumed a particular plant were not falling sick. We adopted this plant into our diet. It is a plant that grows near your settlement— and as I learned over the winterkill, it is used here nearly every day."

My eyes widen. "Almighty," I murmur. After all of these years living in terror of an imaginary beast, we've been protected from a danger that was actually real. By a plant.

I bow my head and rack my brain for which plant she could mean. One we use continually. Might even be one I collected for Soeur Manon . . . the smell of the Healing House, always thick with sage smoke.

I look up at her.

Her gaze is serious. "Your people are safe here," she says.

It is better not to know.

"All right." The unease in my belly remains.

"We will take the remedy as we journey," she says. "If"— she hesitates—"if you still wish to come."

"Course I'm coming," I say, and as I do I remember my dream from this morning—her dying on the Watch flats and me burying her—and a chill wraps around my heart. It's the first time I have dreamt of death. The rest of my dreams, the ones that show life, are about Matisa's home.

Mayhap this death dream was urging me to leave this place; mayhap it was showing me what could happen to Matisa if we stay.

Should I tell her about it?

I look at her worried face, her nervous hands pulling the drawstrings on her pack shut.

No. I'll tell her later—no use adding another worry right now—and I'll make sure she gets home safe to her people.

To the place that offers life.

She pulls her pack off the bed and eyes my bad leg. "Make sure you pack your tincture."

A rap at the outside door draws our heads up.

We hurry back to the common area. Kane is at the door. His ma, Sister Violet, stands behind him. Behind her, Frère Andre peers at us with watery eyes.

"What is it?" I ask.

Kane rubs the back of his neck. The words out of his mouth are the last I expect: "They want to come," he says.

I stand outside the gates and wait for him, feeling a dread deep down in my heart. This isn't right, isn't fair.

The rest of the group waits beyond the Watch flats, waiting for me to say goodbye. Giving me space to do it.

His wheat-blond head appears around the wall of the fortification. He looks at me a mite shy as he approaches, worrying something in his hands. A bow? He's been practicing his aim with all manner of things for months—bow and arrow, Andre's rifle—practicing, because he thought he'd be coming with me out into the wilds. He wanted to be able to help hunt and protect us.

An ache starts in my chest.

As he gets close, I see it's a child's bow, made of willow and gut string.

Tom ducks his head. "Give this to Nico," he says, handing it to me. He shrugs. "He seems nervous. Might make him smile."

I stare at it and swallow hard. "Course it will."

He puts his hands on his *ceinture fléchée* like he's not sure what to do with them and nods at the pack on my back.

"Finally, hey?" he says. "Feel like you've been wanting this all your life. Since we were youngsters, surely."

I force a smile. "Suppose I have." My voice is thick. "Even if I didn't know it."

We look at each other. He's trying to look brave for me, I know, but there's a flash of sorrow in those prairie-sky eyes. Sorrow, and longing.

"This is proving Discovery the real way; the way it should be," he says.

My smile turns real. It's true. Before I found Matisa, Discovery was contained within the walls of this fortification, to things that made our life here a mite easier, without risking the woods beyond. I proved it a new way, bringing her in, showing people there was no *malmaci*. Tom proved Bravery a new way, too: he defied Council and got Andre to open the gates for Matisa and me, even though he was afraid.

He doesn't look afraid anymore.

And thinking on him sitting by his pa's side, spooning him that tea I made, caged in this bleedin' settlement, when he should be with us . . .

My stomach clenches tight. "You should come," I say before I can stop myself. "You belong out there. You—"

"Em," he cuts me off. "We'll see each other soon."

The look on his face tells me he's made his decision. I nod

quick and then, so he doesn't see the doubt, the sadness, in my eyes, I rush forward and bury my head in his chest.

His arms go around me and I press myself tight to him, trying so hard to keep the tears back. Crying does him no good.

He strokes my head with one gentle, scarred hand. I pray to the Almighty he won't scald them on purpose anymore. Pray that he'll be all right here, without me.

He draws back and this time his eyes are determined. Strong.

"Go," he says.

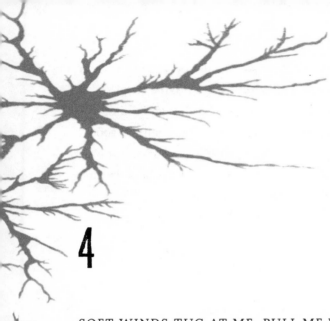

4

SOFT WINDS TUG AT ME, PULL ME FORWARD INTO the dark embrace of the forest. The leaves of the trees are bright, a heartbreaking green that only comes with the Thaw. I stop and take a deep swallow of air. It's like soft, sweet water filling my mouth and chest. It's like breathing in freedom. Life.

This is how I imagined it.

A hot breath blows against my neck.

Well, near to.

I turn and find myself face-to-face with Isi's horse, its soft nostrils speckled with moisture. Above the white blaze on the horse's forehead, Isi frowns down at me. I raise my eyebrows. In response, he looks pointedly behind at the others: Sister Violet and her little boys, Daniel and Nico. Frère Andre with his battered hat and wiry beard. Kane.

They're all walking in the forest with looks of wonderment on their faces. They're all walking . . .

"Too slow," Isi hisses.

"They're just not used to being out here yet," I say,

although we've been walking hours at this pace and I'm not used to it yet, neither. Nishwa is scouting way ahead on his beast, doubling back, scouting ahead. Matisa brings up the rear, scouting behind from time to time, on her own horse.

"We do not have time for *getting used* to things," Isi says, watching them with a frown.

"And how do you suppose we speed them along?"

"I wish I knew. They do not even know how to ride."

"You wish they hadn't come."

"Don't you?" Isi turns his eyes on me.

"Course I'm glad they came," I say.

Isi studies me in that hard way of his, like he's asking me to be sure of my words, be sure of my own mind. I hate that look. It reminds me of how often I used to fail my Honesty virtue. Shouldn't bother me. Ever since I proved Discovery, I've seen the virtues in a new light. They're not so cut-and-dried. Still, I'm relieved when he clicks his tongue and urges his horse back to Sister Violet and the boys. I sigh deep.

Mayhap "glad" wasn't the right word to use. Sister Violet is more determined to keep her family together than I figured. And I know why Isi's irate. When it was only the six of us setting out—Matisa and the boys, Tom, Kane, and me—it was going to take a week, doubling on horseback. Now with so many of us walking, it'll take closer to two. But with Kane showing up like that, all hopeful . . .

A wave of guilt washes me as I remember Matisa's face. She was torn; bringing them wasn't the plan, but she could see Kane didn't know how to refuse his ma.

Isi was unhappy, but she convinced him it would be all right.

And Frère Andre. Well, once Sister Violet was coming with the boys, what was one more?

"Je suis âgé," he said. *"Je n'aurai pas d'autre chance de voir le monde."*

It was true: he *was* old. If he wanted to see the world, coming with us was his chance. I feel a pang, thinking about him saying goodbye to his bird-boned daughter and her life mate and youngsters. She clung to him a moment with her tiny arms, but when she pulled back, she offered him a smile.

"Allez-y voir le monde, papa," she said. Go see the world.

I watch him stomp along, pack on his back with two rifles strapped across it. We had one rifle in our effects already, and Kane has dead-sure aim, but he hasn't practiced much with a gun, preferring his knives. It's good Andre came.

But it should've been Tom.

I watch Nico drop behind his ma and take Kane's hand. Kane smiles at him and my pang disappears. At least Kane didn't have to say goodbye like I said goodbye to Tom. The relief on Kane's face, though, once Matisa convinced Isi—it made me happy and uneasy at once. And keeping the truth about the Bleed from him is weighing on my mind.

Thing is, telling Kane about the Bleed now, and how we're staying safe from it, means asking him to keep it from his ma. Can't do that. And if he tells her, it's not just one person Matisa has broken her vow for, it's three. No. Matisa will keep us safe until we reach her people.

I shove down a niggle of unease.

Isi leans and scoops up a delighted Daniel, setting the little boy before him on the horse's dappled-gray back. He wheels the horse in an about-face.

"Look, Em!" Daniel calls in glee as they trot past. He's beside himself with the excitement of being out here. His older brother Nico is another story, more wary, but right now his eyes, too, are wide with wonder.

I follow after them, *les trembles*—the tall poplar trees—yawning and rustling above us. I press into the brush, stepping on springy new moss, tiny green shoots of horsetail. As I clamber over a log crusted with moss, my good foot lands on something hard—like stone. I hear a clink as my foot grinds down. The new ferns I push aside to get a look at the source are feathery soft. But my fingers touch something cold and solid.

Bones.

I recoil. Looks like a deer, picked clean long ago, washed white with the wind and snow. I step around it careful, wondering how it died. Predator or old age? Or mayhap the winter was that harsh.

I have a sudden thought for the Jameson family, who passed this way months back, with no weapons but a bow and their few belongings in packs on their backs, right after the first snow-bitten winds coursed through the coulees and around the fortification.

No way they survived.

I swallow. It was the settlement's decision to cast them out like that. Brother Jameson killed Pa. He would've killed me, and Kane, and anyone else who stood in his way if Kane hadn't brought him down with his knife. None of the settlement wanted to trust his kin after that. And I didn't think too much on it when they left, neither.

But I know what it's like to feel cast out; I've endured

plenty-enough wary stares in my day. Imagine that feeling being the one you take with you to your grave?

"What is it?" Matisa has appeared at my elbow, silent as frost.

I start and look around, confused that she's here beside me, off her beast.

She throws her head to indicate behind her. "I gave my horse to Sister Violet for a little while. Nishwa can scout behind."

I look back. Frère Andre is now leading Dottie, with Sister Violet and Nico perched atop. Kane walks beside them.

Guilt floods over me again. "I'm sorry," I say. She frowns in confusion. "About this morning," I say. "Had no idea they'd want to come. I'm sorry for putting this on you."

She waves me off. "Refusing them did not feel right."

"But it'll take us near twice as long to get to your home, now."

"We have time."

She sounds like she means it. I raise my eyebrows.

"If we start to lose too much time," she says. "I can send Nishwa and Isi on ahead."

I study her. Only half a day from the settlement and she already looks happier—like a weight has been lifted. "Are you sure you're all right?" I ask. "This morning . . ."

Her cheeks color a mite. "This morning I was a bit frenzied," she admits. "The mapmaker's news unsettled me. And Kane's request was one more surprise. But we are on our way now. And we will reach my people in time."

I step over the bones and we continue walking. "Isi doesn't seem to think so."

"Is that what's bothering you?" she asks, keeping pace with me. "He has always been impatient to get home."

"It's the fact we're here at all. You teaching me to ride didn't sit too well, remember." Matisa spent several days getting Kane and me comfortable on her horse while we waited on Soeur Manon. Isi had watched us circle the sheep paddock, his face a thundercloud.

She sighs. "I know." She gets a sly smile on her face. "But maybe it was because you took so long to learn."

"I did not!" I protest. Except she's right; I don't ride very well.

"Your boy, though, he's another story," Matisa says, appreciative-like. It's true: Kane took to riding horses like it was a memory he'd stored in his bones long ago and finally remembered.

I crane my neck to look at him. Dark eyes, new-shaved head, shirt open at the throat. He looks easy out here, natural. Like he was meant to be outside the fortification all his life. He catches me looking and holds my gaze. He puts his hand to his heart, pretending to adjust the leather pack on his back. It's a secret gesture: *You are here*, it's saying.

My steps falter. I feel his ma's stare and snap my head forward.

"Ah," Matisa says, like I've explained everything.

"'Ah' nothing," I say, keeping my face blank. I pick up my pace.

"'Ah' *everything*," she says. "You two will be field mice under an eagle's watch."

"Well, then," I say, not meeting her eyes. "Need to find a burrow."

"Would you two mice know what to do with yourselves in a burrow?" She nudges me with her elbow.

"I have ideas," I mutter.

Matisa's laugh rings out clear through the woods.

Flames crackle bright and orange, casting long shadows on the trees at our backs. Kane's little brothers sit with their ma. Daniel's head lolls against Sister Violet's shoulder, and Nico rubs his eyes, fighting sleep.

Across the fire, Kane sits next to Andre, who I think is busy describing the strange new birdcalls he heard today. Kane's only half listening; his eyes keep rising to linger on my face. I can't stop the smile that tugs at my lips.

His ma peers at me, so I busy myself with feeding the fire another stick, though it's already roaring good.

Our bellies are full of venison stew and the tea Matisa prepared—the remedy—and we're all wrapped tight against the quick-cooling night. Our tents and bedrolls are tucked away in the trees, waiting for our tired bodies.

Beside me, Nishwa tilts his head, checking the tops of the trees, the sky.

"What are you looking for?" I ask him.

"The clouds will clear soon," he says.

I frown. I'm about to ask how he could possibly know that when a sound rises up from beyond the trees. Shrill. Keening. Like a lost and terrified child. The hair on the back of my neck stands.

The chatter around the fire stops abrupt.

"*Sacrament,*" swears Frère Andre.

Kane is on his feet in a heartbeat, hand flying to his knife.

Matisa raises a hand. "Please, sit," she says, calm.

I throw a look to Isi and Nishwa, who haven't moved a muscle, despite the ghost-cry.

"*Mescacâkan*," Matisa says. Our faces must be comical-blank, because she grins. "Like a wolf, but smaller."

An animal—one that doesn't make its home near the settlement.

"Is it dangerous?" Sister Violet asks.

"They are not." Matisa smiles. "But their song is strange to the new ear."

We listen, and more voices join. Sharp and shrill, coming, it seems, from every direction, all around us. And, true to Matisa's words, as the cries blend and weave they become a kind of song. Sorrowful, beautiful. I can feel my face matching the others' as we stare around at each other, wide-eyed. Daniel is rapt. Nico's brow is furrowed, but a small smile pulls at his mouth.

We sit still as ice, listening.

"The stars," Nishwa says, nodding his head heavenward.

I look up, and my breath stops.

Out here, away from the glare of the burn baskets in the fortification courtyard, more stars than I ever thought possible stream across the dark sky above us. So many stars. Dancing apart and crowding together. Large streaks of white; smears of frost upon a dark wood. Glowing, glimmering. Like they're alive.

Soeur Manon used to describe the night sky as though the Almighty himself had sprinkled bits of silver upon a black cloth. Sitting here, I remember her knobby hands, remember them soothing my brow, and I feel like she's reaching toward me from her resting place.

And I feel the goodness of these woods sinking into my skin. My skin, bathed with the starlight that shines and pulses and echoes the *mescacâkan* song.

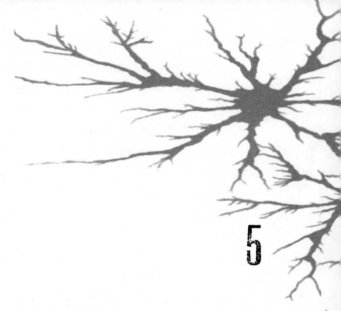

5

AS WE PRESS THROUGH THE DEW-KISSED FOREST, the wild song from last night trills in my mind, my heart. I catch Kane looking at me. The low brush touches our legs and hands with its drenched fingers, drawing soft, wet patterns on our leggings and skin. The trees above stretch tall with leaves that twist lazy in the morning breeze. As we walk, the beauty of the woods becomes dizzying—like one too many cups of saskatoon wine. And seeing Kane out here, beauty in beauty—

"Where are you?" Matisa's voice snaps me from my reverie. I turn my head. She's beside me, leading her horse, one eyebrow cocked.

"Here." I flush, embarrassed at being caught doe-eyed. "Just . . . distracted. By the . . . trees."

"Ah yes, the trees," she says, throwing a glance to our right, where Kane walks. "They cast a spell." Her lips twitch. "On some."

I clear my throat and look around.

To our left, Nico sits atop Isi's horse; Daniel, atop Nishwa's. Matisa's cousin and brother are leading the beasts, casting glances at each other that verge on irritation and amusement at once. The little boys are arguing over which horse is smarter.

Violet and Andre are quite a ways behind, distracted by examining the tall trees and strange new plants that are coming up through the forest floor.

"Are we losing too much time, do you think?" I ask her, in part to change the subject.

"We are slower than I thought we would be," she admits. "But the season of rains is still in the night air."

I hope she's right. Matisa made this decision so I didn't have to ask Kane to refuse his family. I don't want it to mean she's sacrificed anything more than patience, than time we can safely lose.

She notices the worry on my brow. "I have said it before: Isi and Nishwa can ride on ahead."

"Leaving you won't sit well with Isi," I say.

"We will deal with things as they come," she assures me. "For now, we are headed home, and you are with me, and it is a beautiful day." She looks to the blue sky stretching above the treetops.

I follow her gaze, taking a deep breath of the fresh-smelling air, and feel a rush of fierce love for this girl. This girl who followed her heart to find me and brought us the freedom I'd always longed for. This girl who knows so much more than me but never makes me feel foolish.

It *is* a beautiful day.

I risk a glance at Kane again—he's walking with the boys now.

Last night, lying in the makeshift tent with Matisa, I could feel him lying awake like me, far across the coals of the fire, tucked away in his tent. Could feel his breath, soft on the night air, winding over to me, hot on my skin that burned with the memory of that day on the riverbank.

I'll go anywhere with you.

His voice when he said those words, husky, honest. My pulse skips into my throat now, remembering.

And watching him now as he walks in that easy way, watching him throw his head back and laugh at something Nishwa says, just watching him do anything—it's unbearable.

Matisa looks over at me and squints at my face, then looks over to where Kane is walking. She shakes her head. "Still haven't found that burrow."

I flush and sigh deep. I'm not foolish; I know that getting in a family way would be a disaster. But more of those woodshed moments wouldn't be so bad.

Matisa smiles in sympathy. "There is a place, back home, where we go to get away from"—her eyes sparkle—"disapproving eyes. It is a secret place, far beyond the first spruce, back in a crevasse of the mountain. Warm water springs from the rock into deep pools."

"Warm water from the rock?" I ask.

She nods.

"And who is *we*?" I raise my eyebrows.

She laughs. "Not me and someone special. I meant *us*." She gestures between her and me. "My friends. We go to be by ourselves."

Matisa told me many things about her home over the

49

winterkill. She described valleys teeming with animals, warm winds, a glistening lake, groves of tall trees. Surrounding that, huge walls of rocks, capped with snow, dotted with spruce. Some of those things I feel I know from my dreams. Some of them are things I can only imagine.

"I'd like to see that."

"You will." She smiles at me.

I return the smile. Being around Matisa makes me feel like I'm brushing up against the life I was always meant for. She makes me feel at ease and bold at once, like I can learn those things she knows. Like I can decide things for myself.

"Em!" Nico calls from atop Isi's horse. "Watch!" He has something clenched between his thumb and fingers—a leaf or some such—and as he snaps his fingers it leaps into the air, swirling up on an invisible breeze. It drifts, spinning, toward me—a seedpod from an ash tree. He beams. "Isi taught us!" It's the first full smile I've seen on his face since we left the settlement.

Daniel tries to do the same, but he can't snap, so the seedpod falls limp from his fingers. He furrows his brow and pulls another one from a low-hanging branch.

My eyes linger on Isi. Unlike Matisa's easy wisdom, Isi carries himself with a knowing that unsettles me. He's mayhap a bit haughty, and full of pride, which is something I've never felt and don't full understand.

I know, though, that underneath his stony surface is a softness. I've seen it when he speaks with Kane's brothers, when he's helping them do something they can't do themselves. I saw it over the winterkill with Tom's little sister

Edith. Isi would sit in the common room and spin stories from nothing. Matisa told me he's like that with the young ones at their home, too.

"Teach them something useful next time!" Matisa calls to Isi.

Isi waves her off, the ghost of a smile on his lips. Nico snaps one pod after another. Daniel fails again, but his face only becomes more determined.

"He stopped their bickering," I point out.

"I am teasing him because he is teasing me," Matisa says. "I have been dreaming about a tree seed and Isi. In my dream, he follows it in a big wind, even though the places it goes are very dangerous. I've told him about it."

"And now he's playing with seedpods to show you they aren't so scary?"

"Probably," she says, a soft smile on her face.

I've only ever seen that smile when she's looking on Isi.

As we crest a hill, Kane has the spyglass to his eye. "Isi says there are people up ahead."

Isi slaps his horse's neck. The beast's ears are pricked forward, and he nickers, his neck stretched out in the direction Kane is looking.

"Can't see much. A ramshackle camp of sorts. But there's smoke, signs of living," Kane says.

We look at each other.

"Everything looks weatherworn—they have been there some time," Isi adds.

Some time. A flicker of familiar curiosity lights in my chest. Feels like when I used to look out at the woods from the Watch flats. When I finally got out into those trees and couldn't help but go farther still.

"First Peoples?" Sister Violet asks.

Isi shrugs.

"Do you think it's safe?" I ask Matisa.

"We could skirt to the south," she says. "But we would need to backtrack several hours."

We look around—the forest is climbing and dipping with little gullies. We've been pressing west with a large ravine to the south for a long while. The most direct route is straight through that little camp.

Isi says, "I'll go."

"Not by yourself," Kane says.

"We'll go with him," Matisa says, looking at Nishwa.

"What if they aren't First Peoples?" I ask.

We shift, looking around at one another. I can see what's weighing on everyone's minds: If these are newcomers, are they the rogue types Henderson was speaking on? The thought makes my skin prickle, but there's something else starting in my belly: excitement.

"Better in a group," Kane says.

"*Oui*," Andre says. "We go together, *mais les femmes restent ici avec les enfants*. And one man stay with the women."

Matisa shakes her head. She doesn't look angry, just like she has no inclination to stay back. "I go with my family."

"I'm going, too," I say, feeling bold.

"Em can ride my horse," Matisa says, "in case we need to get back here fast."

I look at my foot. It doesn't hurt me so long as I'm on

that tincture, but I'm still not as quick as the others. I look at Andre, expectant.

He sighs. *"Bien."*

"I'll stay with my boys," Sister Violet says. "Kane?"

He looks torn. Andre pulls one of his rifles from its strap on his back and hands it to Kane. *"Reste-ici."* He removes the other gun and fastens it to a strap on his *ceinture*, close to his right hand. "We signal to Kane when it is good."

We start down the slope toward the camp. There's a fluttering in my chest. Seeing someone living outside the settlement like this feels like the day I found a young sparrow with a broken wing on the riverbank. I could cradle it in my hand, look at it up close—this wild thing I only ever saw from afar, winging along the river.

We get to the bottom of the slope. The dwellings are shabbier this close. They're hasty-put-together shacks, logs and spruce bows and bits of bison skin all stuck together like a mended cloak. There's an untended fire smoldering in the center. The camp itself is well protected, I suppose, in this gully, but they aren't exactly hidden here.

Course, they might not need to keep hidden. My heart speeds as we approach. We're a stone's throw away now, and Isi holds up a hand for us to stop. He turns to us to speak.

A child appears from behind one of the shacks.

He stops dead, his gaunt face a mask of fear. One eye is crusted over with a thick, yellow film, his hair is matted, and the bison-skin long shirt he wears is filthy, hanging off his thin form like old bark on a birch.

We all stare for a heartbeat, shocked by him appearing like that, shocked by the way he looks. He bolts. Each of us has the good sense to keep our traps shut as he disappears beneath a flap door in the nearest shack.

A chill starts up my spine.

Blond. Pale. That child isn't First Peoples. He's familiar. He's—

The flap is pushed aside, and a figure stoops low out the door. He puts a hand on one knee as he straightens, like he doesn't quite have the strength. His clothes are tattered and stained, his collarbone and shoulders sharp points through his shirt, eyes too big in his sunken face.

He puts a hand to his brow to shield the morning sun, and his face breaks into a grin, showing dirty teeth. His eyes are hard, though, and the chill wraps around my heart.

"Morning, brothers and sisters," he says.

That voice. I know that voice. I can hear it in my head, reminding me about my Stain, calling me out in front of my age-mates.

It's Charlie Jameson. We've found the outcast Jameson family.

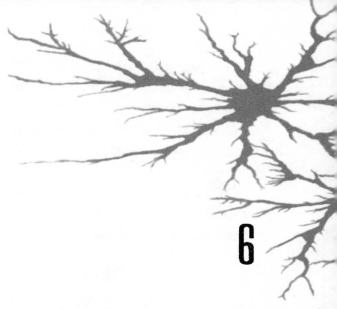

6

CHARLIE STEPS FORWARD, OFFERING HIS HAND to Andre. Andre doesn't move; his eyes skim the camp. Isi is behind us on horseback, a rifle on his back, but I know he can have it to his shoulder in a heartbeat.

Charlie stops. His eyes are bright blue, like his pa's. Piercing.

"*Êtes vous ici seul?*" Frère Andre asks. "Only you? Here?"

"Nah," Charlie says, "but my sister's too sickly to move around much. That winter—weren't she something?"

I stare at him. He barely looks like himself, excepting his eyes. His face has lost its boyish look, and there's a scraggly beard started around his chin.

He jerks his head toward me. "Hiya, Emmeline."

The little boy appears again, crawling out through the tarp. He stands, wraps one arm around Charlie's leg, and hides his face behind Charlie. A pang cuts through me. He's so thin.

"My little brother, Josiah," Charlie says, nodding at him.

"And your ma?" I ask, trying to remember how many were in Jameson's family when they were sent out from the settlement.

Charlie's face goes stony. He shakes his head. *"La Prise."*

The words hang in the air between us.

"How many of you are there?" Matisa asks.

Charlie turns toward her, and his eyes get a gleam, like he's just noticed her and Isi and Nishwa. He pulls his head to the side. "Well, if it ain't the Lost People," he says. "The gift of God."

All at once I'm nervous. I wish I were standing on the ground, not perched here on horseback, though what I could do for Matisa—for any of them—I don't rightly know.

Matisa stands her ground. She's not smiling, but her face is calm. Waiting. Isi's horse sidesteps, jittery, and Isi puts his hand on his neck to soothe him.

The way Charlie's looking at Matisa—like he's figuring something. Deciding something . . .

"How many?" I repeat Matisa's question.

"Three," Charlie says. "We lost three: Ma, my ma's brother, Joseph, and my sister's life mate, Frederick Woods."

When they were cast out from the settlement, his sister, Rebecca, was spared since she was already bound and living in the Woods's quarters. But Rebecca refused to leave her mother and insisted on going, too. Her life mate followed. Bad decision.

"No adults?" Frère Andre asks.

"I'm in charge," Charlie answers, looking past us to Kane and the rest—small shapes on the crest of the hill. "Where you headed?"

"Just passing by," I say.

Charlie's eyes narrow. "Passing by to where?"

He doesn't know about Matisa's people. Doesn't know about the colonies in the east.

"Why you ask this?" Frère Andre says it friendly-like, but there's a warning in his words. He shifts, his hands drifting to his *ceinture* near the sling that carries his gun.

Charlie shrugs. "No reason. Don't much matter, and we don't want no trouble." He eyes the horses' saddle-packs. "You got any food to spare?" He smiles, but it looks like a grimace. "Found out I'm not so good with the bow."

Silence. Frère Andre shifts his stance. I can see by the set of his jaw he's about to tell Charlie no, and I can see on Charlie's face he knows it, too. The air goes still, the desperation in this makeshift camp closing fast around us.

Movement at the tent breaks the spell. A bedraggled, bone-thin girl pushes her way through the flap and rights herself with effort. She stares at us and her right hand goes to her belly, protective-like. I can see by the unnatural bulge: she's pregnant.

Rebecca.

Her sunken eyes fill with tears. She takes a stumbling step forward, looking like she'll sink to her knees. "Thank the Almighty," she says. "You've come."

We sit around the Jameson's fire, now stoked high with wood and crackling orange.

"I don't like this," Isi mutters to Matisa as we portion out bits of dried mutton stew. Twelve servings: three more than we're truly prepared for.

Rebecca sits, chattering to Charlie, who pokes at the fire with a stick. The rest of us are sitting away from the Jamesons—as far as we can get without seeming obvious. Josiah edges close to Nico. Matisa says nothing as she hands Isi a bowl of stew and gestures for him to take it to the boy. He goes with a frown.

Rebecca appearing like that changed Frère Andre's mind about refusing Charlie. I saw it on his face the minute she stepped out of the tent. It was midday anyhow, time for us all to eat something. We decided we could invite them to share with us and then move on.

I watched Charlie's face careful as Kane and his ma and the boys came down the hill. Kane killed his pa, and it was no pretty death, neither. Brother Jameson drowned in his own blood, choking, lying on his back at the pulpit while the rest of the settlement fled.

Charlie's eyes dulled when he recognized Kane. Then he pulled his chin up and offered him a thin smile. He hasn't looked at him since, but Kane has barely taken his eyes off Charlie.

I look at Rebecca's haunted face and at Charlie's, wondering what they're thinking. They carry the burden of their pa's mistake; I know too well how that can wash out. Drove Brother Stockham mad. They can't be trusted; they were cast out to their deaths. Wasn't *our* decision—not truly— but who knows what ideas they're harboring.

Though, seeing how happy Rebecca is, and watching Josiah take the food from Isi . . .

Something twists in my heart.

"You all right?" Kane says. I turn my head to look at him,

feeling a mite dizzy. He frowns, puts a hand on my arm, and pulls me off toward the tattered shack, out of earshot of the others.

"Em?" He puts a hand under my chin and tilts my face up toward him. "You feeling sick?"

"No."

"You don't look good." He brushes a thumb across my cheek.

I look back at the group: one side of the circle hollow eyes and rags, the other staring at them like they're staring at death itself. Rebecca accepts her portion from Isi with a wide smile. Charlie catches my eye and gives a weak smile, like he's embarrassed. I noticed a limp in his gait when we gathered ourselves to share food. Don't know what caused it, and I don't want to know. Watching him limp feels like I'm sharing something with him I don't want to.

I think about the way he used to look at me—like I wasn't fit to clean sheep pens, like my Stain was somehow catching. No way they'll survive much longer out here, and Rebecca's unborn child is as good as dead. I watch Josiah wolf down the stew.

"Em?" Kane says again.

"Need to go for a think." I back a step away from him, toward the trees.

His eyes are dark with concern, but he nods. He knows me well enough to know not to insist on coming along. "Stay close?" he asks.

"Got no choice," I mutter.

Around the trunk of the first tree, I run straight into Andre, coming back from a tour of the woods.

"Where you go?" He frowns.

"Just . . . need to get away," I say.

His frown deepens. "Not alone," he states. He slings his shotgun, hooks his thumbs on his *ceinture*, and leans back. Waiting for me to turn around, return to the group.

All at once I want to scream with frustration. Too many people out here, having a say in everything. Too many eyes watching me. It's like the bleedin' settlement all over again. I wrap my arms around myself and take a breath. It hitches, and tears well behind my eyes.

His grizzled face softens. *"C'est difficil,"* he says. He shakes his head. *"L'enfant."*

Josiah . . . his starving little face. I brush away the tears that come.

He puts a hand on my shoulder.

I lean into his touch, breathe deep, and try to clear my head, but Brother Jameson's cold blue eyes swim in my vision. My pa would be out here if not for him. Anger surfaces in my chest, hot and deep.

"Jameson deserved his death," I say, like I'm accusing Frère Andre of something.

He nods. *"C'était le désir de Dieu."*

Almighty willed it. Yes.

I want to cling to that notion when I think on Charlie. But all those years being Stained by my own grandma'am's Waywardness muddies it up in my head. Her supposed sin was *my* burden, for a long time. Until I washed it clean, until I proved it false.

Nobody's giving them the chance to wash their pa's stain clean. But . . . say we did?

"Frère Andre, Charlie and his family have survived out here so far . . ."

"Oui," he says. "They survive." He raises his eyebrows. Waits.

I hug my arms around my body close. "But surviving and living are two different things."

He studies me. "You have—*comment on dit?—culpabilité.*"

Guilt. I look away, off into the trees. "It's not that." But I can feel that ice in my chest again. It's *not* that . . . is it? When they were cast out, how did I feel? Can't remember. Back then everything was so upside down. Back then my mind wasn't on Brother Jameson's family; it was on my Discovery. What it had brought upon us, what it had brought upon my pa. It was on Matisa showing up and the greater world that lay outside our gates. It was on surviving *La Prise* so we could see that world.

And it was easier to send them out when it wasn't my decision. But casting them away from my own fire—now, that's something different altogether. And now that I know the Bleed might be out here . . .

"Don't know if they can be trusted." I'm not outright asking him what he thinks, but I'd be lying if I said I'm not hoping for an answer. He's quiet. "Don't know how Charlie feels about Kane," I try again.

Andre's eyes soften. "Talk. To *les autres,*" he says, gentle.

I fight back tears. "Yes."

I let him put an arm around my shoulders as we walk back to the fire and realize with a pang that his gruff warmth reminds me of my pa.

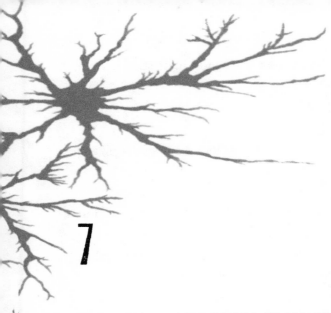

7

"NO." THE WORD DROPS FROM ISI'S LIPS LIKE A stone.

"We can't just leave them here," I say, looking around at the others. Matisa and Nishwa exchange a glance. Kane watches me. I'd pulled him aside, told him first. He didn't have much to say, just asked me if I was sure. Then he put his fingers to his lips, then to mine, and said, "I've told you before: I'm with you." But there was a flash of worry in his dark eyes.

"Your people sent them away," Isi reminds me.

"That was the settlement's say-so. This—this is our choice, now," I say, but Isi crosses his arms. "We'll just get them to the next settlement we see. Leaving them to perish isn't right."

"And if we do not find a settlement?" Nishwa asks. "Do you expect us to bring them to our people?" He's not asking it unkindly.

"I d-d-don't know," I stutter. "Henderson talked about a settlement to the west of the crossing. One that had registered with the Dominion . . ."

"You do not *know* that it exists," Isi points out. "Or if they would accept them if it does."

Matisa leans forward. "Why do you ask this, Em?" she asks, not like she's irate, but like she truly wants to know.

"I just . . ." I trail off and look at her, helpless-like. She studies me. "I just feel like giving them a chance is something I need to do. If we could just get them someplace better—"

"We are delayed already," Isi says. "We will not waste more time searching for a settlement that may not exist."

"It is true that it may not exist," Matisa says, "and even if it does, it could take us days to find it." Isi nods, satisfied. "But," she continues, "the crossing itself is not too far. We could take them there. They could make their own way east—the mapmaker said there was a military outpost that way."

"Matisa—"

"The big river winds to the west," she cuts Isi off. "If we alter our path to the southeast, it would be less than a day out of our way."

"It is a better plan than hoping we find a place for them along the way," Nishwa agrees.

Relief sweeps me. It dulls when I meet Isi's glare. "I know it's a burden," I say to him. "But that little child, that unborn baby—"

"Bring them then," Isi says. "But not Charlie."

"You know they won't go without him."

"That is their choice."

I blow out a frustrated breath and look to Kane.

"Charlie's too weak to think about harming us," Kane says, careful. "And Rebecca's with child."

"So you agree with Em?" Nishwa asks.

"I understand why she's asking," Kane says.

I have half a thought that he didn't exactly answer Nishwa's question.

"Hatred buries itself deep," Isi mutters.

I turn to Matisa. "Do *you* think it's dangerous?"

"I think this is your decision," she says. "His family wronged yours, but he is your people. The weight of that history lies with you. We should respect your wishes." She looks at Isi.

I swallow. "But do you think Charlie is the same kind of person his pa was?"

She turns back, her brown eyes measuring me. "Who can say? We are all walking a new path, now."

"I can't leave them."

Matisa nods and looks to Isi again. He looks away, his jaw clenched.

"Let's get moving," says Kane. "We're losing the light."

Isi and Nishwa are on foot now. It was Nishwa's idea to give their horses to Rebecca and Josiah, who are too weak to keep up. It was a practical decision, but I know Nishwa's soft heart made him speak before anyone else thought of it. Isi's beyond prickly now; he gave Kane's brothers a stiff shake of his head when they asked to walk with him and paced off ahead of us. Matisa consoled the little boys by putting them on her horse, and they look happy enough, but Isi slighting them like that bothers me.

And I can't get his words out of my head: *Hatred buries itself deep.*

I push the thought aside. Surely doing the right thing will help things turn out all right for all of us.

Still, nobody was inclined to sit out around the fire last night; we all ate and turned in quick. There was no *mescacâkan* song; just the thin drizzle of rain on our tarps. I shut my eyes tight and prayed for sleep.

Now I walk with Kane and Nishwa, out of earshot of Charlie, who limps behind us, beside Isi's horse carrying Rebecca. Matisa showed him how to lead the horse and he's doing all right keeping pace. That Almighty-cursed limp doesn't seem to bother him too much; he's stronger than I figured.

They know we're only taking them to the crossing, that they'll have to journey to that Dominion outpost on their own. Even so, Rebecca's face is going to crack from her big smile; it's clear she's so relieved she doesn't know which end is up.

Was a mite surprised Kane's ma was agreeable about bringing them along, considering Charlie might harbor some hate toward Kane. But I suppose being a mother makes her more inclined to help. I notice, though, she's keeping the little boys away from Charlie's lot.

Kane reaches out to lace his hand through mine. My pulse doesn't skip like it normally does—I'm too distracted. We walk, our moccasins whispering on the mossy forest floor.

Long moments of silence. I can't take it anymore. "Do you think we did the right thing?" I say to no one, to Kane and Nishwa both. I toss my head back toward Charlie and Rebecca.

Kane squeezes my hand in reply. "I know why you wanted to do it," he says.

Again, he didn't truly answer the question. "But everyone's skittered, aren't they?" I ask.

"People were skittered to begin with," Nishwa says. I smile at him using our word for feeling scared—sounds funny on his tongue—but his observation doesn't make me feel better.

When I think about Charlie's family, with their sunken eyes and bones poking through their wind-eaten clothes, I feel like we did the right thing. But I also feel like I'm dragging my old life along with me.

"Do you think we can trust him?" I look to Kane.

He rubs his free hand up the back of his neck to his shaved head. "Don't know. But hopefully we won't have to."

"Meaning?"

"Meaning I don't want to get in a situation where our lives are in his hands. We keep him at arm's reach, we shouldn't have a problem."

In the late afternoon, the forest thins out in all directions and gives way to small hills with low brush. We press south, heading back to the river that winds past our settlement in the north.

Our group splinters a mite as we traverse the hills and wander around the pockets of brush. The incline is a bit of work on my foot, and as I pause to take a drink of my tincture, I fall behind Kane and Nishwa. Voices drift through the scrub, coming down the hill. Charlie and Rebecca. For the moment I'm hidden from their view, and for some reason I stay this way.

Rebecca's voice reaches me as they approach. "—do it?"

"No," Charlie answers as they pass by, "ain't the right time—"

Rebecca looks to the side and catches sight of me. "Hi, Em!" she blurts, her hand flying to her belly—a nervous gesture. Charlie cranes his neck around Isi's horse, pulling it to a stop.

"Not the right time for what?" I ask.

Charlie squints. There's a pause. "Just talking about this baby here." He gestures to his sister's swollen frame. "I'm telling her to wait until we get to this 'Dominion' you told us about."

My eyebrows raise. "Don't think she has much choice in the matter." I say those words, but I'm wishing they weren't true. Kane's ma says Rebecca will have that babe soon. She looked at me meaningful when she said it, and I know she was thinking on me helping Soeur Manon with the birthing women at the Healing House. Except I never truly helped, only cleaned up after, whether the birthing went wrong or right. And I don't miss it. My stomach tightens looking at Rebecca; she's so helpless out here. Never want to be like that.

"Suppose you're right." Charlie shrugs. "Just . . . you're helping us so much. Don't want to be any more of a burden than we already are."

"It's fine," I say. There's something about the way they're looking at me that sets my skin prickling. Something about this feels wrong. Feels—

"Em," he says, "we know it was you convinced the rest to help us." He takes a step toward me. "You're a helping sort, ain't you? You help others like it's second nature." Up this close Charlie's blue eyes are burning straight into me, showing me things I don't want to know about: desperate cold and hunger, watching his family starve.

I swallow. "I think everyone should get a new start, if they want it."

"That what you're heading for?" Rebecca asks. "A new start?"

"Something like that."

"Well, that sounds mighty good," Charlie says. "We could use one, too."

The sun shines bright on their hollow faces, making them squint. Like they're looking into daylight for the very first time.

"Going to catch up with Kane," I mumble. I leave them as quick as my foot will allow. My skin doesn't stop prickling for a good long while.

By evening we come upon a sheltered spot in the forest and make camp. Everyone is tired. It's rockier terrain here, and the going was rough. We've skirted boulders and slipped down shale-laden inclines. Henderson described the land changing like this; I hope it means we're getting close to the crossing.

Nishwa caught two rabbits in the afternoon, but they're

not enough for the twelve of us, so once the tents are up, Kane, Isi, and Nishwa try hunting again. Frère Andre heads out on his usual patrol.

"Can I come?" Daniel asks him. The boys are at loose ends without Isi's attention. Nico pouts by the horses, brushing them in a halfhearted way.

Andre shakes his head no but ruffles Daniel's hair kindly.

A splinter of ice pangs in my heart as I watch his shrivelled form stomp away from us, off through the trees. *La Prise* was hard this year, and he's getting up there in his years. His daughter's words ring in my head: "*Go see the world, Papa.*"

I breathe deep against the icy feeling and set to my chores for dinner. As I measure out the bulb flour into a wooden bowl to mix for bannock, my thoughts fly back to Rebecca and Charlie.

When we left their tattered camp, Charlie said he was sorry for the things his pa did. I want to believe that. They want a new start. And I want this new world to help us leave that dark past forever. So why is that ice creeping back into my chest?

Matisa's voice breaks my thoughts: "Where are the little boys?"

I look up from mixing the bannock. She's been skinning the rabbits and her hands are stained pink with blood.

I glance around. It's quiet inside the tents.

Sister Violet is hanging the washing on a thin line of cord that extends between the trees.

"Don't know for sure."

"Did they go with Isi?"

"No."

Matisa looks off into the trees.

"Probably just gone wandering," I mutter, casting a side glance at Sister Violet. "I'll get after them."

I leave the center of camp casual so as not to attract her attention—don't need her getting riled—and head toward the far side of the grove.

It's this moment I notice Charlie's tent is silent and none of his family are milling about. They aren't given chores; Frère Andre thought it best we keep our goings-on separate from them, treat them as guests, not part of us, and everyone agreed: nobody wants them to get the notion we're taking them any farther than the river crossing. But they're usually about, getting underfoot somewhere.

I drop my bowl and stirring stick as I approach the tent.

Rebecca's lying down inside. She raises her head when I look in.

"Where's Charlie?" I ask.

"He wanted to show the little boys something in the woods."

My heart stops. "Which way did they set off?"

She stares at me.

"Rebecca! Which way?"

"Off past those bunches of spruce, I think. Em, what's—"

I spin on my heel, skirt the tent, and break for the woods. I don't rightly know why, but the thought of Charlie alone with Nico and Daniel puts a sick feeling in my gut. The sick turns to a panicked fluttering in my chest when I don't find them beyond the row of spruces. Where could they be? What could he possibly need to show them?

I push farther into the woods, not caring when the branches pull and slap at me, tear at the skin on my arms. "Daniel!" I call out. "Nico!"

I stop to listen. Nothing.

"Daniel!" I call again. I can hear that note of terror in my voice and swallow hard to ground myself, set myself right.

Surely he wouldn't harm them. He's got his own little brother along with . . . He wouldn't . . .

I'm about to holler again when I hear a scream. It's ahead of me, at the bottom of the hill of brush.

"Daniel!" I take the decline in three unsteady strides, busting through the brush and skirting a large moss-covered boulder. There's a little creek—a trickle of water, truly—running between two small boulders, and pools are collecting in the rivulets of mud.

The screams come from down in the creek.

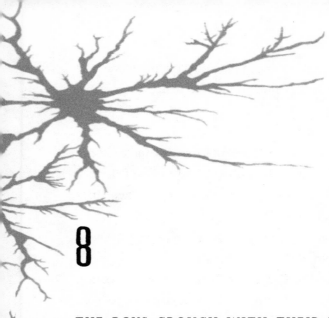

8

THE BOYS CROUCH WITH THEIR BACKS TO ME. Josiah and Nico have sticks. They're fishing around in the water.

Daniel screams again as Nico turns to him, a small something—insect?—in his hand. He holds it out to Daniel, making him scramble away, laughing.

Charlie stands beside them, watching.

As I slip down the bank, he turns to me. Unsurprised, like he knew I was coming.

"Daniel!" I say again.

Daniel starts and looks up. His face breaks into another smile. "We're catching frogs! Look at 'em all!" He points with excitement at the creek.

The water is teeming with tiny frogs. Must've been a tadpole clutch in these pools. Nico swings his hands toward me and opens his palm. The small frog leaps off, straight at me, but I'm hardly worried about that.

"I was calling you!" I say to the boys.

Nico looks at me in confusion. "We didn't hear." He turns back to the pond.

"Settle down, Em. The young'uns were safe with me," Charlie says.

I ignore him. "You don't go off without telling us." I'm admonishing the backs of their heads. "Nico! Daniel!" The boys pull their gazes from the creek and turn. "You hear me? You don't just leave camp like that."

"But we were with Charlie," protests Nico.

"I know," I say, feeling Charlie's gaze on me. "I know that. But . . ." I pause. "But you need to tell us where you're going, no matter what."

"You let us go off with Isi," Daniel says.

I grit my teeth, my face going hot. Can't meet Charlie's eyes. "Just tell us from now on, you hear?"

The youngsters nod, serious-like, and turn their attention back to the frogs. Charlie's still staring at me. I expect him to say something nasty, so I force myself to look at him, brace myself to take it. He should know his place anyhow, and I'm not scared anymore to put him there.

But he uncrosses his arms and softens his look. "Apologies, Em," he says. "I should've told the womenfolk where we were headed. Thought they'd get a kick out of this. I used to look for frogs when I was a young'un."

When he was a young'un. A picture of him as a child flashes in my mind. His pa was on Council, so he didn't much consort with us. I knew him from a distance. He was forever trailing around after his pa's cloak, his face all smug. Like he was better than us.

Charlie was a mean braggart back at the settlement. He

admired his pa—*must* have some bad feelings toward Kane about his death. But of course he was a child once, too—one who shot stones and played jacksticks and caught frogs.

He looks at his brother, Josiah, and smiles, and all at once I feel foolish, charging out here like he was feeding them to wolves.

"It's all right," I say, uncrossing my arms.

We watch the youngsters squeal and dig, get their hands muddy to their elbows. My eyes linger on Nico. He's lost his cautious look—he's happy out here. They all are. My heart swells at their amazed faces.

"Em," Charlie says. "I know we've got some bad blood between us, from the past."

I wait.

"But the way I see it, we can't go backwards. We're out here now, and I know that wasn't your decision. I know you were only doing as you saw fit when you went after them Lost People, when you brought them in."

I swallow. This sounds like an apology.

"Anyhow, I wanted to say I'm grateful you've taken us in. Hope I can find a way to repay you."

And I don't know what to think or say. Soeur Manon told me I would change, that I'd make decisions I never thought I'd have to. Well, mayhap forgetting what happened at the settlement, trusting that we're all moving forward, is part of that.

I still the flicker of doubt in my mind.

"Appreciate that, Charlie," I say. "I want to put the past in the past, too."

When we get back to camp, Kane and the rest are arriving back from hunting.

"Thank the Almighty!" Sister Violet says, hurrying forward to take Daniel by the arm. "Where were they?"

"Just looking at the new frogs," I say.

Kane sets a rabbit carcass on a rock near his ma and sheathes his knife, his eyes on my face. His ma shepherds the boys to scrub their hands. No one takes much mind of Charlie, who's heading back to his own tent with Josiah. No one, that is, except Isi. He's standing with his arms crossed, a strap with two gutted animals on it dangling from his hand. He makes no move to take it over to Matisa, who's getting a rack ready over the fire.

He stares at Charlie, and then at me.

I feel my face start to flame, like it does when I'm embarrassed. I feel a rush of anger. What does he think? That I'd betray Kane with Charlie? The very thought makes me want to either shudder or laugh. I could explain, could march over to him and tell him that the youngsters were missing.

No, that's not what he's thinking. The way he looked at Charlie, and then at me, it was . . . It hits me like a rock in the gut: it was the same.

Mistrustful. Wary.

My heart sinks.

"Em?" My head snaps away from Isi to find Kane. Somehow he's crossed the camp and is beside me. "You all right?"

"Sure," I say, brushing at my tunic.

"Thanks for going after the boys," he says. "I—" He pauses.

"I worry about them doing something foolish out here. But not when you're around." He smiles that funny half smile and my worry over Isi melts away.

I smile back. "Course," I say. "I defended them from those frogs, no trouble." Out here in the sunshine, with Kane standing so close, my panic from earlier seems right laughable.

"Did you now?" His smile widens, pulling up the other side of his mouth. "Mayhap we should put you on frog patrol."

I shrug. "I'm not scared."

He laughs and takes my hand, squeezing it in his warm, strong one. My cheeks flare bright red as I dart a glance over my shoulder, searching for his ma.

Everyone is busy with getting prepared for dinner. Isi is gone.

I turn back to him, and my pulse skips into my throat as he leans close, his collar open, the smooth skin of his throat and the top of his chest radiating a heat that matches the hot breath in my ear.

"I know," he says, his voice low. "It's why I love you."

The Watch flats are empty. Everyone is gone.

I sit beneath the dogwood. The soil shifts through my hands. I am digging. Digging.

The river sings beside me, voices of all those long dead. All those we cast in the Cleansing Waters.

The earth beneath my palm shifts, moves of its own accord. My hand springs back from the movement—away from whatever is coming to the surface.

The head first, shaking—shedding its earth-trappings—and the rest emerges slow. Brittle fingers, grasping at the earth. The soil falls away as it pulls itself up out of the dirt: Matisa, but not Matisa.

One half of her body is whole. Her long hair shines in the sun and her skin glows with health. The other half is only bones; bright white, like they've been picked clean by the wind.

I stare at her. Half life, half death.

The dead under the river sing out loud.

Make peace with it.

I wake in a sweat.

The cool blue of dawn is bright. I can hear the others rising, shaking off the last bits of sleep. Beside me, Matisa's bedroll is empty.

I push from our tent, searching the camp.

Isi stands in the trees, bent at the waist, checking his horse's hooves.

"Where is she?" I call to him, hurrying across the camp.

He straightens and frowns.

"Matisa," I say, though I know he understands. "Where is she?"

"In the forest," he says, moving to the back of his beast and picking up its hind leg. "Gathering wood."

"How long will she be?"

"How would I know?" Isi scowls at me.

I feel a flash of irritation. His stare from last night resurfaces in my mind, deepening my ire. "Thanks for the help." I turn to go.

"Save it for Matisa," he mutters.

I whirl. "Beg pardon?"

His scowl turns into a glower. "Matisa is doing what you want, bringing these . . . *people*"—he eats the word with distaste—"to safety. Now you complain when she isn't at your calling?"

"I wasn't complaining!"

"How much more does she need to sacrifice for you?"

My face flames. I close my mouth, whirl on my good foot, and stalk away.

I feel his stare all morning. Anytime Charlie's anywhere near, if I so much as turn my eyes his way, Isi's gaze burns into my skin. I busy myself pointing out birds and clouds to Daniel and Nico. I try to distract myself with the sound of their chatter and laughter.

But by the time we stop for the midday meal, I'm still wound. Anger throbs deep in my chest as I fumble in my pouch for my tincture. I'm so rattled I don't notice Andre talking to me until he touches my arm. I start and grab at the clay vessel before it falls from my hand.

"Emmeline," he says. "You are troubled?"

"No," I say quick. I look over at Matisa, handing out portions to Rebecca and Josiah. I grit my teeth. "A mite."

"C'est quoi le problème?"

I look over at him: his watery eyes, his wiry mess of beard, that Almighty-lovin' battered hat. He pats my hand. My shoulders drop in a sigh. I contemplate telling him, but I'm not sure what to say: I don't like the way Isi's looking at me?

Isi thinks Charlie and me are the same? It sounds foolish, even if it feels true.

I shrug. "It's just more . . . difficult than I thought. Out here."

He grunts like he's agreeing.

"And I'm having these dreams . . ." I trail off and look at him, helpless. Can't explain Matisa in my dreams, why I'm digging. Or why we're back at the settlement, the place I was so sure we should leave.

His eyes soften. *"Moi aussi,"* he says.

I lean close. He used to dream at the settlement, too, and his dreams urged him out to the woods, like mine. "What are your dreams about?"

"Je pense . . . I think . . . about my new life. Out here." He smiles, a bit shy. "I dream of a cabin. On the river. *Une belle place."* He shrugs.

I smile. "Sounds real nice."

"And you?"

"Not so nice." I take a quick drink of the tincture.

He pats my free hand. "Things are not easy now," he says, "but they get better." He smiles. *"C'est le désir de Dieu."*

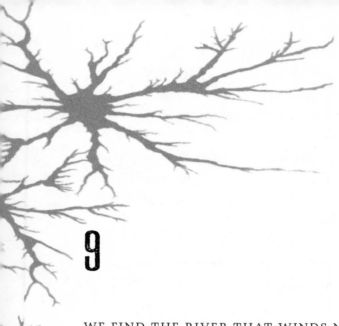

9

WE FIND THE RIVER THAT WINDS NORTH TO OUR settlement in the late afternoon. The waters are wider here than back home, rushing past the rocky cliffs in a fierce roar. Matisa says we'll follow it to the crossing, which should only be two days at most. And then it will only be a week until we reach her people.

We've only been out four days. Feels far longer—the past two days in particular. Again last night, Matisa gave the Jamesons her remedy tea with the rest of us, but I'm not sure how much she has to spare. She didn't look worried, but I'm happy the Jamesons won't add to that burden much longer.

Not that they know what she's doing for them. Not that anyone knows, save me, and even I don't know the whole story. Again, the thought that Matisa alone is responsible for our safety like this starts a flicker of unease in my belly. If we got split up from her . . .

Mayhap I should tell Kane about the Bleed.

I walk with Matisa at the head of our procession. Kane

walks just behind us with his ma, leading Dottie, who is carrying the little boys. The horses with the Jamesons are at the rear with Andre. Behind them, Isi and Nishwa.

I glance over my shoulder and notice Kane's head is bent toward his ma; she's talking quiet and serious about something.

I bite my lip. How would she react to this? Is it worth upsetting her if we're not truly at risk?

I look back once more, to where Charlie leads Josiah on Nishwa's horse.

I draw close to Matisa and keep my voice low. "How do you think the Jamesons survived out here?"

She glances at them. "Luck," she says.

"You mean the Bleed wasn't in their water," I say.

She nods.

"But there's no big water around there," I argue. "They would've had to source it from small creeks." I think aloud. "Suppose it's like Henderson told us: the Bleed's gone?"

"No," she says. "As I have said, it comes and goes. We have observed this cycle for generations. The Jamesons were lucky."

"So those newcomers Henderson talked about—they've been lucky, too?"

"Perhaps," she says, but she hesitates.

"What is it?"

"I've been wondering if they know how to avoid it."

"You mean avoid the shallow waters?" I ask.

"That, or they know to boil their water. Boiling is only a temporary solution, not one a community can exist on for long, but it may explain why they have been surviving so far."

"But wouldn't that mean they've figured out where the Bleed comes from?" I ask.

She clucks her tongue and shakes her head. "It took us many years to understand. Many years of watching. I do not think they could discover such a thing so quickly." Her eyes grow dark. "But I have been thinking: perhaps they didn't realize it is in the little waters; perhaps they were *told*."

"Told by who?"

"There was talk before we left last summer. About some of our people abandoning. There was one group who spoke the loudest. They were known as *sohkâtisiwak*—it means 'they are mighty'—and they wore the symbol of the hawk."

"Abandoning. Why?"

"They were not content living in . . . mystery."

"They didn't like the remedy being kept from them?"

"Yes. They want to break off, lay claim to a different area, and live on their own terms. But . . ."

"They can't without being able to create the remedy."

She nods.

"But why would the *sohkâ*"—I wave my hand helpless-like as my tongue trips on the word—"tell newcomers where the sickness comes from?"

She shrugs. "Perhaps *sohkâtisiwak* have decided to align themselves with a more 'mighty' group. One that can force us to reveal the method for creating the remedy."

"'Force' you," I say.

"We have studied the weapons the Dominion creates," she says. "They are many, and brutal."

The war she's been dreaming. What if it's not just the

Dominion who's bringing it. Could be it's this group of abandoners aligned with people from the Dominion. Fear shoots through me. The thought of these abandoners out here, betraying Matisa's people like this . . .

"You say they don't have the remedy?" I ask.

"They may have stores of the remedy, but *sohkâtisiwak* are not healers from the circle; none would know what it is. All of our people know the sickness is in the waters—that knowledge is common—but they do not know which plant protects us."

"You sure about that?"

"Yes," she says, firm. "And none of my circle would reveal that secret."

I think on this. "But how *is* it that the remedy came to be secret? At one time, all of your people must have known what it was."

Her eyes flicker. "Careful mythmaking," she says. Her tone is flat—like she's telling me an answer she knows is the truth but wishes it wasn't. "Our elders realized how valuable our remedy was when the 'newcomers bringing death' perished without it. Some of them wanted people to forget their knowledge of the remedy."

"Your elders didn't trust their people with the truth," I state.

Matisa's brow is creased. "It was a dark time," she says. "Not everyone agreed."

"But how did they do it?"

"When we left the plains, we took the remedy plant with us to cultivate at our new home. At that time, people were busy adjusting to a new way of life: different tribes had come together, uniting against this threat of newcomers our dreams had foretold. In the chaos, our elders saw a chance to ... obscure the truth. They created a mysterious lore around the sickness, full of superstition and half-truths. A circle of healers was created to know the truth and to create the remedy as a mix of many plants and herbs—all useless, except for one—so that none could identify it. The mythical stories were passed down generations, and the knowledge was forgotten."

Like before, the familiarity of Matisa's tale starts an uneasy feeling in my stomach. "Sounds like how my people started believing in the *malmaci*," I say. I think of how the lore shifted over the years from an evil that caused sickness to a monster that would Take people from the woods. "Sounds like Brother Stockham's pa, perpetuating the spirit-monster myth to keep power."

She presses her lips together. I've upset her.

"But I know this is different," I say, quick.

"Perhaps not so different," she says. She smiles, but her eyes are a mite sad. "But necessary. My ancestors' methods to shroud the remedy in secrecy may have been deceitful, but if *sohkâtisiwak* are doing as I fear, it proves that the fewer people who know the truth, the better."

But if what she says is true, it means that being one of those few people puts you in danger; it makes you valuable to people who would use the truth for their own gain. I glance back again at Kane. He's still listening to his ma, nodding, but his eyes seem troubled.

All at once I wish we'd never found the Jamesons. Taking them to the crossing will only waylay us a day, but even that one extra day makes me nervous. And the fact that I'm the reason we are delayed—

"Do you smell that?" Matisa asks me, tilting her face to the wind.

I frown and shake my head. Don't smell anything but the fresh moisture of the forest. "You know I'm useless at that sort of thing," I say. Matisa and the boys always smell and see things long before I do.

"Yes, you are," Matisa concedes. A small teasing smile lights her face. She reaches over and grasps my arm. "But I am glad you are here, Em. I feel . . . I feel better that you are here."

I look at her fingers, and my dream surfaces in my mind. Her brittle fingers coming up from the soil. Emerging, half skeleton. In my first dream, Matisa was dead. In this last dream, she's halfway to life. Mayhap it's telling me I'm on the right path.

"I think my dreams are telling me that, too," I say. I watch her turn her head again to the wind, wrinkling her nose. I should tell her. She might help me figure it. But . . .

Make peace with it.

It's asking me to accept something, and it feels like it's something I've already done. The settlement, Matisa, life and death—is my dream telling me to make peace with what I've agreed to keep secret? Or is it asking me to accept what I've done by finding her? With what happened after—

"What is that?" Kane's voice comes from behind us.

I look to where he's pointing, off into the trees.

Something hangs in the branches.

A bundle of sticks? Whatever it is, it doesn't look natural; doesn't look like it belongs to the tree.

Looks like it was put there.

Matisa peers into the trees. "I do not know. But I believe it is making that smell."

"Stay here," Kane says to his ma, giving her Dottie's lead rope.

Matisa and I follow Kane into the trees, our eyes fixed on the bundle. The way it twists in the breeze—slow, lazy— puts a chill to my skin. As we get close, I notice the smell. It's sickly sweet, rotten, like deadfall and spoiled meat.

We stop beneath it and stare, putting our hands to our noses to block the odor and squinting into the sun that filters through the poplar boughs. I walk to the far side and shield my brow with my free hand to get a better look. The bundle is held together by a net of ropes. Within those ropes patches of fur and flesh are visible. Bits of white bone protrude from the netting. Flies buzz around its bulk.

"What is it?" Kane asks from beneath his hand.

"A food hang?" Matisa suggests, staring up at it with a curious look. "Perhaps it was left behind by mistake."

"What do you mean?" I ask. "What is a food hang?" The eye of whatever animal it is stares down at me. I think I can make out a mouth.

"We are travelling through big-predator country," she says. "I have heard of people hanging their food to keep it safe." She frowns. "But my people do not do this. We have different methods to avoid big predators, and we know well enough when they are near."

I look at her.

"There are many signs." She waves her hand.

"Looks like it's been there a while," Kane says.

"It is spoiled," Marisa agrees.

I look back at the group.

Isi and Nishwa have started into the brush toward us, their eyes fixed on the sickening bundle above.

There's something that doesn't feel quite right about this.

When I turn to look back at the bundle, I know. From where I'm standing, I can see the mouth. It's caked with black blood. As I look closer, I can see that blood starts at the eye.

This isn't someone's food; this animal had the Bleed.

So why would they hang it—

A scream cuts the air behind us, shattering my thoughts.

We spin to where Isi and Nishwa were walking. They've disappeared—no, I can see the top of Isi's head among the brush, the tall ferns. Matisa sprints off toward them, with Kane close behind.

When I catch up, I find them on the ground, hidden by the underbrush. Matisa is bending over Isi, who's kneeling beside Nishwa. Nishwa lies on his side, his leg twisted awkward beneath him.

"What happened?" I ask.

They're speaking fast and furious in their tongue, and I can't see past Matisa to get a look at what's keeping Nishwa on the ground.

"Get me a strip of cloth!" Matisa calls to me. Nishwa lets out another inhuman cry.

I fumble with my *ceinture*, unravelling its bright length from my waist fast as I can.

"Can I help?" Kane asks.

"It's all right," Matisa says, her voice more calm. "Keep the others back so they do not get scared." Kane leaves to do as she says, and I hurry forward and pass my *ceinture* to Matisa, who is kneeling beside Isi.

Nishwa is an unnatural white, and he's breathing hard. Whimpering.

Below the bright sash Matisa is tying around Nishwa's calf I see blood, flesh—metal.

Oh Almighty . . .

One of Nishwa's feet is caught in a big steel trap. It's huge—far bigger than the traps Pa used to set out for the odd wolf that would venture near the settlement—and the teeth of one side of it are sunk deep into the flesh of his leg, above his moccasin.

The teeth on the other side have caught a small piece of fallen branch and have it pinned against his shin. Blood is spurting out around the teeth that bite his flesh.

His pant leg is soaked dark.

Matisa wraps the cloth below his knee and ties it.

"We need to get it off." I try to say it firm, but my voice is too high. I can't stop staring at the blood. Slick crimson pools coat his leg and the ground beneath.

Isi examines it, running his hands over the hinge real light, like he's scared it'll close harder if he touches it wrong. He speaks to Matisa in their language, his voice low and tight.

She examines it with the same caution, looking over every inch, but not touching it. "He is lucky there was a branch here. Without it catching the trap, his foot would be gone."

Nishwa whimpers again. I don't know what to do, so I go to him and take his hand. He squeezes so hard I think he'll crush the bones in my fingers to nothing.

"If he had been on his horse—" Isi begins.

"Isi, stop," Matisa snaps. "This was no one's fault."

Isi pulls his chin up and looks away. Nishwa whimpers. Squeezes my hand.

Matisa examines the trap again. "We need something strong. To pry it apart."

"A branch?"

"A branch won't do. We need something harder."

"The rifles," Isi says.

Matisa nods. They look at each other, unhappy.

I stare at them. "What are we waiting on? How many?" I push to my feet.

She holds up a hand to stop me as I go past. "It could ruin them. They are old weapons. It might bend them."

I frown. Can't see how she'd care about rifles when Nishwa's in pain like this. Then I realize she's not worried about the rifles; she's worried the others won't want to give them up.

But she's wrong. Course Frère Andre and Sister Violet won't think twice about passing them over so we can save his leg.

"Is Nishwa all right?" Kane hurries through the trees toward us.

The others stand fifty strides away, watching on. Charlie stands off to the side, craning his neck at the scene.

"Almighty," Kane swears under his breath as he gets close. "That trap—we walked right past it."

"That branch got caught in it. If it hadn't, his leg would've been torn straight off," I say. I feel sick.

Kane puts a hand on the back of my neck. "We'll need something harder than a stick to pry with," he says.

"We know," Isi says.

"Need something made from steel," I say.

Kane catches my meaning. "It'll ruin them."

Everyone is silent.

Kane nods. "I'll be back."

Too many moments later, we're still talking about the bleedin' rifles. Sister Violet and Frère Andre have had a look at Nishwa's leg, and they've got their heads together, jawing on the matter.

I can't take it anymore. I push away from the tree Kane and I are standing against, intending to march over and tell them what I think.

Kane catches hold of my arm. "They'll make the right decision," he says. "They're just scared. Best not to stir that hornet's nest."

But I'm not so sure. I can see the doubt in their eyes, and the way Sister Violet flaps her hands, it's like she's trying to conjure a better plan out of thin air. Andre holds two rifles, one in each hand, and weighs them as he speaks. Violet shakes her head, gesturing to the youngsters and horses. She crosses her arms, her jaw set.

And now something real curious happens. Charlie approaches them. He holds out a hand, talking low. I'm desperate to hear what he's saying, but Kane tightens his grip, keeping me in place.

A couple of moments later, Andre's headed back to Nishwa with the rifles. With Charlie.

I rush toward him. "Andre?"

"*Pas maintenant,* Emmeline. We free the boy. *Et après, tu peux aider.*"

He figures I can heal it, except I've never seen such a wound. I look to Matisa, who's staring at Nishwa with big eyes.

I can help. I have to. I pull my satchel over my head and start digging through the roots and bits of herb. I'll need flame and water.

I find a dry patch of ground a few strides from Nishwa and start building a fire with the little twigs and leaves I find nearby. I strike my flint and get a small spark going. I blow on it, coaxing the flames. Before I know it, Charlie's helping me, finding bigger branches to get the flames real hot.

Andre's busy getting them all in a position where they can work the trap. He gets the rifles wedged in at cross angles so that they're dug firm into the ground.

"I'll tell the young'uns we'll be stopped a while," Charlie says to me and heads back to the horses, fast as he can with that Almighty-cursed limp.

"Isi *et* Kane, you take rifles," Andre says. "When I say, pull back, *comme ça*—" He mimes the action. "*Avec toute votre force.*" Hard, he's saying. "We don't have long time. I pull the trap. If branch come also, *bien.*"

Isi and Kane take their positions. Andre gets his hand under the trap in a way I hope means he won't get his fingers snapped off if it springs again.

I pour some water in Matisa's metal cup and stick it in

the fire. I add some yarrow, willing it to boil quickly. I don't want to look, but my eyes drift back to the scene, where Andre sits, all his attention on the trap.

"*Alors*," Andre says, "*maintenant.*"

Kane's forearms strain as he pulls back on the rifle. Isi does the same, clenching his teeth tight. Real slow, the jaws start to unhinge.

"*Un peu plus*. Little more," Andre says, his hand at the ready.

Isi sets his jaw as he and Kane pull away from each other, steady. One violent jerk from either side would mean disaster.

The jaws open another inch and Andre starts sliding it off.

Nishwa shrieks as the teeth of the trap shred along his skin once again, and finally the trap is over his foot and Andre's setting it on the forest floor. Kane and Isi pull their rifles free. The trap snaps shut with a bone-chilling clang.

Matisa rushes to put a cloth to Nishwa's leg. She talks to him in soothing words, pressing into the wound though he shrieks again at her touch. She throws me a wide-eyed look so I nod, trying to reassure her.

The rifle Kane held is bent, I can see that from here. Isi's looks fine. Andre looks Nishwa over, grabs the rifles from Kane and Isi, and slings them over his forearm. He uses the tail end of his *ceinture* to wipe at his glistening forehead. His eyes are satisfied. Relieved. But his face looks older than before.

He walks over to me and puts a hand on my shoulder. "*Doucement,*" he says.

"Course I'll be gentle," I answer. He mops his brow again and turns to go. "Andre," I say, "what did Charlie say to you? To get you to use the rifles?"

"He say he has wooden bow for us. It was—*comment on dit?*—exchange."

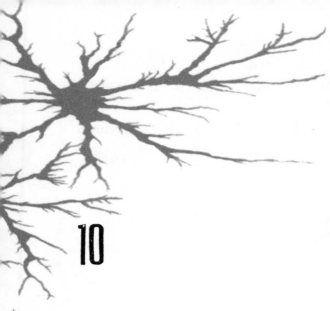

10

"YOU JUST STAY RESTING," I SAY TO NISHWA, laying my hand on his shoulder and squeezing. Matisa looks over her shoulder from the fire, where she is stirring a pot of tea. Once we got the bleeding stopped with my paste of spruce gum and yarrow, I gave Nishwa some of the tincture Matisa made for my foot, hoping it would dull the pain. The bandage looks good, but he lies on his back with his eyes closed, his face an unnatural white. I place the tincture vessel next to his slack hand.

Matisa nods her thanks. "We will make you more, Em."

A pang of guilt hits that she's thanking me at all. I leave Kane with Nishwa and step away, taking deep breaths. Isi paces around the outskirts of our makeshift resting spot. The rest of the group have ventured farther down the rise to unpack provisions for the midday meal. I can tell no one's sure how settled they should get. Nobody's talked about moving on or setting up camp yet.

Charlie sits with his family, watching on. He gave his

most precious implement to help save Nishwa's leg. Still can't quite believe it.

"Nishwa needs better medicine," Isi's voice breaks into my thoughts. I start and turn, find him standing with his arms crossed. "That trap must have broken his leg."

"Couldn't feel anything out of place," I say.

"Breaks can be difficult to find," Isi replies with a shrug.

We look over to where Nishwa lies. Kane is checking his forehead for fever. He notices us looking on, hops up, and joins us. "He'll need time to heal."

"I'm pretty sure if there were a bone to set, I'd have found it," I say to Isi.

Isi waves me off. "He needs to see our *âstehowew*—it means healer."

"I know what it means, and I know how to take care of wounds," I say.

"This is not about you!" Isi snaps.

Anger surges through me. "You sure about that? Because all you're doing is pointing out where I've failed!"

"Easy, Em!" Kane says.

Isi's face goes dark. He spins and stalks away.

Kane crosses his arms. "What was that about?" The curve of his brow is cleft with a deep line, and his eyes are troubled.

"Just standing up for myself," I say.

"Isi wasn't saying you were responsible."

"I *am* responsible. I'm the reason we're headed for that crossing, the reason we passed through these particular woods in the first place."

"Em—"

"Nishwa had to give up his horse for Charlie's family or

95

he wouldn't have been on foot. And now Isi's sure I haven't healed him proper."

"He's just worried."

I look down. Pull my arms close around my body. "It's just—" I force the words out. "Isi's right: Nishwa needs to go back." As much as I want to believe I've helped his leg, I know he won't be better tomorrow. Or the next day.

Kane nods.

We look at each other.

"So we leave Charlie and his family." But as I say the words, I feel sick. I wrap my arms tighter around myself.

Kane's forehead creases.

"It's only another day. If they just follow the river . . ." I trail off. Can't be sure they'll make it. But I can't ask Matisa to keep going this route. She's done so much for us already.

"Em," he says. "My ma—she's skittered."

I nod. Can understand that. "All right. So we'll press on—"

"No," Kane cuts me off. "For a while now she's been talking about what the mapmaker said. About the rogue types out here—the people who can't be trusted. Whoever laid that trap must be nearby."

For a while. I think about seeing the two of them talking earlier.

"Seeing this has made up her mind."

"Her mind?"

"She's talking about that crossing," he says. "She wants to head east."

I draw back. "With Charlie and the others?"

"Not *with* them," he says. "But she . . . she wants to head to that Dominion outpost. Figures she can get help going east from there." He rubs the back of his neck. "We leave Charlie, we're leaving my ma and the boys. And I can't—I can't do that. Not before I know they're safe."

I stare at him, taking in his meaning. "You want to go with her." My stomach twists.

"I want to get to that crossing."

"But—but then what? They'd still have to journey all those days east. Henderson said that outpost was days away!"

"I don't know," he says. "Mayhap you and I would take them?"

I stare at him in shock. "I can't leave Matisa." After all she's done, I can't abandon her now. Bringing Kane's family—that was Matisa making a sacrifice to ensure Kane didn't have to, and bringing the Jameson family along was another: she was helping me live with myself. And my dreams are telling me to stay with her.

"Then she can come with us," he says.

I stare at him. "To the people she believes are bringing war to her home?" My voice is heavy with disbelief.

He scrubs his hands over his face. "We don't *know* that's true."

"No," I say. "I can't ask it of her."

Kane clasps his hands at the back of his neck and looks skyward, blowing out his breath. The poplars creak around us unsettled-like, as though they can feel our desperation.

He won't leave his ma and the boys right now. It's all over his face, in the way he stands.

But . . . no. I need to fix this. Find a compromise. Days ago, Matisa talked about sending the boys on ahead if we were slow. That was before Nishwa was injured. It's asking more of her to stay with us now, but I don't have much choice. "I'll ask Matisa to stay with us till we reach the crossing," I say. "Mayhap we'll find a settlement after all. Or mayhap we'll meet some good people who'll take your ma and the boys east."

Kane drops his arms and looks down at me. "I can't leave them before knowing they're safe," he says.

I swallow hard. "But if Matisa will come with us, and it looks all right for your ma and the boys?"

He looks away. "Guess we'll deal with that when it comes."

I stare at his profile, willing away the tears that swell against the backs of my eyes. That day at the riverbank comes back to me—his skin searing into mine.

I'll go anywhere with you, he'd said.

But it's not true.

A flicker of anger lights in my chest. He knows how much being out here means to me, he knows I've pledged to stay with Matisa.

I swallow and clear my throat. "Let's see what Matisa says."

He nods. "Think that'd be best."

"I will take you to the crossing," Matisa says, and the icy hand around my heart unclenches.

I try hard not to breathe a sigh of relief.

"Nishwa needs to go." Isi's eyes narrow; a muscle works hard in his jaw.

Kane and I stand with them near a dozing Nishwa, out of earshot of the camp, where the rest are busy setting up.

"I know."

Isi stares at Matisa as she bends to Nishwa's foot. Her expression is unconcerned as she turns his foot over, gentle. "I have been dreaming of you, Isi, taking care of an injured bird." She looks up. "Perhaps this is what it meant. You can take him."

"And leave you here? No." Isi shakes his head. "That is not what your dream meant. You will come with Nishwa and me."

"No," Matisa says firm, standing and crossing her arms. "Kane's family needs to get to the crossing, too, now. We will stay the course. You can bring the news to our people about the Dominion."

In this moment, I'm so full of love for Matisa that I want to shout.

Isi launches into their language. Sounds like he's protesting.

"Speak English!" Matisa snaps. "Em and Kane deserve to know what you think."

"Fine!" Isi shouts. He whirls on us, and his voice could tear the hide off a mule deer. "Here's what I think: I think I would be shot by my own mother if I showed up back home without Matisa, telling them I'd left her to a pale death-bringer."

Matisa's eyes widen in horror. She shoots a look at me, grabs at his elbow, and pulls him toward her. "Em is our *friend*," she hisses.

Isi pulls his arm away. "Is she?" he asks. "A friend who adds to the burden of others, then asks them to abandon their wounded family so she does not have to take responsibility for that burden?"

Blood rushes to my face.

Matisa's eyes blaze. "Em was doing what her heart told her. And I am doing what mine tells me."

He turns away, mutters, "I knew this would happen."

"What are you talking about?"

He wheels back. "I trusted you! I have done what you asked. When you wanted to find the settlement, I followed you. When you wanted to stay at that settlement, I stayed. And then you were sure we needed to bring Em along when we finally, finally returned. But enough is enough, Matisa. You can't keep chasing after dreams you pretend show the future."

Hurt flashes in Matisa's eyes. Her voice is a growl. "I never asked you to come with me."

Isi steps back like he's been slapped.

I need to stop this. "Isi's right," I blurt out. "Nishwa can't make the journey with us like that, he needs to go back to your people."

Isi's eyes flicker to me, but he only looks annoyed I've spoken at all.

"I said Isi can take him," Matisa fires back. I've never seen her angry like this. Her eyes have a sheen to them, and two bright spots have appeared on her cheeks.

"And I said I'm not leaving you here!" Isi shouts.

They glare at each other. Matisa's hands are curled into fists.

"Are you two finished?" a voice asks. We look to Nishwa, who is peering at us with one eye cracked open.

Matisa hurries to his side, kneeling and pushing a chunk of hair behind her ear. She helps him sit. "We thought you were asleep."

"Difficult to sleep with all the noise," he says, wincing as he pushes himself up and looks around at us all. "So here is a way to get some quiet: nobody goes anywhere. Matisa, stay with the group, Isi, stay with Matisa, I will take myself back."

Isi snorts, and Matisa starts to protest, but Nishwa cuts them off: "My leg is hurt, I'm not dying. If I rode hard I could be home in four days."

"That is a terrible plan," Isi says. "It's clear there are new-comers out here. No. We come with you."

"I will be on a horse, and I know the route back," he says. "I have Em's tincture. And I'll take a rifle."

We all shift at that. There are two rifles left. If he takes one . . .

"You don't know how to fire it," Matisa protests.

"Andre taught me how to aim." Nishwa waves his hand.

Isi snorts again.

"Isi, Matisa believes she and Em must stay together," Nishwa says. "You cannot ask Em to leave her people, and you cannot ask Matisa to leave Em." He speaks some words in their language.

Isi's jaw works hard, but he stays silent.

"Let me take myself back, or come with me and leave Matisa here. But she is not coming with us."

Isi stares at Nishwa and Matisa in turn. Matisa raises her chin. When he locks eyes with me, his gaze is fire.

"I knew this was a bad idea," he mutters. "I knew it." He turns and stalks off into the forest.

"Matisa—" I start, feeling guilt and relief at once. But thanking her feels foolish. Feels like it would belittle her sacrifice.

Nishwa speaks, saving me from having to continue. "I will need help getting packed."

Nishwa is settled atop his horse, enough stores for four days and one of our precious rifles strapped to the beast. Isi's jaw is in its usual set, and his eyes are narrowed. He leans forward, speaks a few words of his language to Nishwa, who nods. Nishwa bends low to Matisa and touches his forehead to hers. They speak soft, something in their tongue. I can feel their family love for each other in their whispers, plain as day.

His round face goes serious as he looks around at us. "Take care."

He turns his horse to the west and sets out. Sister Violet leads her little boys away, following Andre, who heads to pack up. Matisa, Isi, Kane, and I watch Nishwa until the forest swallows him up.

"Four days?" I ask.

"If that," Matisa answers. "He will be fine."

"You don't know that," Isi mutters.

"Isi, Nishwa will be fine," Matisa says. "And we will all be together again soon."

He turns scathing eyes on her. "Will we," he says, like he's tasting a bitter berry.

She nods. "And you have made your choice, so there is no need to punish anyone for it."

He stares at her a moment. He shakes his head and stalks away.

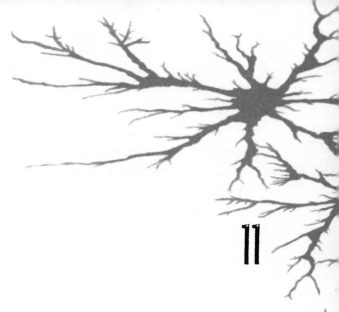

11

THE MORNING LIGHT WASHES OUR TENT IN A soft, warm glow, but I awake with that sliver of ice in my chest. I roll over and stand, careful not to wake Matisa. My bad foot protests with a painful throb. I bend to grab the tincture from my satchel before I remember I sent it with Nishwa. Matisa said she and I would make more, but last night we were all too rattled to do much but move away from the stinking bait, make camp, eat, and turn in.

Least, that's what I told myself. That's how I explained Kane avoiding my eyes around the fire, why he leapt up to help his ma settle the boys to sleep and didn't return. That's how I was able to fall asleep finally, my chest hitched tight with the thought of us getting to the crossing. Getting to the crossing, and Kane heading east with his ma.

I step on my foot wrong as I leave the tent and let the fiery pain wash away that thought. Haven't done that to my foot in a long while. Haven't needed to. But thinking on Kane, and Nishwa heading out alone yesterday, that ice in my chest feels heavy. We'll be slower now, too, looking out for those awful hidden traps.

Least we know to look for the bait. We'll probably smell it first. And we might be slow, but Nishwa will be sure to reach his home in time to warn their hunters.

If nothing bad befalls him on the way.

I head to the river to wash. The willows along the bank are coated with dew still, and the morning sun glimmers over the far bank, chasing the fog on the river away slow. As I look for a good spot, I notice the wide mouth of water drops and disappears from sight about fifty strides downriver. The banks are high, cutting away sharp. And the water just disappears.

A flicker of excitement lights in my belly. On a hunch, I double back to our camp and press south into the woods, cutting parallel to the river. Straight away the pitch gets steep. The ground here is soft; thin trees that haven't kept their grip are lying in jumbled messes beneath the moss. I trip over them, grabbing at branches to steady my diagonal trek across the hill.

When I get to the bottom, I can hear the river again clear.

It sounds like *les trembles* moving in a big wind, but louder. More urgent. I claw through the brush, pushing toward it. The air grows heavy, clinging to my skin and hair like a giant spiderweb. I part the bramble and stumble out onto a rocky shore.

The river tumbles down the rock face above me, a great cascade of white water falling from the heavens, rushing to meet the churning water below. The clouds of mist drifting onto the shore settle on my face, coat my eyelashes like dew. My chest gets tight.

Been wanting to see a waterfall my whole life.

Saw a drawing in one of Soeur Manon's storybooks, once. The river used to flow real fast at spring breakup, and I'd picture it careening over the side of a rocky ledge somewhere, picture myself falling with it. But this—this is so much more powerful than I figured. It's pounding in my ears, in my chest.

I want to take my clothes off right now. Wade in, duck under that silky water, and listen to the pounding from underneath the surface. I shouldn't. The river's moving too fast. It would be dangerous. But mayhap just my feet . . .

I bend and unlace the moccasin on my bad foot. I set it on the rocks and do the second. My heart thumps loud as I shuck out of my leggings, untie my *ceinture*. I'm about to pull my tunic over my head when movement flashes in the corner of my eye.

I freeze.

I'm not alone.

Kane stands on the rocks downshore. Barefoot. Barechested. He has a kerchief in his hands that drips water. There's a stick of something in the corner of his mouth— wild mint, judging by the way he sucks it. His mouth stops when he sees me.

That ice in my chest returns. For months, I wanted to be out here in these woods with him—only him. But now . . .

He holds my gaze, his eyes unsure.

That moment in the woods yesterday floods in: that moment he turned away from me. Uncertainty was all over his body in that moment—the way he stood, the set of his mouth.

My anger returns. Why can't he be sure about this?

About me? I kneel on the rocky shore and cup my hands. The water is an icy shock. I scrub it over my face and drink it down, washing out the night, and sit back on my heels to look at the swirling river. There's an eddy close to the waterfall where the water is more calm. The rest of the river rages past, widening and churning as it dashes itself on protruding rocks.

Kane ventures closer. He takes the stick from his mouth and tosses it at the river. "Morning," he calls, his voice near swallowed by the roar of the water.

"Morning," I mutter, staring out at the waterfall.

"It's amazing," he says, nodding at the falls. I stay silent. Part of me wants to tell him how much it means to me to see it, another part feels like he doesn't get to know.

Kane comes closer still, and now I can hear him plain. "Em . . ." Out of the corner of my eye I can see his hands fiddling with the bandana, wringing it out over and over. "I'm sorry. About yesterday."

"It's fine." I stand and fix my gaze on the mist drifting off the water. "Matisa chose to stay." But my voice catches. I lean into my foot.

"It's not fine," he says. "It was—well, everything was tense already with the Jamesons showing up. And then Nishwa getting hurt like that . . ."

I wait.

He stops wringing the kerchief. "It's different out here, Em."

"It is," I say, my voice still hard. "It is different."

He waits, but I offer nothing more. He sighs. "I know it seemed like I was changing my mind yesterday, but all I was hoping was that you wouldn't ask me to leave my ma and the boys right then. Was hoping there was some way we could sort it out . . ."

"I was *trying* to find a solution."

"I know." He sighs. "I just . . . everything was so upside down."

At this, tears spring to my eyes. I blink them back, my voice tight. "Can't ask you to do something you don't want to do."

"What I want is to be with you." His voice is soft, near a whisper, and it sends my blood galloping around inside me.

I step my good foot into the silky water. Mist coats my bare legs.

"I'm sorry," he says again. "I know how much it means to you, to be out here. I'm sorry it hasn't been . . . better."

And now, *now* I look at him.

He stands in surrender. One hand holds the kerchief at his side and the other is raised—like he wants to reach for me but isn't sure he should. His dark eyes searching my face are anxious and hopeful at once. That ice in my chest melts.

"It's all right," I say. "I'm sorry, too."

He smiles, that funny half smile that makes my heart beat triple time, and for a moment I'm lost in its warmth, in its promise of protection.

He breaks the spell by knitting his brows, feigning a frown, and tipping his head at my feet in the water. "Thought you couldn't swim." He folds his arms across his chest.

The motion draws my eyes, and suddenly the fact he's shirtless comes over me full force. "C-c-can't," I stammer. "Was going to . . . to wade. In that still pool."

He looks over his shoulder, to where the river gets frenzied. His forearms crisscross his chest, his torso is all tight lines and ripples and *Oh for the Grace* . . . I drop my eyes, my heart thudding in my throat.

"Can't go in there if you can't swim. It's not safe." He's playing at being stern; his voice is husky.

There's a long pause. The falls roar. I steel myself, tell the cabbage moths flitting around my stomach to be still. "You said you could teach me."

"Did I?" He steps closer.

My breath gets short. "You did."

Why am I jittering like a June bug? I know him. I know him pressing me up against the walls inside the woodshed, kissing my mouth so hard it stopped my breath. I know his body against mine—it's burnt into my memory for good, but . . .

Right now, it's different. The dark woods and the crashing falls, my bare legs in the heavy air and him standing there with his crossed arms and dark eyes on my face.

It all feels a mite out of control.

I swallow. I can see he feels it, too.

He's nervous.

The underbrush rustles. I glance at the woods, expecting to see someone from the group, ruining the moment . . . No one appears. The noise goes silent.

Kane lets his arms fall to his sides and steps forward again. We're so close now I can feel the heat coming off his bare skin.

"It'll be cold."

"I know."

"Can't wear your tunic if you don't want to answer questions."

I know this, too. I can't show back up at camp with wet clothes that need drying. To answer him, I pull the leather strip from my plait, gather my hair in a knot on the top of my head, and rewrap the tie to keep it in place.

He reaches forward and brushes a stray hair from my cheek. "All right, then."

The water is cold; it sends little slivers of pain up my legs, through my core, into a spot in my neck, below my jaw, where it throbs. I gasp but keep wading, stepping careful on the small stones beneath the water.

"You in?" Kane is standing with his back to me. I felt foolish about asking, but he didn't raise an eyebrow—only nodded and turned around.

I hesitate when the water reaches the tops of my thighs. My bad foot is numb now, but the rest of me feels the ice shooting around in my blood. The next few steps are going to hurt; I've bathed in the river before. Best to get it over with quick. I tighten my arms across my breasts, take a breath, and plunge to my waist. A shriek escapes me. "Yes!"

He's shucked off his leggings; I can hear him splash into the water behind me. The skin on my bare back prickles as he wades near. And he's beside me. I keep my arms clamped firm and risk a glance. He's waist-deep—the murky water blurs him below the surface, and his chest is tensed in the cold.

"We have to stay in this pool—that current looks pretty strong." He nods at the water. "It's warmer if you get all the way in."

He reaches out. I let him take my elbow and guide me deeper. The pebble-caked riverbed becomes soft sand and drops so that the water laps below my collarbone. I shiver deep. The cabbage moths in my stomach have ice shards for wings. I'm frozen right through; he must be, too. And yet . . . I can feel heat coming off of him, searing into me.

He turns me to him. I let my arms drop away, feeling a new shock as the water hits all of me at once. I reach up and grasp the back of his neck. His hands find the small of my back, pulling me close and closer, his eyes locked on mine, his lips parted like he's barely breathing. He stops, his mouth hovering a whisper away.

He closes his eyes tight, as if pained, and dips his head, pressing his forehead into my neck, breathing deep. He grips my waist, and his voice is low, smoke and honey. "Almighty, Em." It's like a curse and a prayer at once.

His thumbs graze the hollows of my hips, setting me to trembling like the trees on the bank. His lips brush my neck and whisper up to my mouth.

He kisses me. Soft, nervous; like we've never kissed. Like the sweetest, freshest breath of air. A small sound escapes the back of my throat, and his fingers respond, tightening on my frozen skin. The kiss becomes sure, insistent.

Desire rushes through me, humming like a thousand bees, stealing my thoughts. I press into him, feel his heart beating hard and fast. The falls crash behind us, and all I can feel is him, his hot breath, his soft skin—

Rebecca and that unborn baby surface in my mind, slamming sense into me.

I grab his forearms and pull back.

His dark eyes are fire as he sucks in a deep breath, searching my face. My tongue grazes my bottom lip, tasting him there . . . But I force a small shake of my head.

"We shouldn't—"

"I know," he says.

My heart is beating out triple time. He pulls away from me, lacing his hands behind his neck as if they're safest there. The curve of his chest heaves with another breath, and I have to look away. The sun is up higher now, and the mist is near burnt off the river.

When I look back, his brow is furrowed. "What is it?" I ask.

"Just wondering if you've got it yet," he says.

"Got what?"

He frowns, like I should know what. "Swimming."

A laugh bursts from me. "Think I'll need to practice a bit."

He smiles—that smile that lights everything, warms everything—and grabs me up in his arms, swinging me about in a wide arc, my bare skin cutting through the silk water like a scythe through soft wheat. When he sets me down, we're twined together, his arms tight around my back. I am a thousand years away from uncertainty and fear. And this is enough.

The falls roar.

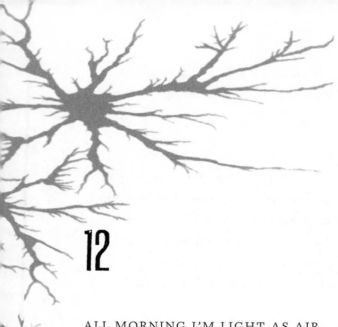

12

ALL MORNING I'M LIGHT AS AIR.

Isi's scowl doesn't needle at me like it usually does. He rides far ahead, our only rifle clutched in his hand. I walk beside Matisa, resisting the urge to look on Kane too long, knowing my cheeks will bloom a telltale red. Matisa says nothing, but her small smile is knowing. I avoid Sister Violet altogether.

Still don't have that tincture, but I don't notice my foot. I'm back at the river with Kane, ice and fire shooting through my body, sweet air filling my lungs. Waterfall roaring in my mind, his skin burning into mine, arms wrapped so tight around me it felt like we were one.

Even with everything else upside down, that moment felt like an answer to what I've been wondering. It felt like the start of our new life. Out here.

I smile, content.

When we stop to let the horses drink in the afternoon, Matisa says we're still at least a day away from the crossing.

Most of us aren't used to walking so much in a day, and we're dragging.

I fight a niggle of impatience, telling myself not to be like Isi. Deep down, though, I can't wait to be free of Charlie and his kin. Rebecca is getting some color in her cheeks but seems more labored with that unborn child by the hour. She and Josiah ride Isi's horse; Kane's brothers now ride Dottie, the rest of us walk, painful slow.

Getting rid of Charlie means we'll also be leaving Violet and the boys, but the thought doesn't put me in a panic like before. The moment at the waterfall felt like it sealed something between Kane and me, something he won't break for anything. Nishwa will get home safe and Sister Violet will head east and Kane and I will go to Matisa's people. Together.

The earth swells upward, emptying us from the rocky forest onto a sweeping grassy plain that skirts the river. In the distance, a line of trees promises the start of a new forest—and shelter. But here, the wind bites at us with no hills or trees to break its howl. We press forward until the forest is far behind—a blur on the north horizon. By late afternoon, we still haven't reached the forest to the south. These plains won't do for setting up camp, and it's clear by the frustrated look on Matisa's face that she thought we'd be well back into the forest by this time.

The sun is disappearing, splashing orange and red through the clouds on the horizon, when Matisa points to some coulees in the distance. It's the closest thing to shelter we can reach.

As we get close, Isi stops us. There's a flare on the horizon, below the first level of hills. We file in next to him,

Dottie nickering soft beneath Kane's little brothers. Daniel reaches out a hand to pat her neck.

"She's nervous," he tells me, pleased he can tell.

I frown. Don't like the idea of Dottie being nervous.

Andre passes his shotgun and pouch to Isi and swings his pack from his back. He digs through it and finds his spyglass.

"What is it?" asks Sister Violet.

Andre gazes through the spyglass. *"Je ne sais pas,"* he says, shaking his head and handing it to Kane for a look.

Kane squints through the scope. "A campfire, mayhap. We're too far to see for sure." His eyes catch mine, and I forget my worry over Dottie for an instant. The wind picks up, whipping my hair into my face.

"We need to get to the bottom of these hills," Matisa says. We press forward.

The land swells and the sun becomes a soft haze on the horizon as we wind our way toward shelter. When we get to the bottom of the first small hill, Isi holds up a hand for us to stop again.

"The big coulees are next, but we're almost on top of whatever was making that flare," he says.

"You sure?" Kane asks.

"It was right over this next ridge."

"Better to see what it is now than chance camping next to it in the dark," Sister Violet says, "and it finding us."

"Dark already," Andre mutters.

"Should we send a lookout?" Kane asks.

Nobody knows what the best thing to do is anymore. I

feel a hand slip into mine and look down. Daniel has left Dottie's back.

"I think it's best to stick together," Matisa says.

We go.

Soon, we can smell burning, but it's a strange smoke. Woodsmoke, sure, but also something underneath the good, familiar smell of charred timber—something acrid and sweet. And a sound . . . high-pitched, not human. Like a lamb bleating.

I look at Matisa. Her nostrils flare, and her eyes widen enough for me to know she's nervous.

"Stay close, Daniel," I say, squeezing his hand.

We traverse the side of the steep-walled coulee and climb up the bank. Nestled before a small grove of trees is a homestead.

Ablaze.

"What on earth?" Sister Violet says.

We get closer, moving slow along the flats toward the cabin. Huge tongues of red and orange lap the sides of the shack, devour the roof. The horses stop in their tracks, nickering. I pace ahead, my mind trying to make sense of the scene. Giant flames gut the shack and cast long shadows along the darkening banks.

I can't look away from the door.

Nailed to it, two limbs extended frame to frame, is a charred figure, near unrecognizable but for the bright whites of his teeth against the orange flame. A man.

Blackened body, mouth open in a mask of terror.

The air roars, but there's a dead calm to it all. Like an

invisible curtain has been thrown over the scene, thickening the air, slowing time. It's not the man screaming. It's coming from somewhere else . . .

Andre steps forward. My eyes snap away to see him shuffle ahead in a daze, staring up at the orange glow.

"Stay back!" Isi barks, but Andre's walking like he hasn't heard.

I dream of a cabin. On a river . . .

"Horse!" Daniel's voice pierces the air.

My eyes shift from the door. There's a horse trapped in a paddock to the side of the cabin. It rears and tosses its head, its high-pitched scream cutting over the roar of the flame.

Kane shouts something. It all sounds so far away.

Daniel drops my hand and darts forward. That's a bad idea—I want to tell him so, but my mind is working slow. The heat on my face, those two shadows, big and small, framed by the orange glare.

Sister Violet stumbles forward to retrieve Daniel. She holds out her hand, grasping for Daniel's little one. She's near caught hold—

The world splits apart.

A hailstorm of loud bangs bursts over the roar of the fire, echoing around in my sluggish brain.

Gunshots.

"Get down!" Kane's voice.

And in that moment Andre is ripped to shreds.

A dozen bullets pepper his chest, a dozen more his face and hands. He jerks backward in a spray of blood and flesh. It's loud, so loud, and his body is like an ash tree dancing on the wind. He pitches to the earth.

Fire in my head. Like the flames are eating up my mind—

Matisa's scream comes from behind, snapping me to. Daniel is staring back at me with wide, terrified eyes. I scramble forward, shoving past Sister Violet, and dive on top of him.

He hits the ground hard as I fall, as I try to cover his little body with my own.

More screams. More gunfire coming from Almighty knows where—how can there be so many bullets at once? There must be dozens—no, *hundreds*—of shooters in the woods. I clap my hands to my ears and look up.

Sister Violet stands stuck in place, her mouth open in a silent scream. A pool of crimson is spreading beneath her breasts, down her tunic to her *ceinture*. More bullets tear through her, tossing her this way and that, riddling her, spinning her to one side.

She drops to her knees and turns a nightmare face toward me: one side the perfect remains of Kane's ma—lined corner of her mouth and dark eye wide open in disbelief—the other side blown clean off, a bloody pulp with glistening cheekbone shining through.

I can't breathe.

She topples to the ground.

And now: riders. Men on horseback appear from the woods to the right, screaming across the homestead flats toward us like the deathwinds of *La Prise*.

I throw my arms over Daniel's head, pressing my body hard onto his. More gunfire. Something tears through the pack on my back. I look under my arm for the others. Kane's trying to grab for Dottie, who's shying and dancing with Nico on her back. He's hollering and grasping at her. Isi's horse whinnies and rears, dumping Josiah from behind Rebecca. Isi stands, fumbling with the rifle and pouch. He loads it, raises it, and fires—fast, so fast—but it's clear he'll get off one shot to every one of their hundred—

"Run!" I scream as Isi lowers the rifle to cock it again. He drops it in disgust and grabs for his slingshot.

The riders stream from the woods, heading for our horses. One rider breaks from the pack, turning his horse toward Daniel and me.

He's got something in his hand—a rifle? A knife? He's barreling toward us fast. Kane hollers my name from far away. I scramble to my knees and pull at Daniel.

"Get up!" But he's curled into a ball, hands clapped to his ears. He shakes his head. "Daniel!" Hoofbeats coming fast for us, can't be more than ten strides away. We've got no chance—

The rider lets out a yell and doubles over, his horse skittering to a stop. He pulls his beast in an about-face, and I see a knife handle sticking out of his buckskin shirt, a pool of blood spreading fast. He heads for the woods.

The rest have disappeared behind a jumble of horses and riders.

Kane emerges from the chaos and sprints toward us. A rider notices and wheels his horse, breaking away from the throng. Wielding a rifle like a club, the man closes in on Kane, black hair streaming out behind him. I try to warn Kane, but my scream is drowned out by gunshots. Kane trips and stumbles to the side as the rider swings. The blow catches his shoulder, knocking him forward.

The rider doesn't slow. I drop on top of Daniel once more, waiting for the horse's hooves to crush us. I hear a shout.

The rider topples from his horse, hitting the earth hard and rolling faceup next to me. His long dark hair falls away from glassy eyes. Eyes like Matisa's. He's First Peoples.

The shout comes again. "Em!" Isi is towering above me, extending his hand. In his other hand his arm goes round in a smooth circle with his slingshot. He takes his eyes off me for a moment to aim and let another rock loose. A rider barreling toward us drops from his horse. The beast rushes past, mouth frothing, eyes rolling.

Isi grabs my hand, and I scramble up, holding on to Daniel, and now we are running, running as fast as our legs can take us toward the blazing homestead. I turn my head from the heat as Isi pulls us along.

Can't find Kane. The attackers swarm our group. A rider emerges from the bunch, something that writhes wedged under his arm. He puts heels to his horse and heads for the trees. Something drops from his bundle as he goes.

And then I see something that makes my heart stop.

Two horses emerge from the chaos. Rebecca on Isi's horse, Charlie on Dottie, Matisa's unmoving body slung across in front of him.

Is she—?

Heat sears into me, and when I whip my head forward again, we're so close to the burning shack I'm sure it'll singe straight through us.

Isi pulls me hard off to the left.

We plunge down the riverbank, and I pitch forward, losing hold of Daniel and slamming my chin into the back of Isi's head. The skin splits, and a hot stream of blood streaks down my throat as we splash into the river shallows. I reach back and grab for Daniel's hand. The river bites cold, and my breath is caught, feels like I'm choking. My mind's going to splinter.

We're leaving them all back there. To die.

I want to shout at Isi to circle back, but I can't get words out. He pulls us forward through the rocky shallows and back up onto shore, where the bank is steep. He gestures at the muddy wall of dirt. "We need to get into those trees."

I'm frozen, looking back toward the glow of the fire and the sound of gunshots.

"If they saw us leave, we are dead down here!" Isi shouts, shaking my shoulder.

But the shouts, the ripped flesh—Matisa, Kane.

Isi shoves me aside, takes Daniel by the arm, and thrusts him ahead, lifting him up until Daniel finds purchase on the shrubs at the top. He pushes at my back, and I watch my hands and legs move of their own accord, scrabbling up the bank, grabbing tufts of grass.

"Quickly!" Isi yells once we get to the top, pushing me again.

I lurch forward, Daniel's hand again in mine, tearing through the brush and into the dark trees.

Gunfire again, coming from somewhere in the woods. I grab Daniel to my side, and Isi hits me from behind, throwing us to the ground. My split chin seeps blood onto the back of Daniel's neck as we wait, facedown. I breathe in dirt and leaves. Isi's arm is heavy across my back, Daniel's form so tiny beneath me.

The gunfire is louder, closer.

A rush of hoofbeats clamors through the trees. I hold Daniel tight as riders stream through the woods, whirling past.

We wait until it's quiet.

Isi pulls his body off mine and hops up. He dusts off his hands and scans the dark woods.

Daniel cowers under me. I try to slow my heart. "Isi," I hiss.

He shakes his head and holds up a hand to quiet me. The forest creaks around us.

And now: someone moving quick through the brush, pushing through. Coming straight for us. Isi crouches again.

As the sound gets louder, I can make out a horse and rider in the dusk. The beast nickers. Isi's horse. And . . . Charlie?

I take in air to call out, but Isi snaps his head my way, flinging out a hand again. His motion stills my tongue. I clap a hand over Daniel's mouth, too. It's like smothering a doll; he's limp with shock.

The beast gets close, and I see I'm right: it's Charlie, with Matisa before him. Isi waits until they are on top of us and then jumps up, lunging for Matisa. His horse shies and dances out of reach, and Charlie swings the rifle in his hand in a wide arc, near catching Isi in the face. A scream is stuck in my throat. Isi dodges the blow and reaches for Matisa again, but Charlie puts his heels to the beast's flanks, and the horse leaps ahead into the brush.

I don't see Rebecca until she's right on top of Isi. She rides like she's been doing it all her life. She barrels up behind Isi, swinging a knife. Isi hollers as the knife connects and tears along his back. He crumples forward, and as Rebecca spurs her horse past, she places a solid kick to his forehead. His head snaps back, and he falls like a stone.

I scramble to my feet, find my voice. "Charlie!" I scream. "Rebecca!"

But they're both long gone. Branches snap, and hoofbeats pound the forest floor as they disappear.

A sickly silence coats the woods.

And we're alone.

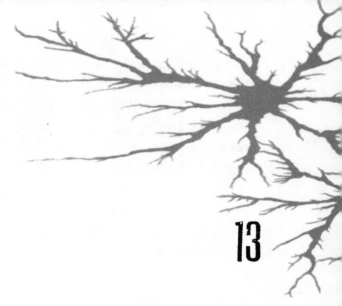

13

I GAPE INTO THE DARK OF THE FOREST, HEART pounding, a wildfire of confusion and fear raging through me. Charlie took Matisa. Why did he take her? Was he trying to get away from those riders, the gunshots?

Andre ripped apart, Sister Violet's pulpy half face; it all swims in my vision. I double over and dry-heave. Going to lose everything in my stomach. The forest floor surges up, and I grasp for the tree before me, trying to stay upright. My head spins. Gunfire, screaming, Kane running toward us with his knife . . . Almighty, what happened back there—

I hear a small cry.

Daniel. He cowers in the brush, staring at me with wide eyes.

Get hold of yourself. Don't let him see you like this.

I take a deep breath. Another one. I put my hands to my face. My chin is matted with leaves and blood. Right. I cracked my chin on Isi's head—

Isi.

I find him facedown in the brush, unmoving. My gut churns. I want to turn and run, but I force myself toward him, knowing Daniel's watching it all.

Keep your head.

I kneel beside Isi. The pack on his back has a large tear on its surface.

I turn his head to the side and clap my hands beside his ears. He doesn't move. I pull at the pack, easing it off his arms, gentle as I can. My fingers come away sticky. Can't see for anything in the dark. The gunfire starts again in my head, the screaming . . .

Just focus on what's in front of you.

I rummage in the pack and find his lantern, grateful Matisa showed me how to use these things. The woods are quiet; no sound, no sign of anyone around, so I risk lighting it.

"Daniel," I call, soft. Force my voice steady. "Come here? I need your help."

He appears in the glow, his face ghost-white and eyes wide as saucers. Did he see his ma—? I push the thought away and force a reassuring smile, handing him the lantern. "Hold it high," I say cheerful, like I'm about to fix dinner.

He extends his arm, and the light reveals Isi's lifeless body. There's a rip in his shirt soaked with dark blood from his shoulder blade to his waist. I put my ear to his back.

Relief floods me as I hear the soft thud of his heartbeat. The pack probably saved him.

I pull his shirt up as high as I can and find a bloody gouge the length of my hand down his back. The cut doesn't look too deep. I strip off my *ceinture fléchée*, wad it up, and press it into his wound as hard as I dare. I focus on my hands, on my task. Can't let my thoughts drift back to what happened at the homestead.

Isi's breath stays shallow, but by and by the bleeding slows. He'll need something to keep the wound closed when he wakes.

If he wakes.

He'll wake.

"Em," Daniel says. He's a specter in the shadows. The lamp lights his face, pale and scared. "My arm is sore."

"Course," I say. "Just set it on the ground over there."

He puts the lantern at his feet. The light casts shadows under his eyes. He crouches near me, silent.

Isi coughs and starts to move.

"Easy!" I say, relief washing over me. "You've got a bad cut."

He tries to raise himself on his hands but drops his head again.

"Hurts," he says.

"I know. Just sit tight a bit."

In my dream, there is a bloody footprint staining the earth. I turn my head, look away from it, and find the wooden walls of the fortification looming tall above me, dwarfing me in shadow. The river dead sing out to me.

My heart beats fast. I can't go back there.

I look back down. The toe of the footprint begins to bleed a small river. This time I let my eyes follow it. It trickles out, staining the earth, getting denser and faster, until it is a tiny brook. Impossibly, it flows up the grassy hills in front of me to a grove of tall trees. Bright green leaves shimmer in the sun, but clumps of white snow are gathered in the branches. The river of blood burbles past, rushing to get to the trees, disappearing into the strange grove.

And deep inside those snow-dusted trees—I can feel it—someone waits for me.

The forest is washed in pale light. I sit up quick, alarmed I drifted off. I meant to guard over Isi and Daniel all night.

I look around. Daniel is still asleep on the forest floor, wrapped in my cloak.

On the other side of me, Isi is stirring. We're all damp with dew from the underbrush. I turn to Isi and put a hand on his arm to let him know it's all right.

He lifts his head and groans, trying to push himself upright.

"Go slow," I say.

"My head—" he mutters.

"You took a kick on your forehead," I say. "And you have a bad gash on your back—don't move too much."

He ignores my advice and sits, wincing as he touches my *ceinture* through his shirt.

"I stopped the bleeding, but moving around will get it going again."

Isi continues like he doesn't hear me. He gets to his knees and searches around in the brush. When he finds his torn backpack, he flips it open and starts to dig through it.

"Isi," I say.

He turns to me, a small metal box in his hand. "Can you sew it?"

First I think he means the backpack. But he touches my

ceinture again. I swallow. I'm terrible at mending clothes; never had to sew a wound. I notice the reluctance on his face. He doesn't *want* to ask for my help; he has no choice.

"You'll have to take your shirt off," I say. I look over at Daniel, relieved he hasn't stirred. Don't need him seeing this.

Isi strips his shirt over his head with a groan.

A shiver cuts through me.

He turns. The *ceinture* is stuck to his flesh with matted blood. I tug gentle, coaxing it off the wound, and hear him take a sharp breath. The gash isn't wide, but the blood starts flowing again. I'll have to do it fast.

I scrub my hands on my tunic best I can. I take the thickest thread in the kit and try to thread the needle. It takes me four tries.

"It'll hurt," I caution.

"I know," Isi says. He leans forward and grasps the fallen tree in front of him with both hands. "Do it."

The mend job is ugly. Couldn't stop my hands from shaking, so I've puckered the skin in some places and pulled it other places. A jagged line of coarse black stitches stretches from under Isi's shoulder blade to his waist. But the blood flow has stopped, and it'll have to do.

I help him into a fresh shirt and watch him repack his supplies in his torn pack.

"Thank you," I say. "For what you did for Daniel and me."

He keeps packing.

"I—I didn't know what to do back there. I was so scared."

He stops.

"Thank you," I say again.

His voice is bitter. "I should've stayed with Matisa."

I swallow and look around the quiet forest. "Think it's safe to go back?"

Isi looks at me strange. He hops up and slings his pack to his good side.

I push to my feet.

"Isi?"

"Do what you want," he says. "I'm going after Matisa." He turns and starts off into the brush, leaving me staring after him.

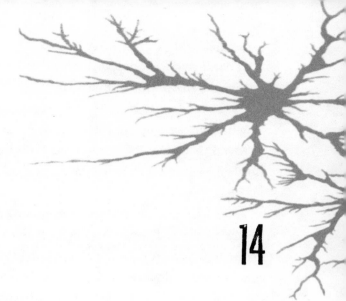

14

"ISI!"

He doesn't stop.

"Isi!" I sprint after him and catch his arm.

He spins, pulling it away. And the look on his face—

My blood freezes. Seen him angry before, but not like this. Looks as if he'll strike me. His eyes are dark, his whole body pulses with fury. And something else: fear.

I step back, my legs shaking and unsteady. "Please don't leave," I say, my voice too high.

"I am going after Matisa," he says again, his voice low and dangerous.

"I know, but . . . what about"—I swallow—"us?"

"Matisa and I are going back to our people. You should do the same."

"But what if there's no one left back there?"

"That is not my concern."

"But—"

"I don't care what happens to you!"

I inhale, sharp. He can't mean it.

"You have done nothing but bring us danger," he spits out. "We need to leave before you bring us death."

My air is closing off. I put a hand on the nearest tree to steady myself. "I—I know you're angry. But we need to stick together," I say.

He scoffs. "Like we stuck together with Charlie?"

My insides roil. Rebecca swinging the knife, Charlie near taking Isi's face off with the rifle. Mayhap they were scared, couldn't see well in the dark. Mayhap Charlie fled the chaos. Could be he had to escape and saw his chance to take the horses. Still . . .

"I'm sorry. I don't know what happened . . ." I cover my face with my hands and scrub at my eyes, determined not to cry. "I'm sorry," I say again.

"Sorry does Matisa no good."

I shove down the panic mounting in my chest. He hates me, I know that. But I can't let him go.

"I know you need to go after Matisa," I say. "Of course you—we—do. But—come back with me to the homestead first? Don't know what's back there—" I stop myself as Andre's and Sister Violet's shredded bodies surface in my mind. Can't think about Kane being among them.

He shakes his head. "Me coming along will not change what you find there."

"But if there's no one, Daniel and I won't survive out here alone."

"That is not my concern," he says again.

Shock surges through me. "Why did you bother saving us?"

He looks away.

"Why *didn't* you stay with Matisa? If you're willing to let us die now?"

"Em?"

I spin. Daniel is awake, and he's fighting with the cloak, trying to stand. He pushes mussed hair from his eyes, and as he focuses on me and Isi, his face breaks with relief. "Isi!" he says.

I look back. The darkness has left Isi's face; in its place is uncertainty.

"You're all right!" Daniel says.

Isi's face loses its hard edge fully. And now I see. He wasn't saving me; he was saving Daniel. Course he was. A strange, hurt flush rises up, but I push it away. Doesn't matter why he saved me; him not leaving us is all that matters.

Daniel kicks free of the cloak, and I hold out my hand for him to come to us. I put on a bright smile. "Isi's all right, Daniel! You did such a good job of holding that lantern last night." I glance at Isi. He looks trapped. And I see my advantage.

"Knew you'd be all right," Daniel says, pleased. His little face is still grimy—tears have dried in large streaks—but it's clear he's so relieved, he's forgetting his fear. He stops and looks at us. "Where are you going?"

I put my arm around Daniel's little shoulders and draw him close. I hate myself, but I'm too desperate. "We're going to see where the others went."

Isi gives me a look that would tan the hide off a deer.

"Good," Daniel says. "I want my ma."

My insides roil. This is awful. This is so awful. "We'll go find her," I say. "All of us together."

Isi's face changes from anger to sick shock.

"All right," Daniel says, and holds out his other hand to Isi.

Isi takes Daniel's hand and bends his head toward mine. "You are death," he mutters.

My hands shake as we head back toward the homestead. The ball of ice in my chest is back, and it's weighing me down like a river rock. I stumble twice as we push through the brush, my heart beating double time when we come to the last row of trees and step out into the morning sun.

The flats are empty. Past the cabin are two unmoving bodies. Unrecognizable from here, but I know it's Frère Andre and Sister Violet—lying where they were gunned down. Our attackers have taken their fallen with them. That, or they weren't that wounded.

I stare past the charred remnants, elation and devastation warring in my heart. Kane's not here—his body's not here. That's good. But . . .

Kane's not here.

The cabin is smoldering in the pink morning sky, just chunks of blackened wood now. The wall with the door has crumbled and disappeared into the rubble, taking that horrid figure with it.

Wind whistles across the flats, stirring the branches of the woods to the west. Thanks be, it's also sending the smell of burnt timber and flesh away from us. I look over at Daniel.

"You stay here while we look around." I point to the riverbank. "See how many skips you can make." I gesture to the rocks. "I see a good one there."

"But where's my ma?" he asks.

"We're going to"—I can't find words—"figure that." I throw a desperate look at Isi. "You just stay here a mite."

Isi stares back, his eyes stony.

Daniel nods, reluctant, and heads for the bank.

Isi turns and paces away. I force myself to follow a few strides but stop, unable to get my feet going again. I should go over there, I should go to Andre, to Violet, but I can't seem to move. Isi walks ahead, staring hard at the trampled grass as he goes. Soon he's past the bodies and headed toward where I saw Kane last.

I watch as Isi kneels and turns something over. A third body—my heart stutters, my breath closes off.

But now I see it's small, with a dirty tunic and straw mess of hair.

"That J-J-Josiah?"

Isi straightens and nods. I breathe deep, washed with shame that I'm relieved. But thank Almighty it isn't—

Stop thinking about it.

Isi continues his careful look through the grasses, disappears around the rise of the coulee a moment, and suddenly he's striding back toward me. "Three of your group are dead. There are many tracks that lead off into the woods, some into the coulees."

Your group. "Tracks?"

"Horses and humans, all mixed together."

"You think Kane's all right?"

"If he were hurt or worse, we would find him here."

I want to believe him. Could have been enough time for Kane to get back into the coulees. But if that's true, wouldn't he come back here? I choke down the panic that rises in my throat.

"What is . . . this?"

"A newcomer homestead."

"How can you tell?"

"We have more sense than to build something like this out in the open, unprotected."

I look at the ruined cabin. He's right about it being unprotected. Whoever built this didn't figure they'd need the shelter of either the coulees or the woods. Which speaks of ignorance, or arrogance. Still, anyone could be arrogant if they thought they were alone out here.

"And the attackers?" I ask. *"Sokaw—"* I fumble with the word. *"Sokawstu?"*

Isi's eyes narrow. *"Sohkâtisiwak,"* he corrects me. "But how—" He answers his own question with a sigh. "Matisa."

"Should . . ." I swallow. "Should we head south?"

He turns away from me. "You are not coming."

"Isi, *please*. Daniel and I are as good as dead out here alone. We need to stay together."

"You will slow me down."

He's right. I'm not fast to begin with, and without that tincture, my foot is getting worse by the day. Won't be able to help carry Daniel like Kane could. Like he used to carry Daniel and Nico—

Nico.

I'd forgotten all about him. That moment of the attack

floods in. That rider was carrying something under his arm, something alive. Something dropped from his horse. I pace across the flats toward the woods, scouring the ground. When I see the little bow Tom crafted for Nico, snapped in two, a wave of nausea washes me. I pick it up, my hands trembling, and turn back to Isi. "They took him," I choke out. "Nico. Those people took him."

He snaps his head toward me.

I hold the bow out, and despair washes over me, so deep that my knees get weak. As I sink to the ground, my head spins, and I drop the bow so I can reach for the earth to steady myself. This wasn't supposed to happen. It was supposed to be different. I look up at Isi for—what? Reassurance? The very thought makes me want to laugh. I can feel it bubbling inside, mixing with a panic that is going to drown me. I gasp for air. I'm losing my senses . . .

Isi's eyes bore into mine a long moment. Then he throws his head back and shouts a word in his language at the sky—a word that sounds worse than any curse I know. He spins in an about-face, shrugging his pack off his back and throwing it to the ground so hard it must split the stitches of his wound. My thoughts stop dead as I watch him begin to pace before me.

I straighten up and stare at him. He's rattled, but something tells me it isn't just the news that Nico was taken. He's pacing, muttering as though he's having a talk with someone I can't see.

Finally he stops and glowers down at me. "Follow the seedpod," he mutters, "take the injured bird."

"What?"

"What can you remember?" he demands. "About when they took him?"

I shake my head to clear my fuzzy thoughts. I can picture the man on the horse, Nico beneath his arm. But why is he asking?

"They headed off that way." I point to the woods. "Two riders. One was bleeding bad from Kane's knife."

Isi's eyes scan the forest. "They will need to stop to close that wound," he says.

I stare at him.

"We could catch up." He gives me a hard look. "How is your foot?"

I shut my gaping maw. Moments ago he didn't care what happened to us; he was determined to go after Matisa. And now—

Doesn't matter. "It's good," I lie.

He nods, his mouth set in a grim line. "We'll go after him."

Relief and confusion wash me. And a flicker of hope springs up. We might find Kane in the forest, too. I throw a glance back to the tracks where Josiah lies. Kane could be around the next bend. Could be headed back this way right now—

"Em." Isi's voice jars my thoughts. "I'm going after Nico. If you head into those coulees, you will be on your own." I swallow and nod. He points to the sprawled bodies. "We need to take care of them quickly."

My heart races as my insides recoil. Part of me wants to flee and never look back. I know Isi wouldn't dream of it, though; last fall he spent hours burying all the bones of his people at the cabin we found, plus the skeletons from the Crossroads—who weren't even his people. I have a fleeting thought for the Cleansing Waters, where they cast my pa—

I shove it down deep.

"We will move them and cover them with whatever we can find," he says.

I look at Daniel, his small form tossing rocks into the river, shining in the morning sun, and that ice lump in my chest moves into my throat.

By the time we've finished, three mounds rest under the first line of trees and the back of my neck is sticky with sweat. Isi sheared off spruce boughs with his knife, and we laid them on top, covering the exposed skin with double layers. We couldn't spare the bedrolls from our packs, or my cloak, so we couldn't wrap the bodies like we would've for the Cleansing Waters.

After laying the branches, we hauled rocks from the riverbank and piled them on top, filling in the cracks with earth and leaves from the forest floor. Never buried anyone to send them to their peace before, so I just did as Isi told me. I worked fast, unthinking, like I was doing some menial task back at the settlement, stacking herb bundles in Storages and Kitchens or some such.

Daniel wandered along the bank, picking dandelions and rock daisies. Then he sat in the sun and waited until we were done. All the while, I kept one eye over my shoulder, hoping Kane would show. He'd know what to do, how to tell if Daniel is going to be all right. Daniel didn't cry when I told him we were burying his ma, just said he'd find her some flowers.

He doesn't understand. Course he doesn't. Death was common in the settlement, sure, but it wasn't talked about. Bodies were disposed of quick, and life went on.

I stare at the mounds of rocks, my stomach hollowing out. Bodies. Andre, Kane's ma, and a little boy who wasn't more than six. Bodies lying there, underneath all that dirt and rock. Useless. Gone. Never coming back.

Andre, who wanted to see the world. Andre, who helped me from the moment he met me, who shared my dreams. Sister Violet, who I didn't even want along on our journey, who I was going to be glad to be rid of. I picture Kane's dark eyes when he hears.

My heart pulses with pain. I sink to my knees, screwing my eyes shut.

"Em?" My eyes fly open, and I find Daniel approaching me slow, unsure. "Found this," he says. He holds out his hands. In one is a handful of limp wildflowers. In the other, Nico's bow.

I sit back on my heels, blinking back tears.

This is your purpose now. Nico. Daniel.

"Hey," I say. "Come on, we're going to get going." I dust off my hands and stand.

"Are we going to Kane and Nico?"

I force a smile. "Yes."

He points at the mounds. "Will—" He starts to ask but stops, looking at the things in his hands. "Will we come back for her?" he asks.

"No," I say. "She's staying here." I force my voice steady. "Your ma is resting now."

He studies me a minute. He nods. He walks past the

graves, scattering a few flowers at the foot of each mound. "Rest good." He looks up at me. "Should I leave this here?"

Nico's broken bow.

"Sure," I say. "We'll make him a new one." As he places it on his ma's grave, I swallow and look away to the river. The wind blows across the flats into the woods, whispering around us.

"We need to go," Isi calls from beneath the spruce trees. "Come." He extends his hand to Daniel, who hurries into the woods to take it.

I have to think my goodbye because I can't bring myself to say it.

Be at peace. I pick up my *ceinture* from where it's been drying in the sun, Isi's blood washed clean from it with river water, and tie it around my waist. I pick up my pack slow, lingering in front of Andre's grave.

I'm sorry you didn't get to see this world, Andre. I'm sorry it ended so quick.

I step into the woods after Isi, taking no care with my bad foot and feeling a backwards relief when it catches on some deadfall and sings with fire.

And as I embrace that pain I wonder if I'm lying to myself. Mayhap Andre got to see this world, all right.

Mayhap this is all it has to offer.

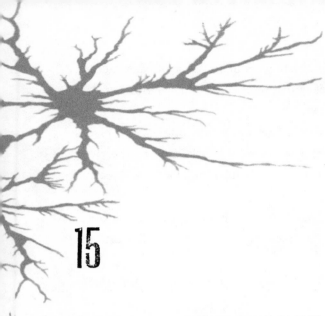

15

WE FOLLOW SOME TRAIL I CAN'T SEE DEEP INTO the woods for hours. In the afternoon we come to a little creek, chattering cheerful-like over a stony bed.

It winds off to the northwest, and Isi climbs into its ravine, beckoning for us to stay on the bank. He stands a moment, looking around. "They followed it." He climbs back into the trees, and we press forward.

As the day wears on, I can see by the frustrated set of his jaw that we are too slow. He carries Daniel on his good side now and again but often has to put him down to pull aside brush or deadfall or to scout ahead to make sure we're still following the creek when it winds. I try to carry Daniel but can only manage for a little while at a time.

It's slow going, and we're walking so close to the creek anyhow . . . "Shouldn't we just walk the creek bed?" I ask finally.

Isi shakes his head. "It's better up here."

I sigh and turn back to help Daniel over a fallen tree. Suppose being on the creek bed would mean walking more than we need to, with all its twists and turns.

When I turn back around, Isi has stopped and is peering at something in the creek.

"What is it?" I join him and follow his gaze.

There's a carcass at the edge of the water.

A deer, but not gleaming white like that skeleton I found days back. Patches of flesh and hair are stuck to the body like some sickly patchwork quilt, skull part-desiccated. Its tongue hangs from its mouth, swollen, caked with black blood. Looks as though it's bled out from somewhere, judging by the stain on the rocks around it, but I can't see a wound. A cloud of flies buzzes about, feasting on its glassy eyes.

I turn Daniel away and draw him behind me, putting my body between him and the sight. Isi hops down the bank and approaches it.

"What happened to it?" I ask.

Isi takes a stick from the forest floor and prods it, looking it over. The creek burbles cheerful behind him, out of place with the carcass. When he straightens, his face is grim. "It was sick."

"What with?"

He shrugs, but his eyes flick to the side. The Bleed. Has to be, but I can tell by his face Isi plans on keeping me in the dark. Is the sickness in this creek? How can I find out if he thinks so? "Should—should we move it out of the water?" I ask.

"Why?"

"Just . . . using water downstream from this seems awful."

"We won't be drinking this water," Isi says, answering my

question. We don't have Matisa's remedy now, so he doesn't want to take chances. He prods at the deer again. The swarm of flies rises and buzzes noisily, waiting to land.

"There are footsteps here," Isi says, pointing at the creek. I lean close. The footprint is solid—human. A boot. It rests beside the deer, and the imprint has filled with bloody water. The toe of the boot leaks slow into the river.

"Like in my dream," I think aloud.

Isi turns to me. "What dream?"

"I dreamt that I found one footprint, bleeding a river. It led to a grove of trees that had green leaves, and snow."

He looks to the sky like he hasn't heard. "It's getting late; we need to keep moving."

We break at sundown. I'm bone-tired, but I offer to set up camp while Isi goes to find something for us to eat. The food packs were on the horses; the pots and utensils, too. Isi doesn't seem too fussed about this, but I have no idea how to manage without our effects. He heads off into the woods with his slingshot and knife. Got no idea where that rifle ended up in the chaos, and I don't want to ask him about it—don't even want to think about the homestead.

I busy myself with doing the one thing I can: making a fire.

"Em?" Daniel says. I look up from the small bundle of twigs. "When will we see Kane and Nico?"

"Soon," I say.

"Good," he says. "They're probably wondering about me."

"Course," I say. "But they know you're with me and Isi. They know you're safe."

He nods. His brow crinkles. "Who were those people? At that big fire?"

I blow and fan, coaxing the flames. "Those men weren't like anybody we know. They were bad men."

"But what if we see them again? What if they find us again?" He's shifting from foot to foot now, looking around at the trees. He's working himself into a state—

I hop to my feet and take his hands in mine. "You don't need to worry about that. You're safe. Isi and I won't let anything happen to you."

He stares up at me, his dark eyes unsure.

I try to smile, but it occurs to me this might become pretty regular, him getting riled. I didn't have brothers or sisters, so I'm not used to soothing them. The only child I ever had underfoot was Edith, Tom's little sister. She liked songs. And I used to sing my ma's song when I was scared, when I was alone.

"Hey," I say. "Did your ma ever sing you songs? At night?"

He nods.

"Which was your favorite?"

"The rabbit song."

Got no idea what that is. "Sing a little bit for me now."

"Don't remember the words." His face crumples like he's going to cry.

"That's all right!" I say quick, squeezing his hands. "Just hum it."

He frowns, thinking. Finally he starts in a halting little melody. Full out of tune.

"That's so pretty," I say. "I bet you felt real good when your ma sung that song, all safe and snug in your bed?"

He nods.

"So here's what you do. Anytime you're feeling scared or nervous, you just close your eyes and hum that song. And even if you can't hear her, your ma will be humming it along with you from her resting place."

His eyes widen. "Truly?"

"Course. And then you'll know everything's going to be all right." I jostle his hands, tugging at him, playful. "Now come on." I point to the packs. "Let's see what we've got for eating tools."

As we look through the packs, I realize Daniel isn't the only one who'll need a song to hum. Been trying not to think about Kane all day, but now that we're stopped and dusk is falling, a panicky little fluttering is starting in my chest.

Where is he right now? Did he get away? Was he taken by those men? Is he still alive—

Stop it.

Kane is all right. I'd know if he weren't. I'd feel it.

Wouldn't I?

The partridge roasts slow over the campfire, letting off a mouthwatering smell. The dark woods are quiet, but Isi hasn't stopped making quick tours of the outskirts of our camp. He returns now and again to turn the meat.

"I can do that," I say. Daniel is huddled in my cloak in the crook of my arm.

Isi waves me off and pulls the spit away from the fire. "It is ready."

We tear into the flesh before it's cool, burning the tips of our fingers and roofs of our mouths. When we're done, the ache of hunger has dulled.

Isi stokes the fire high and Daniel falls asleep straight away. I pull off my *ceinture* and wad it up, tuck it under the side of his head.

Isi watches the flames.

"Thank you," I say. "For the partridge."

He shrugs. I look at the fire and study him from under my brow. He led at a determined pace today, stopping only when Daniel complained or I asked for a rest. It's clear he believes we're on the right trail. Somehow . . .

I poke at the fire, look over at Daniel, sleeping quiet beside me. Clear my throat. "How can you . . . track them?" I ask.

Isi raises his eyebrows. "There are many signs if you know where to look."

"What are they?"

He shrugs. "Broken branches, footprints. There was blood in places, from the one man's wound. They stopped to tend to it."

"Oh," I say. All I saw was that bloody footprint. *That footprint.* Isi ignored me when I talked about my dream earlier. Like it meant nothing. But I know different. Could feel someone waiting in those trees. "My dream . . ." I hesitate. "It was the strangest thing. Tall green trees—like in summer, but capped with snow."

Isi squints. It's slight, but it's a tell: I've spoken something significant.

"What?" I ask.

He shakes his head like he doesn't know, but he's not being truthful—I can see it.

"You know those trees?"

He shrugs. "Our purpose is Nico." His eyes shift. He's keeping something from me.

Off in the trees, a night bird calls.

All at once I'm uneasy. Isi's sudden change of heart, us following a trail I can't see, this snowy forest. None of it makes any sense. My skin prickles. "Why?"

Isi's gaze snaps up.

"Why are we coming after Nico? Why are you helping us?"

He studies me a moment. "You don't trust me," he says.

"It's not that."

He's giving me that look I hate—that hard look that makes me double-guess my own thoughts. Well, so what if I don't trust him now? Why should I? "You were ready to leave Daniel and me. You would've if he hadn't woken. And you were planning to leave us at that homestead and go after Matisa yourself."

"So?"

"So what changed?"

He looks away into the trees. "Matisa's dream," he says.

"Beg pardon?"

He's quiet so long I wonder if he's heard me. I'm about to ask again when he sighs deep. "She dreamt that I was following a tree seed—drifting on the breeze. In my hand I held a bird with a broken wing." He stares into the fire. "Follow the seedpod . . ."

Take the injured bird.

Matisa thought the injured bird was Nishwa. I look at my foot. *I'm* the injured bird. Least, Isi thinks I am. My cheeks flush. I'm not worried about how people see me anymore. Haven't been for months. So why's my face getting hot?

"Matisa was sure the seedpod was one of the little boys. She made me promise to follow that path if it were set before me." His eyes are unhappy. "When you told me the men took Nico, I saw it clearly."

I study him, sitting with his arms on his knees, his face grave. Seems like he's telling the truth. And if he is, his change of heart and constant prickly manner make sense. Besides, what reason could he have to drag me and Daniel out here?

Still, he's keeping things from me, too. He knows more about my dream than he's letting on. I want to press it, but there's no way to force him to tell me; Isi is not the sort. He's the sort who goes the opposite way you're hoping, just to show you he can.

"So here we are," I say. "Because of Matisa."

"She asked me," he says, like it explains everything.

Something in his voice makes my heart race, and I realize I'm wrong: Isi goes the opposite way when *certain* people press him. Matisa is another matter.

She asked me.

Desire tugs at me. What on earth? Can't be desire for *Isi*—that's addled. Desire for someone to feel the same about me—do whatever I ask? Kane hovers at the edges of my mind. I wanted him to be sure about me. I was so hurt when it seemed he was choosing his ma and the boys over me. I won't have to worry about him choosing his ma anymore.

The thought makes nausea rise in my throat, smothering the desire.

I push it all away and keep speaking to distract myself. "You don't *think* you're doing the right thing, though." I don't tell him that I understand. Doing the right thing isn't always clear; it doesn't always feel good.

He shrugs, but his eyes shift. I can see he feels guilt over the way he was with Matisa these last two days.

"You're so sure of everything else," I say. "So sure what happened with Charlie at that homestead."

Isi's face darkens. "Anyone could see what happened there. Charlie is exactly what I warned you he was," he says.

"But—"

"He has every reason to betray you. Kane killed his father. And you are the reason his family was sent out to starve."

I pause. "But we showed him mercy."

"That was why you helped him?"

"Y-y-yes."

Isi looks at me hard, that bleedin' look that asks me to think again about what I'm saying.

And now, of all foolish things, Brother Stockham's gray eyes surface in my mind. The scars on his bare shoulder, stretching across his back. I knew about his father's teachings branded there.

I swallow hard.

Stockham's pa showed him no mercy at all, and Brother Stockham ended up harboring that awful secret, and dying because of it. Charlie had to shoulder his own pa's transgressions when he was cast out of the settlement. But me showing him mercy could save him from repeating his pa's mistakes. Couldn't it?

I flush and close my eyes, trying to focus on the matter at

hand, but all that comes out of my mouth is "It's not what I thought, out here."

Silence.

I open my eyes and find Isi looking at me. He frowns and hops up. "I'll take first watch," he says, and stalks away into the woods.

I watch him go, knowing full well he won't wake me for "second watch." We aren't in this together; I am his burden to bear, and he's bearing it for Matisa. I settle behind Daniel and curl my body around him, shoving aside the hurt that rises in my chest. What matters is that Isi's sudden change of heart makes sense. He's helping us for Matisa. Doing what she asked. But—

Take the injured bird.

Why did she have that dream? Did she know what was ahead for us? Did she know that not five days into our journey, everything would go to hell? If that's true, why wouldn't she tell me? She would. Unless . . .

Unless she's keeping more than the remedy secret. Mayhap there are lots of other things she didn't tell me.

The frozen feeling in my chest throbs and the dull ache of my foot echoes into my hip. I pull up my head and look around at the dark trees. Used to find them so beautiful. Used to think they hid secrets I couldn't live without.

Now they hide enemies. The long branches are pressing on me, trapping me here, in this unfamiliar land. Bloodied carcasses, madmen appearing from nowhere, horrific weapons.

I wish with every part of me that Kane were here, but the thought of him starts an ache in my heart so painful—

I search for something, anything, that might ease me and find myself repeating the virtues ritual. *I am Honesty. I am Bravery. I am Discovery.* These things have had new meaning for me ever since last fall, but the chant itself feels familiar, comforting. *I am Honesty. I am Bravery—*

My thoughts stop there. I've never been Honesty. And telling myself Kane's all right . . .

Well, mayhap I'm lying to myself, like I lied to myself about Charlie. Mayhap instead I should be preparing myself for the worst: that we'll never find Kane again.

Least, not alive.

My breath leaves me in a rush.

Stop it.

Can't keep on like this, I'll go mad.

I take the image of Kane and wrap it in the threads of my mind and bury it deep, deep in my heart. He's safe there. I'll take him out again after we find Nico.

I feel Daniel's little chest rise soft. I send a prayer to the Almighty that he has a dreamless sleep.

Don't bother doing the same for myself.

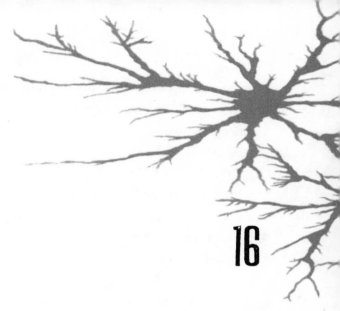

16

THE DREAMLANDS BEYOND THE GROVE ARE DRY
and dusty, the hills cracked with sun and age, rising tall
against the deep blue sky. Heat glimmers off them like river
waves. Inside the grove, where someone waits, the snow on
the trees glints brilliant in the sun. The river winds past,
stretching north and south.

Back on the Watch flats, the dead under the river sing
out. And through it all I hear my pa's voice, clamoring above
the rest.

Make peace with it.

Matisa is here beside me. She is as before: one half of her
living and whole, the other brittle bones. Her movement is
jerky as she bends and scoops up a handful of soil and plant.
It's the plant that protects against the Bleed, I know. But I
can't remember the name.

I lean forward, reaching for it, but she plucks it from
her palm with the brittle fingers of her fleshless hand and
crushes it into dust.

✝

As we pack up to leave in the morning, I decide to tell Isi the first part of my dream; the part about the grove, where someone waits.

He frowns as I speak but doesn't stop packing.

"It's important," I say.

I watch him put the pack on his back and adjust it, then head over to Daniel.

"Twice, now, it's felt like someone is waiting there," I say. "Just can't figure those snow trees." I pull my pack onto my back.

He picks Daniel up and heads off. I hurry to catch up.

"Isi?"

"Perhaps you should 'figure' longer," Isi says.

I scowl at his back and watch him as he walks, off balance a mite with the added weight of Daniel on one side but moving sure-footed, even so. It irritates me that even with stitches in his back and an extra burden, he's faster than me.

I follow him in silence but can't get the dream out of my head. That second part in particular, the one I didn't tell him about—it's eating at me.

"Do you think Charlie took Matisa back to the settlement?" I ask, like I'm changing the subject.

"Not if he values his life."

I think on this. What he says is true. Charlie was banished. Showing back up there would be foolish of him. No. It's not why Matisa is there in my dream.

Make peace with it.

Is my dream asking me to accept what I brought to the

people I love when I found Matisa? Life *and* death—exactly as she appears in the dream.

Except, that part about the remedy. What does that have to do with it?

I stare at Isi's dark head as he moves through the brush, quiet and sure.

Should I tell him about it?

I labor to draw alongside him. "It's just—I'm dreaming on the settlement, too," I venture.

"You are homesick," Isi responds, like he's amused and annoyed at once.

I frown. "What's 'homesick'?" I ask.

"You miss home. You are unhappy because you wish to return."

Irritation spikes through me. "That's not it."

He raises his eyebrows.

"It's *not*," I insist.

And it's true. It's not sadness I feel when I think on the settlement, when I think on my dreams. It's . . . like I've forgotten something there.

I've fallen behind Isi. I hurry to catch up.

"My dreams show me things," I say.

He shakes his head. "Things you don't understand."

"No. Things I haven't figured yet. Following my dreams is the reason I found Matisa in the fall."

He stops and turns to me. "That was luck," he says. "You know nothing. You think the green trees in your dreams hold *snow*."

"They do," I say.

He shakes his head. "You are dreaming of *mâyimitos*,"

153

he says, like he's explaining it to a dull-witted child. "Your 'snow trees' are just trees that have seeds that erupt in a soft fluff. It is a tree you do not know."

I stare at him, my face growing hot. I want to tell him he's wrong, but I don't rightly know that he is. Everything out here is new to me. "Well, they don't grow in the north," I mutter, but as I do, I realize something: me dreaming on trees I haven't seen, with someone there, waiting for me— it's like the dreams I had last fall, when Matisa and I dreamt of each other.

And that's something.

Isi shifts Daniel to his other side and paces off ahead. I hurry to catch him again, but my foot snags an exposed tree root and shoots pain. I suck my air so I don't cry out.

Isi doesn't slow. Course he doesn't.

I want to shout at him, but I take a few deep breaths instead to calm myself. Arguing won't do us any good. "These mah-yee trees," I say to his back, forgetting the exact word he used. "Where do they grow?"

He picks up his pace.

"Isi?" With effort, I draw alongside him.

He doesn't look at me. "Many places," he mutters.

"But in my dream, they're next to the big river."

He grunts. "There is a large grove along the river, just before the crossing."

"Mayhap we should head there. I mean, once we find Nico." *If* we find Nico. "Mayhap—"

He stops again and turns to me. "I am doing as Matisa asked. After, I will go back to the homestead and follow

Charlie's trail." He shifts Daniel again, his movement quick and angry, his jaw clenched. The movement makes him wince. He puts Daniel down. The stitches I put in are pulling, no doubt.

I gesture to his back. "I can help—"

"I don't need your help," he spits out.

"But I know—"

"You know nothing!"

"I know more than you think!" I shout back, my temper boiling over. I bite my tongue against the rest of the words, but Isi's eyes narrow.

"*What* do you know?" he asks.

I clench my jaw and look away.

"Em."

I turn my head. "I—I know that"—his dark look trips my tongue—"that deer back there died of the B-B-Bleed. I—" I draw my shoulders back, straighten up. "I know the Bleed is in this creek."

A flicker of disbelief lights his eyes.

Best to get it over with. "And I know about the remedy."

His mouth drops open.

"Matisa had to tell me," I say quick.

He finds his tongue. "She shared this?" he says, like he can't believe his own words.

"Only with me. She needed me to come and—"

"She betrayed our secret so *you* would come along?" Now he's angry.

"I didn't ask her to!" I snap.

"Why *else* would she do that?"

"Because she believes I can help!"

"You *can't!*" He spins away from me, his body pulsing with anger.

"Only because you're too bleedin' stubborn!" I glare at his back. Almighty! What am I doing out here with him? How are we ever going to find our way?

There's a long silence. The poplars creak around us.

"Can you tell me a story?" Daniel's voice cuts the quiet. He steps forward and tugs at Isi's leathers. "Isi?"

"I can't think of any right now," Isi answers, his voice sullen.

"You can tell me one you told before," Daniel offers.

Isi draws in a breath, like he's gathering patience. "We are trying to keep quiet as we move."

Daniel peers at him. "But you and Em were shouting at each other just now."

I flush as I realize how we're acting in front of this child. "We were just speaking on some things," I say.

Daniel looks between us.

"It's better to move quietly," Isi says.

"All right," Daniel says, nodding his head serious-like. "You can whisper it."

I press my lips together to hide a smile.

Isi sighs. Daniel's hit his weakness. Telling stories to the youngsters was the one time all winterkill he looked happy, not fit to bust through the walls of our quarters and hightail it back to his people.

Isi swings Daniel up into his arms again and brushes the boy's hair off of his forehead with one hand. "Fine," he says.

Daniel's eyes light up.

We resume our pace, but I can feel Isi's anger crackling over to me. I raise my chin and look up at the trees as we walk.

Isi begins: "When I was a boy and I was out wandering the forest one day, I found a small bird—a baby—that had fallen from its nest."

"Was it alive?"

"Yes, it was not damaged. It had perfect fuzzy wings, like this"—I steal a glance and see Isi raise his free hand; he spreads his fingers apart to show a small space—"and a tiny beak and soft fluff on the top of its head."

"Was it scared?" Daniel says.

Isi nods. "I was gentle, and I caught it and held it in my hands. But it was so small I could crush it with a quick fist."

Daniel lets out a small gasp of horrified delight.

"I wanted to help it," Isi continues. "I wanted to put it back where it belonged, so I spent all morning searching for its nest."

"Did you find it?" Daniel asks.

"I did. I climbed the tree, careful not to drop the little bird. But because I was using one hand so that I could take the baby bird up safely, I missed a handhold and was speared in the neck with a tree branch."

Daniel's eyes widen. "You got hurt?"

"The cut was deep, but not too deep."

"And then what?"

"And then I put the baby bird back in its nest and climbed down."

Daniel laughs with delight. "You saved it. You saved that bird."

Isi shakes his head. "That's what I thought, too," he says. "But when I got home, my *moshum*—my grandfather—told me that because I had held the baby in my hand, there was no way the mother bird would accept it."

My skin prickles.

"What do you mean?" Daniel cranes his neck to look Isi in the eyes. "Its ma didn't want it back?"

Isi nods. "It would've been better to leave the bird there, alone and scared, than put it someplace it didn't belong."

He looks over at me and holds my gaze.

I flush. Clear my throat. "You shouldn't carry Daniel," I say. "It worries the stitches."

"We are too slow with him walking," he says. He looks at my foot. "And we are too slow already."

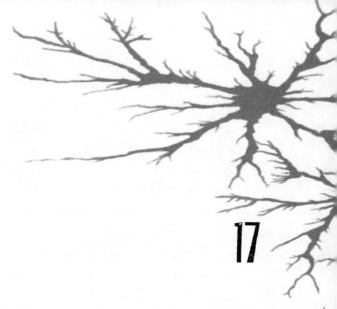

17

THE MAN AND WOMAN APPEAR FROM NOWHERE.

Daniel and I are sitting on a rock next to our packs, and they emerge from beneath the spruce boughs, silent and pale—like ghosts.

Isi moves lightning quick, leaping in front of Daniel and me, his hand flying to his knife. I jump to my feet.

The two start and pull up short, seeming as surprised as we are, but I see the woman's hand also dart to her side. A long knife is sheathed at her belt.

"Wait," the man says, grabbing the woman's arm. He holds up his hands to show us there's nothing in them. His right hand is bandaged with a brown cloth. "We mean you no harm," he says.

Isi doesn't move. His hand stays on the handle of his knife. "Turn around and walk away," he says, his voice low and deadly.

"You first," the woman states.

I stare at them. They're about the same height, and their

skin is pale—like the girls who worked indoors at the settlement. Their clothes are something like Henderson's were but seem a mite more battered and dirty—like they've been journeying without stopping for several days.

Or like they've just been in some sort of skirmish.

My breath gets short as I look them over. First Peoples attacked that homestead. Least, I think so. Don't remember a woman in the mix, but everything happened so fast.

I can tell by the way Isi's standing that he's not taking any chances. His hand hovers near his knife's handle.

The four of us measure one another in heavy silence.

A humming starts up, filling the space with random notes that make up no kind of tune.

What on earth—

"Hop. Hop. The bunny hop, hop, hopped."

Daniel. Almighty. He's either remembered the words to that bleedin' rabbit song or he's making them up.

"And it hopped on up a tree."

Making them up.

Isi shifts, ever so slight, and the man looks at Daniel, his brows knitted in confusion. The nonsense song continues, warbling high and all out of tune.

"Shhh," I hiss, throwing a glance over my shoulder. Daniel just closes his eyes and sings louder and less tuneful than before. I pull myself straighter and turn back to the man and woman, trying to look intimidating.

"Bunny, bunny, bunneeee, hop, hop, hop."

The woman's nostrils flare, and her lips quirk. She's trying not to laugh.

I can't take it anymore.

"Daniel!" I admonish, turning around and kneeling before him. "It's all right. Shhh! Look." I grab his hands. "See? We're just talking." I reach out and smack the back of Isi's leg.

He drops his hand from his knife. The woman drops her hand from her side, too. Daniel stops singing. He looks up at me. Peers around Isi at the man and woman.

"We mean you no harm," the man says again. "How about you go on your way and we'll go on ours?" These people aren't interested in us. Curious as I am about them, I'm happy for us to part without any sort of trouble.

Isi nods. He turns and picks Daniel up, swinging him onto his back. "Let's go," he says to me.

As I turn to follow, I notice the leather case dangling from the man's pack. It's long and cylindrical—like the one Henderson had in his effects.

I can't help it. "You mapmakers?" I ask them.

The man nods. "Unofficially."

I squint at him.

"We're not contracted," he explains. "We've been scouting this land on our own, drawing up maps to sell back east."

Now Isi turns around. "On foot?" His voice is hard and full of disbelief.

"We lost our horses," the woman says, but the man's eyes dart nervous-like.

Isi's eyes narrow. "How?"

They share a glance. Something isn't right here.

The woman clears her throat. "How about you tell us what you're doing out here?" she asks.

"I think not," Isi says. "Come, Em." He jerks his head and hoists Daniel farther up on his back, turning away.

"You're headed up this creek?" the woman asks, her eyes widening. "You know where this leads?" There's fear in her eyes. And all at once I realize she's not asking us for her sake. She's asking us for ours.

Isi turns around again.

"Do you?" I ask her.

"Yes." She looks at Daniel. "And it's no place for a little one."

I look at Isi. His eyes are scanning her face. I can tell we're wondering the same thing: does she know the men who took Nico?

Isi swings Daniel to the ground and crouches next to him. "Find as many fiddleheads as you can," he says, and I realize he's giving Daniel something to do so we can talk to these people. "But stay where you can see me."

Daniel nods. He eyes the woman and man and heads for the base of the nearest tree behind us.

The four of us look one another over again.

"Sit?" the woman finally says, gesturing to some fallen logs that crisscross one another.

I settle myself across from the strange pair. Isi does not sit; he stands beside me, his arms crossed over his chest. Up close, the woman looks about ten years older than me. I thought her hair was tied back, but now I see it's cut strange, just below her ears. The man has a scraggly, dark beard and deep-set eyes.

"I'm Em," I offer. "This is Isi."

"I'm Elizabeth Sharapay," the woman says, and it strikes me odd that she speaks first. "This is my husband, Ulysses." The man inclines his head.

Husband. I search my brain for the word and then realize by how familiar they sit beside each other it must mean life mate.

I clear my throat. "You said you lost your horses?"

Again the man's eyes dart, but the woman's face remains calm. "I will tell you about that," she says. "But first, can you tell me why you're heading up this creek?"

I feel Isi stiffen. He doesn't want me to say too much to these strangers, but I don't have a choice. The only way we'll get information is by offering some.

"We are going to get one of our own back," I say, careful. "He was taken by some men off this way."

"Just the . . . two of you?" she asks.

I sit up straighter. "Isi's tracked them this far."

Again, Elizabeth and Ulysses exchange a glance. Ulysses gestures at his pack, and Elizabeth nods. He fumbles with the cylindrical case, unlatching it and pulling out a parchment like the one Henderson had.

As he spreads it open for us to see, I notice the rough brown cloth is darker in the spot over his little finger—like it's seeping blood.

I take a deep breath and study the parchment. The map looks something like the one Henderson showed us—with the large river on the east side and the mountains on the west—but it's missing all of the symbols to the south. Ulysses points to a winding line running east and west that wasn't on Henderson's map. With a finger on his good hand, he traces to a series of *X*s. Next to those symbols, a bigger line winds, but it's incomplete. Another river?

"What is that?" I ask.

"That is where you're headed," Elizabeth says. "You're a few hours away yet." Her mouth twists in a grimace. "They call it Leon's Keep."

"Who is *they*?"

"The bastards who run it." She says it mild, but her voice contains a tremor. She clears her throat. "I'd advise you to steer clear of them. If they've taken one of your people, they aim to keep him."

"How do you know this?" I ask, though now I'm not sure I want the answer. That bandage on Ulysses's hand draws my eyes. "Did your . . . mapmaking take you there?"

She nods. "We were trying to map west to the mountains and came upon their camp two days ago. We didn't realize what kind of men they were until it was nearly too late."

I look to Isi. His eyes are measuring the truth of the woman's words.

"Lucky for us, they wanted a map drawn up." Her voice is bitter. She doesn't sound like they were lucky. "They let us go on the condition we'd return with it."

"A map of what?"

"This area to the north. They want to know if there are any new settlements up this way."

"Why?"

"They're carving out territory. Trapping the big predators that pose a threat." I think about Nishwa's leg in that giant steel jaw. "Running people off who settle on the land they want for themselves."

That homestead. Our attackers were men from this Keep she's talking about. My throat gets tight. My fortification is to the north.

"We . . . found a burnt homestead a few miles back," I say. "By the big river. I think the owner was among the . . . mess."

"They'd make an example out of anyone who refused," Ulysses says, and I see Elizabeth sit up straighter. An example. I look at his hand. The hair on the back of my neck rises.

I think back to the raid. Think about that man rolling faceup next to me.

"These men," I say. "Are they *osanaskisiwak*?"

Both of them squint at me like they don't know the term.

"First Peoples?"

"Ah." Elizabeth's face lights. "Yes, there were a few in the mix. But Leon and the rest are Cormorant."

Now it's my turn to look lost.

"From back east," she says. "Cormorant Bay?"

I'm still lost but decide they don't need to know that. "What do they want?" I ask instead.

"Claim to as much land as they can get before the Dominion arrives," Ulysses answers. "They're setting to make their own governance, starting with establishing their boundaries."

"Where are these boundaries?" I ask.

"Well, they're expanding," Ulysses says. "But so far"—he points at the map—"they seem to be laying claim to everything from this big river near the Keep they're building"—he indicates the larger line, the one I assumed was a river—"east to the Snake." He points at the river that was on Henderson's map—the one I assume winds past my settlement.

I frown. "The Snake?"

"We're calling it that because of the way it winds."

"And how far north and south?" I ask. The trap we ran

into was a day north of the crossing. It was the first sign we'd seen of anyone, save the Jamesons. Even so, that boundary is only four days' travel from the fortification. From Tom.

"That's harder to say. It seems they're more interested in expanding north than south— maybe because the land south of the river crossing is pretty inhospitable."

I look at the blank parts of his map and raise an eyebrow.

"Or so we hear," he says. "Haven't made it that far." He begins to roll the parchment.

I risk a glance at Isi. His face is all closed down. I make a decision. "We met a mapmaker days back," I offer.

"Oh?" Elizabeth's eyes get keen.

"Called himself Henderson," I say. "Said he was working for the Dominion."

Elizabeth and Ulysses look at each other.

"Do you know him?"

"We know of him," Elizabeth says. "We're his competition." Another word I'm not sure of. "He just doesn't know it yet."

"He talked about rogues, people like this Leon—people who like it out here because there is no law."

"No law *yet*," Elizabeth says. "Once the Dominion's law arrives it's going to get nasty."

My skin prickles. The thought of these men laying claim out here and the Dominion showing up, contesting it, sets my blood running hot. Is *this* the war Matisa was dreaming on?

I focus on what matters to us right now: "What could they want with a child?"

"Sorry?" She squints at me.

Right. She's asking me to come again. I look at Daniel and lower my voice. "Those men took his brother."

Elizabeth's face goes dark. "Probably plan to raise him as their own. They're populating any way they can." The heat in her voice, the hate in her eyes when she says this . . .

I force myself to ask what I've been wondering all along. "You said they let you go. What happened to your horses?"

Ulysses snaps the latch closed on his map case and moves closer to Elizabeth. He puts his arm around her shoulder, pulling her close with his good hand.

"Leon kept our horses as collateral. Took my necklace, too," she says. "It was a locket with"—she falters—"with a picture of our daughter in it." The way she says it tells me the drawing was all she had left of her child. She clears her throat. "Said he'd give it all back when we returned with the map. He wanted me as part of the bargain, but Uly wouldn't go without me." Ulysses squeezes her shoulder, protective-like.

"Why did they want you?"

"There are too many men there; not enough women," she says.

I frown for a moment, trying to figure her meaning. And then I see.

They're populating any way they can.

A sickness grabs my stomach, and I reach out a hand to Isi nearby, for balance or reassurance, I'm not sure which. I sense him stiffen and draw my hand back.

"How did you escape?" I ask.

"They wanted that map more than they wanted me." She puts her hand on Ulysses's injured one. "But they gave Uly a reminder to return."

I can't look at the seeping bandage. "And will you?" I ask.

"Of course not," she spits out. "They're getting nothing from us."

"But—"

"They'll have to hunt us down." Her eyes are full of fire. "All my life I've been dreaming of coming out west. Dreaming of seeing these wild lands for myself. Ulysses and I planned to make our fortune by mapping it. When we lost Charlotte, it was time to come west, to start fresh." She looks at him, and her face gets soft. "I've already found the place we should settle. Just south of that crossing. It's so beautiful—a little valley tucked away among the pines." Ulysses smiles at her, and they share a moment that makes my heart pang with longing.

When Elizabeth looks at me, the fury is back in her eyes. "If you think I'm going to help those rodents claim this land for themselves, you can think again."

I stare at her. Never known anyone like this woman. Sister Ann at the settlement was outspoken and opinionated; she ran her household. Soeur Manon also had her own mind—she lived on her own terms, and even Council left her to herself.

But this Elizabeth is different. She doesn't just have her own mind; she has a dream. She's determined to start a new life out here in the unknown, and she won't let the horror they've just lived through break her.

All at once I want these two to succeed. To survive, at least.

"The water out here," I blurt before I can stop myself. "It might be . . . unclean."

"Oh, we're boiling all the water we use," she waves her hand. "That's survival tip number one in my wilderness guide."

I can feel Isi's eyes boring into me, so I don't ask her what she's speaking on. I change the subject. "This Keep," I say. "Do they guard it at all times?"

"They're still building it," Ulysses says. "It'll be a huge fortification when they're done, with posts for sentries. But for now they've got a camp outside the walls. I'd say half a dozen men keep a lookout at night."

"And they have weapons." I state this; the disaster at the homestead proved it.

Elizabeth raises an eyebrow. "And then some. I'm guessing Leon took advantage of the black arms trade before he pressed west. They all carry Rosses, and I saw a fully automatic bipod. Wouldn't be surprised if they've got their hands on that poison gas."

I can't figure any of this but decide Isi probably can. Best to get information we don't have. "How many men in Leon's group?"

Ulysses scratches his beard. "A couple hundred? Though some of those aren't there by choice. Some are prisoners, being kept for labor."

"Prisoners from where?"

Ulysses shrugs. "Not sure where they came from—some tribe to the west, maybe?"

I look to Isi. A muscle works in his jaw.

"Did they have a red hawk symbol on their sleeves?"

Ulysses frowns. "Not that I noticed."

I think about Nishwa, heading southwest from where that trap was. He was heading direct into Leon's men.

"Em," Isi says, nudging me with his elbow. Daniel is back, his hands full of fiddleheads. Isi takes them from him and messes his hair, affectionate-like. But the look he gives me is grave and impatient.

"We should get on," I say, standing up.

"You never did say where you're from," Ulysses says. This pulls me up short.

"Yeah," Elizabeth says. "Where is your home?" She tilts her head. "Why are you out here?"

I open my mouth to respond. Close it. Don't know what to say. And with that realization, a panicked fluttering starts in my chest.

Isi's voice breaks my thoughts. "We are headed west once we find the boy." He says it like it explains everything.

Elizabeth studies his face. She shrugs. "Well, I suppose it's none of our business. I'm telling you to steer clear of that Keep, but I can see you'll do as you please." She stands. "Sorry we can't help you further, but we've got our maps to see to."

"Beth," Ulysses says, "they're just kids."

She levels him a look. "They're kids who've got along this far," she says. "And you know as well as I do, out here if you're not looking out for yourself, you're borrowing trouble."

They hoist their packs onto their backs.

"Thank you for warning us," I say.

"Hope you get your small one back," she says, and offers a quick smile. "Good luck."

Her smile, though, isn't one of hope. It's to hide the look in her eyes—the look that betrays what she truly thinks. She thinks we'll need more than luck; we'll need a bleedin' miracle.

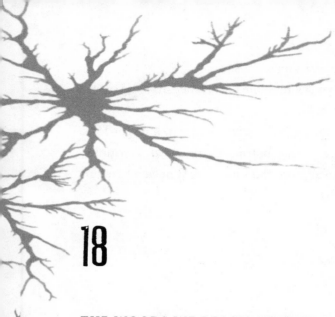

18

THE WOODS WE REACH AT DUSK HAVE BEEN RAV-
aged by fire; skeletal trees and bright purple fireweed remain
in the tall grasses.

It's eerie quiet. We press through as silent as we can,
Isi carrying Daniel and me trying hard not to hobble
on my bleedin' bad foot. Soon we can hear the rush of a
river—probably the headwaters of this little creek we've
been following—and the forest starts greening again. The
grasses are long, hiding the deadfall and making it tricky to
traverse.

Isi puts up a hand to stop us. As our noise quiets, I hear
something new: sawing, pounding. Like back at the settlement when we'd replace parts of the wall or build a new
shack.

We move forward cautious-like and soon can see the forest emptying out to a flat area near the rushing river.

My eyes widen. I'm staring at the fortification.

Except different: new. The walls aren't weathered posts;

they're gleaming flat boards, planed and standing tall. Sounds of construction come from within. There is a scattering of several large white tents outside the walls, and a dozen or so people mill about, too far away to see clear. A fire roars in the center of it all. Half a dozen horses are tethered to trees at the outskirts of camp, toward the river.

Isi touches my arm and tilts his head, telling me to retreat.

We take Daniel back several dozen strides and set him on the far side of a fallen log.

"Stay with him," he says. He begins to check his pack, taking stock of his knife and slingshot.

I ignore Isi and say to Daniel: "Wait here. Be silent as a field mouse."

He grasps at my arms. "What if it's scary?"

"Remember? You have the rabbit song."

"But I thought you told me to be quiet?"

Almighty. Couldn't I have given him a pinecone to hold or something more practical? I grit my teeth and force a reassuring smile. "You hum it *inside*, all right?"

Daniel nods up at me, his eyes wide.

"I will go alone," Isi tells me.

"No," I say.

He crosses his arms. "You're slow and loud," he says.

"And you're bleeding," I say, pointing to the pool of crimson staining the side of his shirt.

Isi looks down, swearing in his language, and I take my chance, spinning around and striking off ahead of him. He catches up to me in a heartbeat, giving me a dark look and tugging me off to the side so we cut close to the river. When

I turn a questioning look on him, he makes a circle with his finger. I'm guessing this means he wants to see the camp from all sides.

We position ourselves so that we have sight of the riverbank and the tents. It's difficult to hear anything with the river rushing past in a torrent, but the sounds of sawing and pounding have stopped. It's getting too dark to work.

At the fire in the center of camp, a dark-haired woman tends a spit, roasting what looks like a dozen small animals.

Isi's eyes scan the banks, the camp. Ahead, there is a small area where the rise from the shore is gradual, emptying up to the clearing they've chosen for the fort. The tents are positioned in a half circle on the opposite side from us. Behind the walls to the north and to the west, the forest holds young trees.

A big man with braided black hair pushes out from a tent on the far side. He cuts a circle, walking the perimeter of the camp, and when he turns I see a red symbol on his sleeve. Can't make it out from here, but I know he's First Peoples, like the woman. He's carrying a gun, but it's big and strange looking—not a buckshot rifle, surely.

He patrols the perimeter once and returns to the fire.

I glance back toward Daniel, but dark has cloaked the woods, and I can't see him anymore.

Isi shifts beside me, drawing my attention back to the camp.

People are emerging from behind the walls of the fortification. The first is tall and broad shouldered, and even from here I can see the settlement women would find him attractive. His blond hair glints in the light of a lantern he carries in his fist. I squint—sure it was a trick of the light—but next to the first man, he looks pale, like a ghost.

A woman appears behind him, red hair a bright flame down her back.

The Cormorant people Elizabeth spoke on.

The blond man and the big man speak. More men appear from the walls, trudging with slouched shoulders as if they've been working hard and are near exhaustion. But I see at least ten are—

Almighty.

Shackled.

They're shuffling slow, their feet bound so they can't run, and the two men who follow last have guns in their hands. As they leave the shadows and step into the glow of the firelight, I can see the shackled all look like Isi—dark hair, tawny skin—and the men carrying guns look like that broad-shouldered man: pale.

I search the line, my heart in my throat, before I realize what I'm looking for—*who* I'm looking for. I'm terrified I'll find Nishwa. The tightness in my throat eases when I don't.

The blond man and the man with dark braids disappear into the big tent and the red-haired woman heads for the small tent beside it. She ducks inside and emerges leading a dark-haired child.

I bite back a cry.

Nico.

The woman takes him to a bucket by the horses and motions for him to wash. They're alone, but we're too far away to try anything—that woman would raise the alarm and the men would be over to us in a heartbeat.

The flap on the big tent opens, and the dark-haired man backs out, awkward. Like he's struggling. He's carrying something—no, someone.

The red-haired woman turns Nico away as the big man emerges.

The blond man is helping him, and as they leave the tent I see what they're struggling with: they're carrying another man. From here it's hard to say what's wrong, whether he's sleeping or dead. They shamble across the camp, heading for the river. Toward us.

We duck lower, watching from beneath the branches. When they reach the riverbank, they set the man down none too gentle. Drop him, more like.

He's not sleeping.

His skin is riddled with angry, bloody welts, his eyes are rivers of blood. His mouth is open, his tongue is black.

The river roars loud in my ears, drowning out their talk, but it seems they're arguing about something. Finally the big man grabs the man by the legs and nods his head at the blond man. The two haul the corpse up and position themselves parallel to the river. They swing their arms, once, twice, and on the third they let go.

The body drops into the water with a violent splash. It bobs, blackened face breaking the surface, and then it is washed away in the torrent.

Nausea sweeps me.

We used to do this at the settlement—put the dead in the Cleansing Waters. There is no ceremony here, though. No final goodbyes.

Isi touches my arm, gestures with his head, telling me to retreat.

We return to Daniel and lead him farther away, back into the fireweed of the dead forest, before we speak again.

"That man," I say, "he had the Bleed."

Isi nods.

"Those two helping—are those the abandoners from your people? I thought I saw a crest on the man's sleeve."

Isi shakes his head like he doesn't know.

"What about those people who are shackled?"

"I do not know," he says, taking his knife from its sheath and holding it out to me, handle-first. "Keep Daniel here."

"I'm coming with you!"

"Not this time."

"There's at least a dozen of them, probably more. You can't just walk in there expecting a welcome."

"I won't. I will watch. Learn the camp, learn where everyone is."

"And then?"

"Then I'll do what my *moshum* would," he says. "Wait for night. Then get in and out like a fox in a pheasant's nest. They won't know until they look for Nico in the morning."

Fear rises in my throat like bile.

"Stay here." He presses the knife into my hand. "If I'm not back an hour after dark, go and do not look back. I will catch up."

"Your wound—" I start to protest, but he cuts me off.

"My wound does not slow me. But you are very slow now." He looks at my foot. My bleedin' foot! I scowl, my heart sinking as I realize he's right. He nods at Daniel, who is now blessedly out of earshot. "He needs you."

I open my mouth to protest, but he wheels and is gone, silent as anything.

We wait in the dead forest. I sing Daniel songs in a half whisper, making little puppets out of twigs on my palm, all the while keeping one ear to the woods around us. I try to distract myself from the quickening in my chest. I wanted to talk it through with Isi, make a plan. But he makes decisions so bleedin' quick.

That blood-riddled corpse surfaces in my mind. The settlement tales described the evil of the *malmaci* taking hold exactly that way. The Bleed is here, in the forest. And these people don't have the remedy.

We eat our supper of berries, and the sky turns twilight. I cover Daniel in my cloak, wrapping him against the chill that descends.

And suddenly there's a sound off in the trees: a ringing.

My heart speeds. I grab up Daniel and run several strides to a fallen log. I tuck the both of us down behind it.

Has Isi been found out? Is the camp ringing an alarm?

The ringing trills toward us. Tinkling. Cheery. It's halting now and again but getting louder. It isn't a big bell ringing at a distance; it's a small bell ringing real close—like the jingle of brass we used to put on the sheep we'd graze out atop the cliffs in the summer.

I peer over the log and see something large shift behind the dead spruce. A deer?

No.

A horse.

Fear turns to elation. A horse!

I push myself up.

Did it break its tether? Surely Leon's men wouldn't chance grazing their horses out overnight?

"Em!" Daniel scrambles up and grabs at my arm. "It's the horse from the big fire, I know it!"

"Shhh." I pat his hand. "Stay here a minute. We don't want to spook it."

He nods, clasping his hands together and bouncing on his toes. I turn and head toward it, slow. It's moving funny, jerking as it steps. As I get close, I notice its front legs are bound together, like those men at the fort. The strange, halting rhythm of the bell is made by the horse trying to take a bigger step than the bindings will allow. It has to move both forelegs at once. I frown, anger heating me and disappearing as I figure the strange sight: it's a way to graze a horse out without it running away.

Still, seems like these men wouldn't want to risk having it taken by someone else. I notice it's a she—her belly is swollen with a foal. Mayhap they thought she wouldn't stray far in her state. I smile at the notion she wandered farther than they thought she would. There's no way this is the horse from that burning homestead, but I won't tell Daniel that.

He can believe in whatever gives him hope.

I coo as I approach her, hand out for her to smell. She huffs out her air, her nostrils flaring, but doesn't bolt. Her eyes are calm. I inhale her earthy, familiar scent and rub a hand along her neck.

She has a halter on. Could be led. Could be ridden? I pat her neck, run my hand over her huge, tight belly. She must be close to having her foal—not fit to carry my weight. But Daniel weighs next to nothing.

I swallow and look at the sky. Getting dark now, the sun has long disappeared through the skeleton branches.

I unclip the bell from around the mare's neck and drop it into the deadfall. Freeing her legs isn't too hard; the bindings aren't fussy.

She takes no notice, stretching her neck to reach some long grass on the far side of a stump.

I fumble with my long *ceinture*, stripping it off and tucking Isi's knife into the side of my leggings, under my shirt. I tie the *ceinture's* tassels to the halter—it'll have to do as a lead rope—and walk her back to our spot in the fireweed.

Daniel is still bobbing with excitement.

"Don't scare her," I say.

He sidles close and touches her shoulder. Rubs her nose. She snorts, speckling his hand with snot, and mouths his arm up to his shoulder. He giggles as she rubs her lips through his hair.

Kane's voice, telling me about Daniel and Dottie that day by the river, comes over me. My heart clenches tight, despite my relief at seeing Daniel smile like this. He bends and grabs some of the grass at his feet. The mare takes it from him, her lips flapping against his palm and leaving a trail of saliva. He wipes his palm on his pant leg and looks up at me in delight.

"You want to see if she'll carry you?" I ask.

He nods, eager.

I hang on to her lead in one hand and pick Daniel up by the armpits. "Just put your leg up gentle," I instruct.

The mare bends her neck for more grass as he settles on top of her. I let her get a mouthful first, then cluck my tongue like Matisa used to, pulling her head up. I lead them in the small circle around the clearing. Daniel holds tight to the mane, like Isi taught him on his horse. His little legs are stretched wide across her huge back, but he's steady enough up there. And she doesn't seem to mind. She also responds real well when I tug her this way and that. She's trained— like Matisa's horses.

After several minutes of walking around in circles, I stop and help Daniel off.

He's grinning wide.

"I'm calling her Lucky," he tells me.

I nod and let him take the makeshift rope in his hand, settling myself on the ground.

Isi said to wait an hour.

The horse can't carry us both, so she would be pretty well useless if we needed to get away quick. Still, I feel better having her around, knowing Isi won't have to carry Daniel anymore.

Or Nico.

Unease rises in my chest. As darkness falls around us, it grows. I listen to Daniel talking soft to the mare, but I can't stop thinking about that camp. About all of the people Isi needs to get past to get to Nico. Would've been better to create a distraction so he could get in and out unseen. He didn't allow us any time to speak on it at all—he just went. Bleeding from his side, clear in pain. Typical. Rash. Stubborn.

I jump up and start to pace, digging into my bad foot on each turn.

Daniel would stay here alone, now this horse is here. I could convince him, I know I could. Mayhap I could steal another horse while Isi gets Nico. We'd be able to get away from here fast. The mare seems dependable, calm, for being about to give birth and all—

Bleed it!

Don't know if Isi thought of stealing a horse; don't know exactly what he was planning. He might only have time to rescue Nico and get away. *If* he can rescue Nico. I stamp my foot in frustration. Why did he up and leave like that? I grab my pack.

"Daniel."

He stops petting the horse and looks at me.

I make my voice bright as I approach. "You're going to stay here with Lucky." I take the *ceinture* from him and untie it from the base of the halter, retying the tassels on the sides of her face.

"Stay here?" he asks.

"Yes," I say. I fold the sash in half lengthwise and loop it over Lucky's nose. I loop it through the halter on the opposite side, trying to fashion something like the harness on Matisa's horse. It's bulky and ugly, but it'll have to do. Best to have her ready. "When I get back, you can ride her."

"Back from where?"

"I'm just going to help Isi."

His face crumples. He's going to burst into tears.

"Daniel." I make my voice stern. "You need to be a brave boy."

His eyes brim. "But I don't want you to leave."

"Hey," I say, kneeling in front of him and grasping his arms. "You remember that story Isi told you? 'Bout him helping that bird back into its nest when he was a boy? Even though it was scary to climb that tree?"

He stares at me.

"It'll be like that."

"Isi said it wasn't good that he did that," Daniel says.

Almighty. "Well, he was keeping the baby bird safe from wolves, wasn't he? So you need to be brave and stay with Lucky. She's going to have a baby soon."

He looks at the mare's swollen belly. "She is?"

"She is. And you need to stay with her and make sure she's safe." I make my voice firm again. "You need to be brave like Isi. You sing that rabbit song." I hum a bit of it, to remind him. "I bet Lucky will like that song."

This coaxes a smile from him.

"Stay right here." I give him the loop of the *ceinture.* "Don't let her take a notion and wander off for grass."

"But you'll come back? Soon?"

"Straight away." I smooth his hair and squeeze his shoulder.

He nods, his eyes wide.

I don't think another thought about what I'm doing. I turn and head for the Keep.

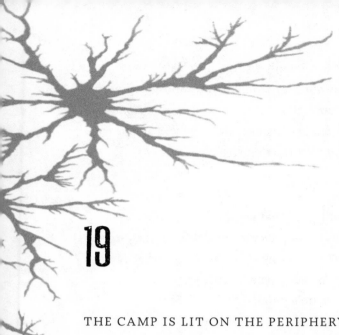

19

THE CAMP IS LIT ON THE PERIPHERY WITH LAMPS like the ones Matisa brought to the fortification—the ones that need a kind of liquid to burn. I crouch low in the brush Isi and I were hiding in earlier, searching for him. The fire in the center is blazing, and I count seven men and one woman sitting around it, including that big man with the symbol on his arm. Those shackled men are gone, and there's no sign of the red-haired woman who was with Nico earlier today. One of the pale men leans forward, his body shaking. As he straightens, wrist to his mouth, I see he's coughing.

His body convulses as he pulls himself to his feet and heads for the tents.

The tent Nico was in this afternoon is quiet; nothing stirs. The nearby river seems louder in the quiet, drowning out the campfire talk. It'll hide any ruckus in the tent, that's sure. I just can't figure how Isi will get in without being seen.

My attention goes to the horses that are tied to a spruce

tree nearest my side of the camp. The trees there are sparse; the beasts are too out in the open for me to untie without being seen. If Isi had waited for me, I could've created a distraction while he freed the horses. I could have—

A flicker of movement to my right catches my eye. A dark shape is crouched low by the big tent on the outskirts. Isi.

Mayhap I should make a loud sound in the brush or some such—so they'll come and investigate and he can skirt the camp to Nico's tent. But I see Isi has a light in his hand—one of the lanterns from the periphery. He's taken off its glass housing and is bending it toward the fabric of the tent.

He's creating his own distraction.

But why? I thought he was going to get "in and out like a fox in a pheasant's nest"? My heart races even as I feel a wash of frustration. What should I do? Wait until the men are distracted with that tent and break for the horses? Or stay and make sure Isi gets Nico out unseen? What can I do if he doesn't?

Bleed it!

Suddenly there's a loud whine from the woods on the far side of the tents—behind Isi. Isi freezes, and the men's heads snap toward the woods.

"Leon!" the big man shouts, leaping to his feet and raising that impossible gun to his eye. The blond man appears at the door of the big tent, his shirt unbuttoned, a wicked-looking gun like the one the big man carries in his hand. The whine comes again.

"Shore up!" he shouts at the group.

The men scramble to their feet, grabbing for their weapons, forming a semicircle that faces the woods.

Silence.

The blond man—Leon—nods at the huge man, who picks up a lantern and turns to the woods. He stalks forward, one hand holding his weapon, the other shining the light at the woods beyond.

Another whine. The big man stops in his tracks. The rest of the men swing their guns, searching the dark for something to shoot.

The river rushes. The men shift as the big man casts his lantern high. Isi crouches out of the light.

And now, a sound I've never heard, like a thousand woodpeckers drilling holes into metal. It rattles out from the trees in a deadly roar—loud, so loud I throw my hands to my ears.

The big man's lantern crashes to the ground and ignites in its own oil. He follows it face-first, his body shredded to bloody pieces.

The scene before me explodes.

Leon dives behind the big tent as the rest of the men shout and duck, firing their weapons at will, at nothing. The dark-haired woman at the fire turns to run for the river but makes it two strides before pitching forward, shredded the same as the big man.

The men scatter, firing their weapons into the dark. Don't need to reload or draw a hammer back, they just fire. Over and over. And from the woods, more deafening noise. Another man is hit and falls, tossed like a bloody leaf in a whirlwind.

I cast a frantic look around for Isi.

He's gone. The lantern lies on its side near the tent, and a small flame is starting up the side.

The hailstorm of bullets is loud, but there is shouting over top of it all—cries of anger and elation at once—in a language I don't know. I squint into the darkness.

And now, with the flames casting light onto the woods, I see them. They're hidden in the trees on the far side of the newly built wall, moving forward. Long dark hair, clothes like Isi— First Peoples.

I scan for him, but there are people running and shouting and long shadows dancing on the walls of the tents and loud bangs and—there! He's slipping along behind the tents to the north. His dark shape appears and disappears in the orange haze.

I want to shrink back into the safety of the trees, but I force myself to move. Now is the best chance I'll have. I dart forward to the horses, who are pulling at their lead ropes, eyes rolling. With Isi's knife, I saw at the lead rope of the first horse, grasping it firm in one hand. When the fibers split, I'm hauled off my feet as it throws its head back and rears. Hands burning, I hold fast. As the beast lands on all fours, I take one running step and leap with all of my might from my good foot, throwing my bad leg over its tall back and clinging for all I'm worth. The horse leaps into the forest, away from the chaos.

At once I realize my mistake: I have only the lead rope, no reins; no way to stop it or turn it about. As the beast crashes through the dark forest, a low branch races toward me. I put my face to the horse's neck so it doesn't take my head off.

The horse stops abrupt, and I near pitch to the earth. It snorts and dances back, its body trembling beneath me.

We've stopped at the river, and it knows the water is flowing too fast to cross.

I need to turn it around. Go back. Find Isi. I smooth a hand along the beast's neck, cooing to calm it. The gunshots have ended, but I can hear hoots and hollers from the camp, sounds of some kind of victory.

Oh Almighty. Did Isi get to Nico? Did he get away all right?

The hollering stops and there are new sounds: shouts of alarm. I hear "Don't let it spread to the Keep!"

The fire. The tent is burning fierce now.

This is good. I think. I hope.

If Isi got to Nico, which way would he try to leave the camp back toward us? Not toward the burning tent, surely. But the alternative is riverside, and wouldn't those people head for water to douse the flames?

What was his plan? What should I do?

I sheath my knife in my waistband, under my shirt. I slide from the horse and put a hand to its neck, fumbling with the rope. Trying to keep myself calm, though my heart is pounding in my throat, I put my head to my task, making reins from the rope like I did for Lucky, talking to the horse soft. I throw the reins over his head and am about to remount when I hear a hiss.

I drop to the earth and search the darkness.

The hiss comes again. "Em!"

It's coming from over the bank, by the river.

I crawl to the edge and look over.

In the moonlight, Isi's wide eyes stare back at me. He's got Nico on his back and a pack strapped to his front. He's clinging to the unearthed tree roots that line the wall. I bite back a cry of relief. Branches snap behind me.

"Where do you think you're going with that horse?" says a voice.

I freeze. Isi's eyes go wider still.

"Get up," the voice says, but it's not kindly. It's nowhere close.

I get to my feet and turn toward it. Standing in the dark beside the horse's rump is the foulest-looking man I've ever seen. His clothes are stiff and close-fitting, and his hat is caked with sweat and dirt, too small for his round, white face. He's got a gun that fits in his hand, and it's pointed at me.

His mouth breaks into a grin. "Well, look here," he says. "Aren't you a nice little surprise." His eyes rake over me, top to bottom.

My skin crawls. I will Nico to stay quiet down below the bank, but even as I do, a soft wail starts up. Nico is crying. *Almighty!*

The man's eyes snap to the river behind me. "You got a friend?" He takes two quick strides, keeping his gun on me, and peers down. I know Isi's still there by the way that awful smile reappears on the man's face.

"Well, now," he says. He sucks his teeth.

My heart is beating loud, so loud, with fear. But something else, too.

Anger.

The man jerks his head at Isi and Nico. "Help them up."

I don't move. *Anger.* I can feel it starting in my fingertips, gaining strength as it moves up my arms and into my chest, my throat, my eyes.

He swings the gun so it's pointed toward Isi and Nico. Nico wails louder.

"Help them," the man says again. "Or I'll shut that young one up right now."

All at once the events of the last two days are barreling through my mind, everything these men—this man—is responsible for. Nishwa's leg, Andre and Sister Violet gunned down, shredded to bits. Kane lost. Nico torn away from us—I take a step toward the man.

"Too slow," he spits out. He brings the gun up to the side of his face, like he might just shoot them without looking.

I can feel Isi's knife tucked in my leggings, under my shirt, and its weight makes me calm. So calm. My anger dies. I take two more careful steps toward him, my eyes on the ground.

When I see the tops of his boots, I stop.

And let it flood back in.

Rage. White hot. In my heart. In my mind. Blinding me.

I tear the knife from my side with my right hand and lurch forward, slashing at the man's foul mouth. His eyes widen in surprise, and he fumbles the gun and drops it, throwing up his arms to ward off the blow.

He's too slow. My knife connects, and the skin of his cheek splits in a long crimson tear.

He hollers and staggers back. I lunge again before he can reach for his gun, tearing and shredding at him. He gets hold of my left hand, twisting my wrist so quick and hard a bright pain shoots through it. It ignites my rage anew. All I feel is a searing-hot nothingness as I draw my arm back and hammer the knife forward. I'm aiming for his chest. I will split him in two.

He grabs for me again, dodging the blade, but the movement throws him off balance and he slips backward on the dewy forest floor. His hands are busy fighting me off, can't break his fall—

Crack!

His head snaps forward as it connects with a rock. His eyes roll to the whites and his body jerks once. Then he's still.

I stand over the man's body, my chest heaving with breath.

"Em!" Isi's voice behind me. I turn and find him pulling himself over the edge. "Are you hurt?" He leaps to his feet and strides forward, reaching out for me.

I don't feel his touch. "No," I say. My voice is a thousand strides away. I look back at the man again. He's not moving.

"We need to go," Isi says. I turn my head and watch him hurry back to the riverbank. He kneels and lifts Nico up, setting him on the forest floor a few strides away from me.

Nico's face is white, his eyes wide and terrified, but he's stopped crying. He looks at me as if he doesn't know who I am.

I can't get my feet to walk to him. Can't reach out a hand. Everything moves so slow. That rage is gone. It's gone, and there's a sickness crawling up into my throat, making it impossible to speak. Everything is hazy, like some terrible dream.

"Ceril?" A voice calls through the trees.

My dream state shatters. I see Isi's eyes now. Wide. Looking at me. He snaps forward, grabs Nico, and hoists him on the horse. He beckons furious at me and makes a loop with his hands to help me climb up. I settle on top of the beast and wrap my arms around Nico, biting my lip against the sudden reappearance of pain in my wrist. Isi leaps up behind us and reaches around me for the reins.

"Ceril!" the man calls again. Close. Too close. I look back—can see a shadow coming through the dark trees.

Isi puts his heels to the horse. It leaps ahead with a jerk.

I press my face into Nico's little neck as we crash through the forest.

Will myself to wake from this nightmare.

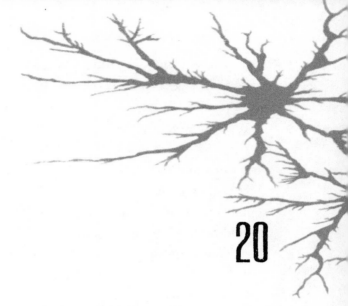

20

"YOU SHOULD NOT HAVE LEFT DANIEL," ISI SAYS for the thousandth time. He stomps alongside Lucky, his eyes scouting the brush ahead. Daniel is draped over the neck of the horse, his legs stretched to either side of her bulging belly, asleep.

Nico lolls against my chest, his head bobbing along with the soft rhythm of the horse's footsteps.

I don't answer. Strange thoughts filter through my head like sunlight through the boughs of the trees above: bloody footprints, bodies peppered through with dark red holes. I see Rebecca with her hands and feet hobbled, like that mare— about to give birth. My hands are numb. An hour ago all I could feel was the knife tearing into that man's face, the shard of pain running along my wrist. Now I feel nothing at all.

Now I'm thinking back on that moment from a strange sort of distance. Thinking: I could've been shot. Thinking: if I hadn't surprised that man the way I did, I'd be dead. But that idea doesn't scare me.

In that moment, everything spun away. There was nothing left but anger. Nothing but that fiery need to harm. It's like Isi said:

You are death.

"Em." Isi's voice breaks my thoughts. I focus on his face. He looks at me hard. "Stop thinking about it."

"I wanted so bad to be out here," I reply, but my voice sounds like it belongs to someone else. "Since the moment I found Matisa last fall, I wanted to be out here." I wait for the icy feeling in my chest, but it doesn't come. I'm outside myself, looking in. "But look what being out here's done."

Isi frowns and looks away.

We continue in silence until the dark becomes blue light.

Daniel wakes, rubbing at his eyes and messy hair. Isi stops and steadies him as he sits up and looks back at Nico and me. His eyes widen with delight, like they did when we found him last night. He was singing that Almighty-lovin' rabbit song and feeding Lucky handfuls of grass, and when he saw his brother, his face shifted into a mask of sheer relief. He asked about Kane, but I couldn't respond. Couldn't speak. In that moment, I felt nothing.

Now Daniel points to his brother. "Nico's still sleeping!"

"He's tired."

Isi clicks his tongue to get the beast walking again. Daniel puts one little hand on Lucky's neck. "Good girl," he says, like the horse was obeying his command.

I watch his dark head bob along with the horse's gait. On top of the beast, he looks so small. Helpless. Isi's right; I shouldn't have left him. That was foolish.

He looks back at me and smiles, pleased. "I like riding Lucky," he says. "Do you like riding Blue?"

He's already named the blue-black horse I stole.

I nod. He turns around, and I'm suddenly washed with relief so deep my throat gets tight. Foolish decision or not, we have the little boys back. And we have Lucky and Blue and we aren't so slow.

Mayhap things will be all right.

We reach a small grove by dusk and set up camp. The pack Isi stole from the Keep contains a few useful things: a pot, some dried meat and several hard cakes of some kind, rope, and a blanket. There's also a strange device that looks like two spyglasses joined together. Isi says he'll show me how it works in the morning.

I can tell his wound is bothering him. He moves slower than usual, kneels careful. I insist we eat the stolen provisions so he doesn't have to hunt for something for our dinner. Afterward, I tuck the boys together in my cloak and the blanket. They fall asleep straightaway. Nico stayed wide-eyed and silent when he woke this morning, but at least now his skittishness is directed at everything, not just me. He hasn't asked about his ma at all, and I can only assume it's because he saw what happened at that homestead and is trying not to think about it. Mayhap he's buried it deep.

I know how that feels.

Daniel is so pleased to have Nico back he hasn't mentioned their ma. He spent the day chattering on about Lucky and how he knows exactly what she's thinking at all times. Nico didn't respond, but Daniel didn't seem to mind.

I settle myself on the opposite side of the fire from Isi. The boys are asleep, and we can speak plain, but it takes me long moments to find words.

The firelight dances and casts fierce shadows on Isi's face, but as he meets my gaze, his face changes, becomes softer. He waits for me to speak, but this time it's without his usual air of impatience.

"I . . . have never felt anger like that," I say finally. I don't clarify which moment I'm speaking on.

He studies me. "It bothers you," he says.

I nod.

"But your anger was useful in that moment," he says.

I look down. "Suppose."

There's a pause.

"That man. Ceril," I say. "Do you think he's . . . dead?"

"It does not matter," Isi says, firm.

I nod, but I can't help but feel Isi's wrong. I feel like what we've done—what I've done—matters a great deal.

I clear my throat. "What happened when you went back to get Nico?" I ask. "I thought you were going to get in and out of that camp without being seen."

"I needed a diversion."

"That was dangerous," I say.

He snorts. "But running away on that horse was not."

"I was trying to help. I was . . . worried about you."

I expect him to dismiss this, but instead he tilts his head and studies me.

"What?" I ask.

"I expected you to wither." His eyes are curious as he looks me over.

"Wither?"

"Out here." His eyebrows knit.

Course he did. He'd never assume I could keep up with him. Do anything useful.

I change the subject and ask something I know the answer to but want to hear him say it. "Nishwa. He wasn't among those prisoners?"

Isi's eyes darken. He shakes his head no.

"Were those First Peoples who attacked trying to free them?"

He nods.

"You think they succeeded?"

"No. I think your kind were taken by surprise, but in the end they fought them off."

"They're not my kind," I say.

Isi raises his eyebrows.

"They're not," I insist, irritation washing me. "They are people from the east. They've joined together with people who have left *your* people." I shake my head. "And I'm nothing like them." But my cheeks heat because the words sound hollow even to my ears. That moment on the riverbank when I lost my senses . . .

Isi's face softens. "I chose the wrong word," he says.

I hold his gaze and hope I don't sound desperate: "*You* are my kind. I am yours."

He studies me a moment. He frowns. "No one would guess you are my kind with the way you ride a horse."

I start to retort but see his eyes flash. He's teasing me.

He also didn't say no.

My lips twitch as I pull my gaze away, to the fire.

"Are we—are we going back to that homestead?" I ask. Haven't had the courage to ask Isi this all day. But something about his manner in this moment makes me bold. He's warmer somehow. Probably so relieved, knowing Nico is safe.

"No." He shakes his head. "We are headed to the forest you dream about."

I gape at him. "Truly?"

"Yes."

"Why?"

He sighs. "Because I don't know what else to do with you. Because you believe your dream means something. Because it, at least, is out of this Leon's territory. Because I hope—" He catches himself short.

"You hope Matisa will be there," I finish for him. If my dreams help find her, will he finally admit I belong with Matisa?

He says nothing, but the look he gives me—like he's hoping *I* might have some answers—somehow scares *and* pleases me. It's the first time he's looked on me as an equal since we set out from the settlement.

"Been thinking the same thing," I say, trying to make my voice reassuring. I don't say what's truly in my heart: that the first dream about the grove gave me a hope I couldn't bear to speak, that it would be Kane waiting in those trees. Waiting for me.

And, for the first time in two days, I let myself think on him.

Let myself imagine finding Kane in that grove, burying my face in the warmth of his neck, his arms tight around me.

And then he'd tell me everything was all right. That he was with me; that he'd go anywhere with me—

Isi's eyebrows raise, and I realize I'm staring at him.

I clear my throat. "Thank you," I say. "For getting Nico back."

He shrugs and reaches forward to poke at the fire. His movement is quick, and he winces.

I hop to my feet. "Show me," I instruct, crossing over to him.

Isi snorts, like he has no intention of doing what I ask.

I cross my arms and stand my ground.

He looks up at me.

"Show. Me."

Reluctant, he turns his back to the coals and draws up his shirt. I kneel. The smooth of his skin glows in the fire, the jagged scar of stitches dancing a pattern from his waist to his shoulder blade. It looks strange in the firelight—beautiful, almost. Blackened blood cakes his side. When I touch the stitches, Isi shudders. I pull my fingers back into a fist. "They hurt?"

"A little."

"All the time?"

"When touched."

My hand unclenches. If the wound wasn't healing, it would feel hot and uncomfortable always—the damaged skin is still sensitive, no doubt. But it's been bleeding from somewhere.

"Wait," I say. I get a kerchief and a small clay pot from my pack. I dip the kerchief into the pot on the fire—water we boiled to warm the boys before bed—and return to him.

Careful, I wash the caked blood away and find the open stitch. The clay pot contains the remainder of the sap paste I used to close the wound on Nishwa's leg. Gentle as I can, I pat it to the open skin, sealing it.

I sit back when I'm done, but my hand doesn't leave Isi's back. Instead, I trace the side of the wound with two fingers. His undamaged skin is smooth. I remember seeing a different man's scars in the light of flame. Seems a lifetime ago. Brother Stockham had taken me to the ceremonial hall and showed me his father's teachings, branded into his skin. My fingers still have that memory. Then, too, I wanted to touch—

I snatch my hand away and stand up.

Isi drops his shirt and turns around. "What is it?" he asks.

"Nothing," I say.

He tilts his head.

I turn to hide the heat creeping over my cheeks and cross back to the boys. Isi's bare skin shouldn't unsettle me; I don't feel that way about him. It's not that. It's . . . the scars look so violent, but the moment feels so gentle. Just like in the ceremonial hall that day. How would things be different now if I had stayed gentle, if I'd shown Stockham mercy instead of risking everything to uncover his secret?

I make a show of checking on the little boys, smoothing Daniel's hair and pulling at their blanket. When I brush back Nico's hair from his face, my hand touches fire.

He's burning up.

"Isi!" I hiss. He's at my side in a heartbeat. I take his hand and lay it on Nico's brow. Nico moans, soft.

The whites of Isi's eyes grow in the dark. "How long has he been like this?"

"I don't know. He hasn't talked all day."

Isi's jaw works. He puts fingers to Nico's neck, checking his heartbeat—*checking his heartbeat?*

No. This is a fever. Seen plenty of fevers. Soeur Manon taught me that when someone's body goes this hot on its own, you have to get it cooled other ways. "We need more water to cool him down. We should head back to that stream—"

"No!" Isi snaps, straightening. He hops up and begins to pace, muttering—sounds like swearing—in his language, under his breath. Now he's counting something on his hands.

"We'll just use it to bathe him," I say. "He won't be drinking it."

Isi doesn't answer, just keeps pacing.

I bite my lip in frustration. Can't carry Nico all the way on my own. But there are other ways to get him cool—willow tea. That's what we need. Soeur Manon taught me how to make the willow tea years ago. Probably fed me it when I was sick with the fever last fall. "I can make him a tea. I just need my satchel."

Isi is still swearing, or counting, I'm not sure which.

"Isi! I can make a—"

"That will not help." He paces back and forth.

"You didn't even let me explain!"

"Because it doesn't matter—"

"But when people took fever at the settlement—"

"Em!" he shouts. "It will not help!"

"Course it will!" My voice is hysterical. I know what he's worried about. He's worried Nico has the Bleed. But he can't. He can't.

He's pacing again, muttering, swearing. Paying me no mind.

I leap to my feet. "Tell me how to make the remedy!" I shout.

He stops and looks at me. "What?"

"The remedy. Tell me how. Tell me how she does it." I don't know why I say it—course he doesn't know. But I'm so desperate.

His shoulders sag. "Em," he says, his voice soft. "Even if I knew, it wouldn't matter. It cannot heal it."

I stare at him. "Yes, it can," I whisper, but as I say the words, I realize he's right. Matisa never told me she had the cure; she told me they had a remedy to keep the sickness away. Two very different things.

He shakes his head. "If this is what that man at the Keep died from, nothing will help."

No. No. This isn't the same.

The sadness in Isi's eyes makes me realize I've spoken the words aloud. He's sad for me. For Nico.

Dread creeps cold fingers along my chest. But—no. No. I have to fix this. Have to set it right.

"I'm making the willow tea." My voice comes out a growl, a challenge. "Now help me move him away from the fire."

Isi watches me as I struggle to get Nico into my arms. Finally he brushes me aside and picks him up without effort, moving him to the cool, exposed roots at the base of a giant elm.

"Get that blanket off and give him some water," I instruct.

Isi stares at Nico's pale face, his shoulders tense, hands bunched into fists.

"Get to work!" I snap.

Isi bends and begins pulling the blanket from Nico, but his movement is too slow. Like it won't matter if he goes fast. I whirl away. Course this will work. Course . . .

I grab my satchel and dig through it, watching as Isi takes off Nico's moccasins and woolen socks, opens the collar of his tunic. I bend my head to my task, stripping the few sticks of willow I have, getting the water to a boil. I watch Isi dribble water onto a square of cloth and wash Nico's face with it.

It takes an excruciating long time for my tincture to boil.

As I set it beside Nico, he opens his eyes once and gives me a glassy stare. I spoon the tea into his mouth in small sips while Isi washes his face and arms with a cloth. When Nico's had a cup of the bitter brew, I lay his head back and cover his legs with the blanket.

And wait.

Long moments pass. Nico moans in his sleep once. Twice. And he's quiet.

My hands fly to his brow.

He's cooler.

Cooler.

I sit back on my heels, feeling a relief so intense I'm dizzy. Isi steps forward and checks Nico. His chest heaves with a relieved sigh. He looks at me with a smile.

I don't return it.

I lean forward and fuss around with the blanket, straightening and restraightening. Finally Nico begins to breathe easy; he's in a restful sleep. I touch his brow for the hundredth time. He's much cooler now, but I need to check—

Isi reaches out a hand and puts it on mine. "He will be fine," he says. "With the sickness, fever rises. He was probably tired."

I snatch my hand away and leap to my feet, pressing into my bad foot.

Isi frowns, and pulls himself to stand.

"What?" I demand.

"You were right," he says.

"I know." I cross my arms and look at him.

His forehead creases. "I—should not have said what I did."

"Doesn't matter."

Isi tilts his head, measuring me with that look. That Almighty-lovin' look that makes me doubt my own words. "It upset you."

"I'm not upset!" I shout.

He raises his eyebrows.

I spin away from him and pace off toward the trees. I stop just outside the glow of the fire, trying to calm my mind, trying to get hold of myself. But all I can think is how bad I wanted to come out here.

And look what it's done.

I knew how much Sister Violet needed Kane, but I'd decided long ago that I was more important—that *this* was more important. I'm the reason they're out here. The reason Daniel and Nico no longer have a ma. Tears blur my vision, fill my throat.

Where is your home? Elizabeth Sharapay asked me. *Why are you out here?*

And I couldn't answer. I couldn't answer because . . .

I don't know anymore.

And if Nico'd had the Bleed—

"Em."

I swipe my hands over my face quick, brushing away the stream of tears. Cross my arms.

He's behind me. A dark, unwanted shadow.

"Come back to the fire. The night grows cold."

"So?"

"So there is no need to grow cold with it."

"I feel like it."

Silence.

"I know what you feel," he says.

"No, you don't."

"You feel that if you don't bring these boys back safe, you will never forgive yourself."

I scrub at my eyes again and stare off into the black forest.

"You wanted this to be the start of your new life, and now you feel—"

"What do you care?" I snap, wheeling around. "I *am* death, remember? My new life has only brought disaster. It brought it to the settlement, it brought it to all the people who followed me. I'm the injured bird, the one you should never have helped. It makes no difference to you what I *feel!*"

He shifts his stance, like he doesn't know what to do.

"Go away," I whisper, fierce.

He drops his arms to his sides. "You are right to ask me to leave."

I stare off into the dark trees, trying to swallow around the lump in my throat, trying to breathe around the cold in my chest.

"But the things I said—those were wrong."

My eyes go wide, and I blink furious, trying to keep back the tears that want to spill.

"I said them because I was angry and afraid," he says. "As you are now." I glance at him. He's looking at me in that way of his, the way that infuriates me but right now washes me in desire. Not desire for *him*, but . . .

Desire to be better. To be braver. Stronger.

I swallow.

"Come back to the fire," he says. His voice is unfamiliar. Gentle.

I look into the black of the woods. Into those shadows that now look inviting because they make things disappear.

Think about the boys. About Matisa. About Kane.

We head away from the dark, back to the soft glow of our camp.

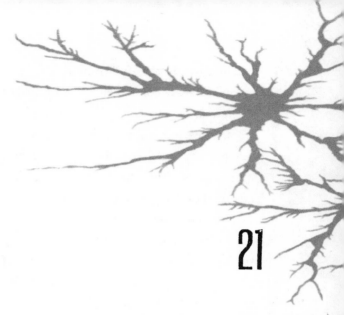

21

NICO MOVES AROUND LIKE NORMAL IN THE MORN-
ing, but he's still quiet, withdrawn. I ask Isi if we should
be worried, but he says he'll come around. We set out, and
today I'm real grateful for Daniel's chatter.

By midmorning the spruce forest thins out and gets
marshy. We have to dismount and lead the horses, who are
stumbling in the mud. Our moccasins make sucking sounds
as we push through tall tufts of marsh grasses and willow.

I'm helping Daniel over a grass-covered fallen log when I
notice that the mud is a strange orange color. As we continue,
the orange gets deeper, like the sun sinking on the horizon
on a hazy day. Soon we're passing through little streams of
bright yellow and orange.

"Isi!" I call out, forcing him to stop and turn back.

I point to the ground.

"Paint mud," he says, as though it explains everything.

I frown at him. Daniel takes a stick and drags it through
the yellow muck and into the orange, blending the two.

"The earth here is full of minerals. The soil and water—the mud—create colors when the air strikes."

I stare at Isi, amazed.

Both boys are stirring the pools now, and there's a small smile playing on Nico's lips. The first I've seen.

Isi studies him a moment. "Come, I will show you." He leads his horse to the trees and wraps the lead rope around one. I do the same with the mare, and the boys and I follow Isi into the woods, stopping where the spruce thin into a large circle. Here, there is an entire clearing full of little pools of different colors. Several shimmer with the orange that caught Daniel's eye. A couple nearby are yellow. The pool nearest us is a brilliant green. And on the far side, there's a red like the rose hips in autumn.

Daniel looks up at us, his eyes round with wonder. "Can we . . . ?" he asks.

"Is it safe?" I ask Isi.

He nods.

"Go on, then," I tell Daniel.

He grabs Nico by the hand and pulls him closer to the pools. They find sticks at the edge of the marsh and soon they're off, digging in the colors, pulling them out, and painting them on nearby trees and leaves.

Isi and I settle ourselves on fallen debris to watch. My foot is aching with the trek through the marsh, and I can't help but rub at it as I sit.

"You need that tincture," Isi says.

I shrug. "It's fine."

"It's not fine."

I glance over at him, trying to figure if he's concerned or pointing out where I'm wrong.

"Em!" Daniel calls from across the orange pond. He holds up his hands. He's dipped the tips of his fingers in the paint mud. Nico stands beside him, and Daniel reaches over and paints a stripe on the arm of Nico's tunic. Nico squeals in delight and darts away.

My heart swells as I watch the two take turns decorating each other's sleeves. "That going to stain their clothes?"

"Yes," Isi says. "But it does not matter."

"True," I agree. The youngsters are off to the green pool now. I put a hand to my brow to shield the glare of the sun, watch Nico's big eyes, his smile. And all at once I feel lighter, happier. "Rather them be laughing than clean," I say.

"It is something Matisa would say," Isi says, his face lighting in a rare smile. But a cloud of worry chases it away.

"How far to the grove?" I ask.

"We should reach it this afternoon," he says. "Did you"— he dips his head—"did you dream about her again?"

"No," I answer. "But we're meant to go to this grove, I'm sure of that." I don't tell him what I've decided: that the part of my dream that concerns Matisa is asking me to account for what happened in the settlement. Feel like it's reminding me that I'm running off into the wild looking for my new life, but I haven't made peace with what happened in my old one.

He nods, but I can see he's trying to look unconcerned.

"Isi, if she's not at the grove . . ."

"I will find her," he says, firm.

I don't ask what he plans to do with us. We've slowed him enough already; he'll want to go on his own. And what will happen when he does find her? Will he tell her where he's left us? Or will he pretend he doesn't know, insist she go home to the safety of their people? What will I do then?

I realize with a pang that what's also bothering me is that *he'll* be gone. Even though he's prickly. Even though he makes rash decisions. So used to having him near now, having him watching over us.

"You love her." It's out of my mouth before I know I'm saying it.

He doesn't answer, but his silence tells me everything.

"I thought you were family," I say, thinking about how such relations were forbidden in the settlement.

"Because she calls me her cousin?" He laughs. "I think we have a different idea of family. Family isn't only about being blood." He picks up a stick and drags it through the mud beside him. "When we were children, I was trouble for my mother. Matisa's *moshum* was not of my direct blood, but he welcomed me like I was his own. He would find things for me to do. Matisa always talked to me and listened like she understood, like we were equals, when we clearly were not."

I look him over careful, his strong nose, his long dark hair gleaming in the sunlight. Most times he looks ready to leap up at the slightest provocation, but right now he looks relaxed, gentle. And, right now, he is the equal of anyone I can imagine.

"Are you . . ." I don't know his words to describe it. "Life mates? Meant to be together?"

He draws a circle with the stick. "Matisa has always been lit from the inside with purpose, and it is not finding another to share her life. Many"—he smiles—"many have tried. They call her *âmopiyesîs*."

"What does it mean?"

"It is a small, beautiful bird that moves from flower to flower so fast you think your eyes have played a trick. Impossible to catch."

"Well, I'm grateful you love her."

He looks at me.

"Otherwise, Daniel and I would've been on our own."

He is quiet.

The silence is broken by the distant laughter of the boys.

He puts the stick down. "When Matisa started telling us about her dreams, I liked the idea of the adventure." He looks over at me. "And when she was determined to come find you, I came to make sure she would be safe, but"—he hesitates—"I didn't want her to be right."

"I know that," I say. "Just can't quite figure why."

"I didn't understand how a girl from a group of Lost People could matter. You were the newcomers from our stories. The ones who brought death. And I . . . had ideas about what kind of people would be so lost, so stuck in time, to begin with."

My eyebrows raise.

He shrugs. "I thought you were fearful and backward."

I chew on this and realize the truth in it. "We were. Always thought I was so different from everyone, but I wasn't: I wasted a lot of time being afraid." I don't mind admitting this to him.

"No. You weren't afraid; you risked death to find Matisa. You did it again to free the people you loved."

I shake my head. "I *thought* that's what I was doing—freeing them. But I don't know anymore. My pa—"

"Em." He cuts me off. "When you decided to go back to the settlement for your father and friend, you were choosing freedom. And that moment I saw you with new eyes. I've . . . been telling myself I didn't."

Heat creeps into my face. "You've been pretty clear that who I am has put us in danger, time and again."

"I told myself that because I was afraid."

"Of what?"

"You."

I swallow hard. Afraid of me? Can't be right. Isi always knows exactly what to do; he's the one who makes me feel like I don't know up from down.

"I sensed you had a rare strength. You have proved it."

I snort. "Proved it by limping painful slow or proved it by pitching a fit in the trees in the dark?"

He laughs and shakes his head. "You mended my wound, buried your people, then walked days into the wilderness to help rescue a child." His face grows serious. "Matisa was right to come after you. You belong out here." He's leveling me a look I've never seen.

A shriek calls our attention back to the ponds. Daniel and Nico are racing toward us with hands full of bright orange, mischievous grins on their faces.

I push to my feet. "Don't!" I call in mock horror. I point to Isi. "Get Isi!"

The boys shift their path and barrel toward him, but at

the last second Nico swerves and jumps at me, getting his orange hands all over. I sink to the ground, laughing, trying to deflect the mucky hands from my skin. Daniel tackles Isi in a similar manner, swiping his cheek with the paint and getting it in his hair.

We tussle with the youngsters, who are hooting and hollering, until I cry mercy so Nico gives up. Isi grabs Daniel's hands in one and tickles him with the other until he yells for the same. We all roll onto our backs, heaving deep breaths and staring at the white-blue sky.

I look over at Isi, and his eyes meet mine. The heat from the earth rises, causing the air between us to shimmer and dance.

Something has shifted between us, like an invisible thread connecting us, heart to heart. Something like the way Matisa and I are connected. Something, also, like the way Kane and I are connected.

I can see he feels it, too.

In the afternoon, we come upon a field. In the distance are rolling hills and, beyond them, the glint of a river in the setting sun. My heart leaps at the familiar sight of those waters—the one marker that grounds me in this vast land.

Isi passes me the spyglasses and directs my gaze to the south. A short way along the river lies a forest of tall trees. Green. Dotted with white.

"*Mâyimitos*," he says.

My dream rushes over me, making my breath fast, my heart gallop in my chest.

As we crest the last rolling hill, the big trees from my

dreams stretch tall to the sky, bunches of soft white tufts in their crooks. My stomach drops through my feet when I see movement. The flash of a spyglass.

I hop from my horse, leaving Nico. My foot cries out fiery pain, but I hardly notice; I'm too busy watching the figure stepping out from the trees. I can tell by the way he stands.

It's Kane.

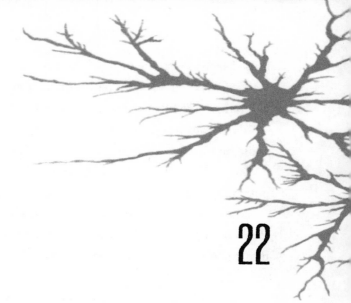

22

KANE.

I break into a run, fast as my foot can bear, across the velvet prairie grasses. He's so near, he's a lifetime away.

But he's running, running for me fast as he can, crossing the long days, reaching out for me . . .

Reaching me. Reaching me, catching me in his strong arms and whirling me around. I cling to him, dig my face into his neck, his warm skin, breathing him in, holding like I won't ever let go.

He pulls back, hands on my face, eyes wide and searching over me like he can't believe what he sees. "Em . . ." His voice is hoarse. "I thought . . ." He brushes his thumbs over my cheeks, tucks my hair behind my ears. And kisses me on the mouth. Hard.

Breath and thoughts leave me. My hands flutter out, grasp at his forearms. He steadies me as I break the kiss and pull back. "I'm all right," I gasp. "We're all right."

He looks past me. The boys are hollering in excitement.

Daniel leaps from the back of the mare and Nico follows. I step aside as the boys run pell-mell for Kane, diving for him and tangling themselves up in his arms.

I look back at Isi, who stands holding the horses' leads, a smile on his face.

Kane frees himself from the boys and steps toward Isi, putting out his hand.

Isi drops the lead ropes and takes it, but Kane pulls him into a hard embrace, clapping him on the back before letting him go. We gaze round at one another. The boys huddle near Kane.

The wind blows and a soft white fluff appears before me, drifting on the breeze. I turn my head to look at the trees, capped in white and shedding their down into the air, and my heart swells.

"Matisa?" I look back at Kane.

His forehead creases. He shakes his head no.

My eyes fly to Isi, whose smile disappears. He looks as though he's been punched. I take a deep swallow of air. His face hardens into a mask.

"Isi—"

"This mare needs rest." He throws his head at the grove. "You have a camp?"

"A fire ring, more like," Kane says. "But yeah—just in those trees."

Isi nods. "Daniel—help me with Lucky. Nico?"

Daniel nods serious-like and takes the lead rope, but Nico looks like he doesn't want to leave Kane. Isi convinces him by asking him to carry a pack. I try to catch Isi's eyes, but he's not looking at me.

"We'll be right there," Kane tells his brothers.

I watch them go, my heart flip-flopping. Relief is still washing over me in waves, but I was wrong about Matisa, and Isi will leave soon as his horse is rested . . .

I shove all those thoughts aside and turn back to Kane, wanting that first moment back. That first moment of joy.

His face is exactly Kane: black eyes and eyelashes, strong nose, mouth that pulls up at one corner. But his eyes aren't laughing like they used to. He has a new scar; a small crescent-shaped cut at his chin. I touch my fingers to it, raise my eyebrows.

"Falling shale," he says, taking my fingers in his hand and pulling them away. "I hid in the coulees during that . . . that . . ."

With my free hand I grab the front of his shirt and pull him to me.

His hands fumble forward, reaching for me, grasping my shoulders. He brings his mouth to mine, desperate. I press into him, trying to bury myself in the memory of this: of how perfect we fit like this. His scent and mouth . . .

He pulls back, staring at me with a force that makes my blood run hot. "I worried you were dead," he mutters.

"I worried the same thing."

He draws me to him, wrapping his arms around me and holding me tight against his chest.

"I didn't know what I was going to do. I saw you and Isi escape past that homestead with Daniel. Didn't know where Nico went. Thought I might be following you if I kept to the river. But I didn't find you, I didn't . . ." He trails off, and I feel him swallow, hard.

"I'm here now. The boys are safe."

He nods. But I know what he isn't saying.

"Kane, I'm so sorry . . ." I swallow. "We . . ." I force the words: "We buried her."

His chest and arms stiffen.

My breath hitches. "Andre, too." In reply, he tightens his arms around me. I bury my head beneath his collarbone and breathe deep. His heartbeat thuds beneath my ear.

After a long while I say, "We thought Matisa might be here."

He releases me, pulling back so I can see his face.

"I knew someone was here, but I was afraid to hope . . ." I say.

His brow creases. "How did you know?"

"I dreamt it."

A shadow flickers across his face.

"Kane, we have to find her."

He glances at the grove, then back at me, but says nothing.

"I think I can convince Isi to wait the night, but he's waited days, tracked Nico first. I—I can't ask him to wait longer than that."

Kane squints. "What do you mean, 'tracked Nico'?" he asks. He doesn't know. Course he doesn't. Everything was such a blur in that fight.

"Those men took him," I say. "But we found him a couple days northwest of here."

"Was he hurt—"

"No," I assure him, quick. "But we got there just in time. They had weapons, and a fight started."

"What kind of weapons?" he asks.

Bodies shredded to pieces. Explosions of dirt. Limbs. "Bad weapons. Like nothing I've ever seen," I say.

"Who are they?"

"They're led by a man named Leon. Near as we can figure, they're those 'rogue' types Henderson was speaking on. They're running off people who settle on land they claim as their own. They're keeping First Peoples prisoners, forcing them to build their fortification. And . . ."

But I can't say it. Can't tell him that they're keeping women, too.

He takes this in, his jaw working hard. "We should get the boys someplace safe," he says.

"We will," I say. "Once we find Matisa, we can get to their people."

He pulls away farther.

"I can help find her," I say. "My dreams led me here to you. I know they'll lead me to her . . ." I trail off because his face is closing down.

"What is it?" I ask.

"We should head for that crossing, for the Dominion outpost."

Now I step back. "What?"

"Going back to the settlement means heading back into the mess. With this Leon running people off . . ." He shakes his head. "The safest place I can figure is east. With the Dominion."

"We don't know that it's safe—"

"That mapmaker spoke of law. Said the Dominion wanted order. Right now, that's safer than out here."

"But Matisa's people will offer protection." Even as I say the words I realize the problem: we'd have to get there first. I press on with the most important thing. "I have to find Matisa. She and I—"

Kane looks at the sky and breathes out in exasperation, clasping his hands behind his neck.

And now I see. Now I know.

This whole time I thought that moment at the waterfall was the start of our life together. Even though I was nervous about parting with his ma and the boys, I felt near certain he'd come with me. And ever since the homestead, I assumed the choice was made for him.

I was wrong.

"You weren't planning on staying with me."

He looks back down, his eyes dark. "I want to stay with you more than anything. It's not about that."

"You don't believe my dreams."

"Em—"

"You never did."

"It's got nothing to do with that."

"Then what?"

"I have a family to keep safe! You don't!" His eyes blaze.

My mouth opens. Closes. Did he really say that?

"Didn't mean that," he says, shutting his eyes. "It's just . . ." When he opens them, I see the fight is snuffed out. He looks . . . helpless. "Should've been me, Em." His voice is thick. "Should've been me who got the boys back. *You* back." He sinks to the earth, pulling his knees up and putting his head in his hands. "I didn't know what to do."

"Kane—" I drop to my knees beside him.

"I was near out of my mind, thinking I'd lost you. And all I could do was wish we'd never come."

I suck in a breath.

"I don't even know what I'm doing out here, save following after you." He raises his head and stares at me, his face miserable.

And the truth of it all hits me full force: being out here isn't *his* dream. It's mine. Only mine.

What I want is to be with you.

He meant what he said at the waterfall. But he followed me out here into Almighty knows what because *I* wanted to be out here. And now his ma is dead and his little brothers are in danger. And he doesn't believe the path I'm walking is one he can follow.

I stare at the prairie grasses, the wind blowing my hair into my eyes.

"I need to get Daniel and Nico somewhere safe," he says after a long silence. "You want to go after Matisa, I can't stop you."

A sliver of ice cuts through my heart.

He pulls himself up and stands. When he speaks, his voice is hoarse. "Should see to the boys."

My chest is heavy. So heavy. I follow Kane into the first line of trees but halt, unable to force myself a step farther. I put a hand to the nearest trunk, bending over with the cold deadweight. He doesn't wait for me.

The ice is working its way into my throat, behind my eyes. Tears blur my sight as I watch him walk away. I turn and sink my back against the tree, staring up at a circle of white sky that peeks through the leafy branches. Tall trees around me used to feel like hope. They used to feel like a promise.

Now they feel like broken things. No promises; just failure.

Last night when Nico took sick, I wanted to walk out into the black woods, wanted to let them swallow me, give myself over to whatever this is I've brought upon us.

And I want to do it now.

Right now, it feels like the only thing *to* do.

Almighty, I wish Tom were here. I need someone who understands—

"Em." Isi's voice jars me from my thoughts.

I push off the tree and turn to face him.

"We are waiting for you in the grove," he says.

I don't answer.

"We will need to talk with Kane," he says.

"Think he's done talking," I say.

He folds his arms across his chest. "He has lost his mother and only now found his brothers. He needs time."

I bark a laugh. "So *now* you're being patient?"

Isi looks at me with that infuriating new calm.

"Kane wants to go east," I say, my voice dull.

"Why?"

"Thinks it's safest for the little boys there."

Isi blows out a long breath. He paces a few steps before me. He draws back his shoulders and turns to me. "Keep him here until I return."

I frown. "What?"

"Convince him to stay here, in the safety of this grove, while I find Matisa. We will come back for you and talk about this then. Perhaps Matisa can change his mind."

"I need to come with you," I say. "My dreams can help."

"I do not need them. I will start back at the homestead and track her the way I tracked Nico."

"And if you don't find her?"

A flash of desperation lights in his eyes. They harden. "I will."

"You know it would be better if I came."

"Kane will not go. Stay here, we will return."

"I can't let you," I say.

"Why not?"

"Because . . . ," I say. "Because I was . . ."

"What?"

I move to turn away, but he grabs my arm and keeps me in place. *"What?"* he demands.

I swallow hard. "Wrong. I was wrong about being out here."

He frowns at me. "Why do you say this?"

I pull away, wrap my arms around myself and look into the trees, swallow the cold shards in my throat. If I look down, the tears behind my eyes will fall. Can't let them.

"Em." His voice is stern. "Why?"

"Because . . . ," I say. "Because it was selfish. I thought my—Kane's—new life was out here. I thought we deserved it. Thought this new life was my reward for bringing my people freedom. But I didn't bring freedom. I brought . . ." I can't finish. My voice is closing off with tears.

"You brought what?"

I shake my head. The ice in my chest is heavier than it's ever been. It's going to weigh me down into this forest floor. Never let me up again.

His look is hard, like he's seeing straight through to my thoughts. When he speaks, his voice is soft. "This is a new world, Em," he says. "It brings things we cannot help." His voice gets softer still. "Andre, Sister Violet . . ."

I hold my breath. Will him to stop. To stop speaking.

"Your father . . ."

Don't say it.

"Their deaths were not your fault."

The ball of ice shatters. Like the frozen river smashing on the rock banks, it bursts, shooting pain through my chest, my core, into my throat. The trees before me blur and dance through my tears. I lean forward, press my face to my hands. Let the tears stream hot down my face. Let myself cry for everything I've lost.

My pa. Andre. Sister Violet.

The life I thought I was starting out here, that foolish dream. Hope.

There's a shrieking in my head, like river currents rushing over me, battering me, drowning me. I want to dig down, down, bury myself here under the rot and the moss. I want to scream down the tall trees, the pink sky, as I drown here on the forest floor. I can feel the forest around me splintering, the trees and sky spinning away as I bury myself in this sorrow that chokes, that blinds—

Isi's hand touches my back.

Warm. Strong.

Not of this dark place.

Not wanted in this dark place.

But.

Familiar. Something like my pa's hands, when I was young.

Something like Matisa's hand in mine when they buried him. Something like Kane's hands that held me at that waterfall a lifetime ago.

Make peace with it.

I will Isi away, will myself back under, back into the icy blackness, but his warmth won't allow it. It burns through my clothes, pulling at me, dragging me back up from the depths. Sets my feet back on this forest floor. Anchors me to this world.

This new world.

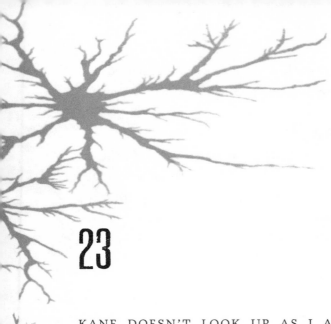

23

KANE DOESN'T LOOK UP AS I APPROACH THE camp in the grove. It's little more than a campfire, as he said, but Isi has laid out our supplies, and there's a pot of water bubbling over the fire. I steady my racing heart and kneel beside our provisions, busying my hands with making a thin soup out of the water. Isi hangs back in the trees, checking his horses' hooves for rocks and scrapes.

Nico is huddled close under one of Kane's arms, his face tear-streaked. Even Daniel is quiet, his face grave, tucked on the other side of Kane. And by the look of pain on Kane's face, I can see they've been speaking on their ma.

I will him to meet my eyes, but his eyes are locked on the flames.

There's a heavy silence as I add grains and salt to the water. Finally Nico looks up at Kane and asks, "Where were you all this time?"

Kane's eyes flick up to mine for a heartbeat. His chest

heaves with a deep breath. I secure the pot over the fire and listen to a halting account of his past three days.

He searches for words as he speaks, like he's trying to either remember or forget things, but manages to tell us that during the gun storm, he took cover back behind the first coulee. A man came after him, but he got back between the crevasses and headed northwest, where the man's horse would have trouble with the terrain. The man was persistent, tried to wait Kane out. Took until the next morning for the man to leave, for Kane to get a chance to head back south to the river. He was off course, though, and missed the homestead. By the time he returned, there was no one left. He decided it best to keep heading south to the crossing, where he hoped we'd gone.

I study him as he talks. Here in this grove, the shadows of the trees and the fire cast his face in a new light, and I see the days of worry on his face. Dark smudges of sleepless nights ring his eyes. And all at once, I see what I'm asking of him.

Almighty—what is wrong with me?

Course he'll want to find safety for his brothers straight away. Asking him to help us find Matisa, those little boys in tow, is plain selfish. I listen with a heavy heart as he finishes up.

Nico presses close, and as Kane smiles down at him, my insides twist.

Isi joins the boys around the fire as I ladle out the soup. It's the first hot thing I've eaten since the rabbit that first night out, but somehow, I'm not hungry. The boys are; they eat like they haven't in days.

And they haven't. Not truly. Watching them tuck in, their hands so small on the bowls, their eyes shining with happiness looking on Kane, my heart grows heavier.

I rub at my eyes in frustration and press my fists to my forehead.

They finish eating as the light disappears from the sky.

Isi rises. "I will check the mare," he says, taking the lead rope of his horse. He'd let Lucky out into the trees to find a spot to foal, but I know what he's truly doing. He's got his pack, and he's headed in the opposite direction; he's leaving to find Matisa and not giving me a choice in the matter.

"Leave it a bit?" I say. My eyes plead with him to take my meaning. "The night?"

"Can we go?" Daniel asks Kane. "Lucky's *my* horse."

"Stay put," Kane says, his eyes on me. "You can see her in the morning."

Isi shakes his head. "I can't."

My stomach tightens. I throw a desperate look to Kane and push to my feet.

"Em." Isi's voice snaps my eyes back to his. He shakes his head. He's telling me not to come. But it's not unkindly.

"Stay here," Isi says, firm. "I will return." He disappears into the dark trees, and I have to fight the urge to run after him. I press into my bad foot instead and look at the forest floor.

There's a silence. And now Kane's voice, tight and quiet: "You sure you want to stay?" His eyes measure me. He knows where Isi is truly going, knows how twisted up I am watching him go without me.

"Course," I say, but my voice catches. "Can—" But I stop. I see on his face it's not the right time to convince him to wait with me for Isi and Matisa. And what will I do if he refuses? Will I go with him to the crossing or stay here? What if Isi can't find Matisa? "Can we talk in the morning?"

"I'll find some pine boughs to sleep on," he mutters, untangling himself from the boys and pushing to his feet.

As he circles past me, I want to reach out for him, want him to take me in his hard, warm arms. But the way he moves—he's further away from me than he's ever been. A cold hand settles around my throat as I watch him cross the grove. The woods around us have gone silent. Or mayhap they always were; mayhap we've stopped making noise.

Kane stops at the edge of the trees and turns back to me. "You're wrong, you know," he says, his voice tight. "I always believed your dreams." He shakes his head. "Just not sure they ever included me."

My heart plummets to my feet. I take a breath to rebuke this, to tell him he's dead wrong, but a movement behind him catches my eye.

And a blur crashes out from the woods.

I have time to scream his name, but Kane has no time to react, no time to turn around—it's a man, club in hand, and the club is whistling through the air, smashing against Kane's temple. Dropping him to the earth like a stone.

The little boys' screams echo around in my head as I scramble to my feet and over to them.

Another man steps out of the woods. The rifle in his hands is trained on us.

I grasp for the little boys, making sure they're behind me. Kane lies facedown, unmoving.

Is he—

The man hisses at us through his teeth. "Don't move now," he says.

The man with the club nudges Kane with his foot and turns his gaze on us. "What is this?" he demands. He's huge—easily twice my weight and stands shoulders above me. Blond hair, blond eyebrows, high cheekbones—familiar, but I know I've never seen him before.

"He never said anything about young ones," the big man says.

Why is he familiar? My mind is fuzzy. I try to place him. He looks . . . He looks . . .

The man with the rifle stalks forward. He's scrawny, light skinned, and blue-eyed, with a mat of dirty brown hair sticking out from under a battered hat. "Where are the others?" he demands.

My breath starts again, heaving my chest as I gulp air.

"I asked you a question!"

I force my tongue to work. "Oth-oth-others?" Violet and Andre? Why would he be wondering about them? I crane my neck to look past him, see if Kane has moved. "Is he all ri—"

The man's free hand shoots out. I see bright white sky as pain explodes in my face. Staggering back, I put a hand to my mouth, tasting salt and iron as blood seeps onto my teeth. My hand finds a sticky valley—my mouth is split at the corner.

"Don't talk unless you're answering questions." He looks

at the big man. "Now she knows, hey, Julian?" He turns to me. "So?"

I try to remember the question, but there's a ringing in my ears, muddying my thoughts. I fight the urge to gag as I swallow my own hot blood.

"Leave it," the big man, Julian, says. "Let's get this half blood in the cage before he wakes. He looks strong." It takes me a moment to realize he's talking about Kane. Relief shoots through my hazy fear. Kane's alive.

"Get up," the scrawny man orders the boys. "Walk." He waves his rifle at the trees.

My head spins. I stagger over and take the little boys' hands. We push through the trees, back toward the riverbank flats. My body is numb, but my mouth throbs.

My dream feeling deepens when we get out past the trees. The full moon lights the banks, clear as day, washing the whole picture in an unearthly glow.

Standing on the flats is a cart, bigger than any we had back at the settlement, pulled by two enormous horses. They're near twice the size of Lucky, strong necks and huge feet covered in soft feathers. In the back of the cart is something that looks like a box, made from the kind of iron that the gibbets at the Crossroads were. *The cage.* Where they plan to put Kane. Panic courses through my body, but it stops dead as my eyes travel the length of the cart.

Tied to the back, in a heap on the ground, is a bundle of rags.

No, not rags.

Matisa.

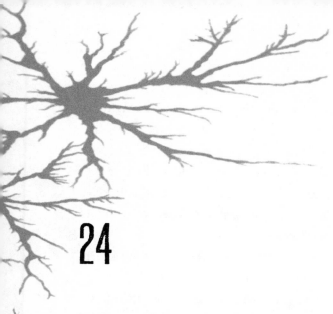

24

I SWALLOW A CRY. THE TEARS IN MY EYES BLUR the scene, and she becomes two figures for an instant, dancing in my vision. I blink furious and again bite back the urge to call out to her.

Beside me, Daniel is crying. I squeeze his hand, will him to stop. Nico is in shock, I can tell by the way he's stumbling, face blank.

Squinting back at the cart, I see there *are* two figures. They're bound by a chain to the back of the cart. The second one moves, pulling a head up and pushing upright.

It's Charlie.

"Hold up," the man says. He steps around me and looks between us. "See someone you know?" he asks, peering at me.

The hair on the back of my neck rises. *Lie. Lie to this man.*

"N-n-no," I stutter, trying to keep my face blank. I will the boys to keep quiet.

"You sure?" The rifle is leveled at my chest. He jerks his

head toward Charlie. "He told us there'd be people coming for her," he spits. "Never said pales and half bloods, though."

I stare at him. Charlie told him we'd come for Matisa? Here?

The confusion on my face must convince him because he spits again. "That's a shame," he says. "Least, for him."

"Get them tied and come help me, Emmett!" a shout comes from back in the trees. "He's dead weight."

My thoughts are fuzzy, and my heart is pounding up into my throat.

Keep your head. Don't panic.

My thoughts fly to Isi. He left moments ago. Please let him be somewhere nearby. He'll know what to do. He's probably planning something right this moment.

But something shifts on the far side of the cart, and the two big beasts lay their ears back, like horses do when they're annoyed. There's another horse, tied near them, and it's shifting about uneasy-like.

It's only a shadow in the dark night—its coat so black.

Blue.

And I notice there's someone lying inside the cage.

Isi.

I am back on the Watch flats with Matisa. She is whole: her glossy black hair hangs in a curtain around her face, and her skin is smooth.

Her movement is fluid as she bends and scoops up a handful of soil and plant.

It's the plant that protects against the Bleed, I know. But I can't remember the name . . . I lean forward, reaching for it, but she plucks it up with her other hand and crushes it into dust with one strong fist. She holds the soil out to me, a mound of black on her pink palm.

The dead in the river sing out, and I turn my head to look at the shining waters.

And now Matisa is at my feet, but her skin is mottled and bruised, swollen with blood.

I fall beside her and dig, pulling up handfuls of soil and pressing them to her, covering her in the earth. Burying her.

A rush of hoofbeats comes. Gunfire. Horses. Screaming.

The voices of the dead call out.

Make peace with it.

The voices drift over me like currents. They ebb and flow, seeping into my mind, filling the night air around me.

"—said there'd be a half-dozen reds."

"Damn liar. You see that cripple? She had no idea—"

"—either that or as stupid as a mule."

"—not just gonna sit here and—"

"But if she's what he says—"

My head snaps up. Moonlight streams down from high above, washing my hands and the rough bark before me in green light.

For a moment I can't figure where I am, but as I twist and feel the leather bindings dig into my wrists, feel my arms ache with the force of being held shoulder-height too long, it floods back. The men. Taking me. Putting each arm around either side of this tree and tying me here. To my left is Charlie, bound the same way. To my right, the little boys. They've been allowed to sit—their shackles are on a length of rope that gives them leave to move around the trunk. I shake my fuzzy head. Have I been asleep?

"—take our chances. What else can we—"

"Take them back to the Keep."

My thoughts sharpen. The Keep. These are Leon's men. I take a couple of deep breaths and crane my head to look over my shoulder.

Toward the riverbank the two men stand, heads together. Gesturing at us. Arguing.

A fire crackles before the wagon, lighting the dark shapes of Isi and Kane inside. Kane lies motionless. I squint hard and hope I'm not imagining that rise and fall of his chest. Matisa is in the same place, still in a heap on the ground. She coughs, rolls to the side, and throws up.

I fight the panic that builds and try to uncloud my thoughts.

I know better than to ask a question, but I need to figure what's going on.

The men wander around, chewing something and spitting it out now and again, checking the horses, checking their weapons.

Checking the hills to the north.

They're watching for something.

Where's the rest?

If they aren't talking about Andre and Violet, could they mean Rebecca? No. They were surprised we were "pales and half bloods." They're looking for a "half-dozen reds"—Matisa's people.

Julian stops dead, peering into the forest behind us. He

hisses, gesturing for the smaller man to come near. "You hear something?" he asks, pointing into the trees.

The man tilts his head, listening, for a long while. He shrugs and shakes his head no.

They resume their walk about the camp.

When they bend their heads together to talk again, there's a hiss at my left shoulder. Charlie's trying to get me to look at him.

I turn my head and wince. His bright blue eyes, the ones that remind me too much of his pa's, are shot through with crimson spiderwebs, and there's a purple bruise on one cheek. He looks awful—thin, like when we found him. Weak. He takes a deep breath and coughs. It sounds wet, like the people who'd come to Soeur Manon with that "water on their chest" sickness.

"Why—why are you here?" he rasps.

I frown. "Came—" I stop abrupt as the split at the corner of my mouth cracks with a stinging pain. I drop my chin to my shoulder, close my eyes, and press the cut into the sleeve of my shirt. Can't let the men know we're talking, but I need to get a handle on what's going on.

"Where's Rebecca?" I breathe.

"They sent her to that Keep," he mutters.

Charlie is the men's prisoner, too. So did he try to trade Matisa to them and get taken himself? Or was he truly trying to get away that day?

That small flicker of hope that Charlie didn't betray us tugs at my heart again. Mayhap it's not what Isi thought.

Course, that does us no good right now.

"You speak English." For a minute I think the words

are directed at me. I crane my neck. It's the blond man—Julian—speaking through the bars of the cage at Isi. Isi sits motionless, his face blank. "You want to be stupid about this, we can find ways to make you smart." He stalks to the back of the wagon, reaches down, and grabs Matisa by the arm. She ragdolls in his grasp. Isi leaps to the back of the cage.

Julian grins at him. "Find your tongue?" And now I see why he's so familiar. That blond man at the Keep—Leon—Julian looks so like him, they could be kin.

I watch him tug at Matisa. Her bloodless face, her limp body. Throwing up like that—might be what Soeur Manon called *la maladie de la chaleur*: heat sickness. Sometimes the gatherers in the gardens would get it if they hadn't covered their heads proper on a real hot day.

How long has she been tied behind that cart?

"Yes, you found it," the man continues. "We just need to get it workin'—"

"He's not one of them!" Charlie calls out in a wheeze.

Julian stops and straightens. He cocks his head like he's considering something, drops Matisa, and starts toward us. The way he moves spikes cold through my chest. He gets close and bends his head to Charlie. "Then where are they?"

Charlie swallows. "They're—they're coming—"

Julian places a hand on Charlie's back and shoves him into the tree. He leans his weight on his hand.

Charlie lets out a horrifying, strangled scream. I pull my head to the side, press it into my arm so I don't have to see.

"You better be telling the truth," he says. "If this was a lie to make yourself more valuable than that sister of yours, you're going to regret it."

Charlie's scream turns into a half sob, half choke. There's something inside his chest that's broken, I know it by the sound. I swallow the bile that rises in my throat.

"They're coming!" Charlie gasps.

"They'd better be," Julian says. He turns his sharp eyes on me. "You want the other side of that loose mouth split, you keep talking." My insides twist. He knew Charlie and I were conversing. But he steps back and turns away, speaking loud for the other man to hear. "They don't show by noon, we're moving on. Ceril will be happy with those two in the cage."

Ceril. The man I attacked. My blood thrums in my ears. Julian nods at me. "And I know someone who's looking for females." The blood rushes louder, putting a sickness in my gut. He runs a hand through his hair and smiles that dead smile. "You"—he looks at Charlie—"can stay here and rot."

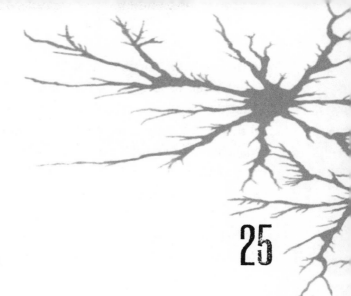

25

THE MOON HAS LONG DISAPPEARED, AND THE black of night is softening into an eerie blue. Trails of mist come off the river, creeping over the bank like ghost fingers. Dawn comes.

The men have dozed, taking turns patrolling the hills to the north, the forest to the south. In the blue light, they sit around their fire, drinking something out of metal cups.

My tongue is stuck to the roof of my mouth, and my arms are numb. I'm so thirsty. My skin is prickling all over me in an itchy heat. I'm losing touch with what's real, I know it. Twice these past hours I felt the forest move and breathe at my back, like the trees had come alive and wanted to reach out, carry me—us—to safety. Like that presence from my dreams—the one that was waiting for me in the grove—is there. Coming for me.

It's plain addled.

Kane and Isi are in that cage, the boys and I are tied here, and the men have got those bleedin' weapons at the ready. I force myself to look at Matisa, lying in that pitiful heap behind the wagon. She had reprieve from the heat for the night, but that sun'll come up, and it'll come up fierce. No way she'll last too much longer like that. For hours I've been trying to figure what to do, but all it's done is distracted me from worrying about Kane.

He still hasn't moved. And Isi's acting so strange. Hasn't gone to him once. Doesn't look at us.

My heart sinks. Does he blame me for this?

As the light grows, the smaller man stands and takes something from the back of the wagon. It's a long satchel of some kind—about the size of his gun.

"Goddamn it, Emmett, not that thing again," Julian says. He turns his head to the side and spits into the dust. He cocks his head at the trees. "You hear something?" he asks.

The little man—Emmett—shrugs.

Julian grabs his gun. "I'm going to look around."

"I'll keep an eye on them." Emmett fumbles with a catch on the satchel.

"If something happens, fire a shot," Julian says. He spits again. "Try not to hit one of them." He laughs and stalks off into the woods, leaving Emmett at the fire.

I look around. The little boys are asleep, tangled together; a mess of limbs and chain. A low melody starts up, thin and scratchy but nice—and all out of place with this filth. My head snaps toward the sound.

Emmett has a fiddle, but he's not playing it like the men from my settlement. Instead of resting it on the crook of his arm, he's got it tucked under his chin. He stares into the fire

240

as he plays. Never seen anyone play like that. Never heard a sound like that, neither. Can't reconcile something so beautiful made by someone so . . .

My mouth throbs. I close my eyes, try to pretend for a heartbeat we're somewhere else, somewhere good. My thoughts go to the Harvest dance. I think about dancing with Tom, with his wheat hair mussing into his eyes and his pa's too-big shirt. My troubles seemed so big back then, but I'd give anything to be back there right now. Safe inside those walls. Staring at Kane from across the hall, hoping he'd ask me to dance—

"Em." It's a whisper. Charlie again.

I keep my eyes closed.

"Em." More insistent.

I turn my head toward him, real slow.

"Why are you here?" he whispers.

I risk a glance at the fire. Emmett's eyes are closed now, and it's clear he's lost in the sounds he's making. He's paying us no mind. Still, I keep my voice low. Emmett may not be able to hear us, but if Julian is anywhere nearby . . .

"What do you mean?" I whisper.

"Why did you come here? To this forest?"

I frown. "I dreamt it."

His eyes narrow, like he can't figure my words. They widen. "She knew you'd come." His face contorts, like he's going to cry.

"Who?"

He shakes his head. "She lied to me," he says.

"Who?"

"Matisa."

The fiddle stops abrupt. I glance back, heart in my throat, expecting Emmett to be striding toward us. He's bent over the fiddle, fussing with the strings. He pulls and plucks at them before putting it back under his chin to start again.

"We're in trouble now," Charlie whispers. "Such trouble."

"What are you speaking on?"

He rests his forehead on his arms. "She told me to bring her here. Said they'd be here." He looks at the forest floor, like he's talking to himself. "But it's because she knew *you'd* come. They're not coming."

"Who's 'they'?"

"Looked like her: black hair and eyes, weapons I've never seen, riding those beasts like the wind. Spoke English rough. Came through my camp not more than a week before you showed up. They told me if I found her and brought her to them I'd be safe."

A week before. Looking for Matisa. What tale is he spinning?

"I don't understand," I say. "Why—why did you leave us? At that homestead?"

"I did the only thing that made sense." Charlie turns his head to look at me. "She was my guarantee of safety."

So he did take her. Shock and anger flare in me. "We helped you!"

"Helped us?" Charlie laughs low. It's an ugly sound. "You planned to cut us loose soon as you could. You would've sacrificed us to save your own hides in a heartbeat."

"That's not true."

"Ain't it? You saw how they hemmed and hawed over your

friend's trapped leg. Imagine if that had been me? And if I hadn't offered up my bow, you'd still be there while it withered and rotted off."

"You only offered your bow to win our trust. You did it so we'd drop our guard around you."

"I was trying to do something useful. Something you might remember favorable if the going got rough. But I could tell you weren't never going to accept me, even after all that." I fight down a pang of guilt that surfaces, but it deepens as he mutters, "Was just looking out for my family."

His family. Josiah gunned down. Rebecca, so close to having that baby, a prisoner at the Keep.

Now's not the right time—Charlie said that to Rebecca. I straighten up. He wasn't talking about the baby.

"You were planning to take Matisa all along," I say.

His eyes drop away from mine. The gesture speaks his truth. My insides twist, and I realize how bad I was hoping Isi was wrong. How bad I was hoping that me doing the right thing would help Charlie do the right thing. Why did I think that? Why did I even want that?

Brother Stockham swims in my vision again, raising the gun to his mouth. *You have lifted the burden*, he'd said, right before he pulled the trigger.

I press on my bad foot. Why is he in my thoughts again? What does he have to do with any of this?

When we found Charlie, I told myself I was giving him the chance I never got, the chance to choose a life without the shame of our family's actions shadowing it.

And now I see how wrong that was. Charlie doesn't deserve it.

I rest my head against the rough bark of the tree. Can't look at his pitiful, lying face.

At the fire, Emmett is lost in his fiddle playing. The high, strange melody fills the space around us.

"Em, you would'a done the same th—"

"Stop talking," I hiss. "Or I'll get them to bust your mouth so that you can't ever again."

I turn away from him, the drumbeat of my heart drowning out the fiddle.

No, not drowning it out. The fiddle has stopped.

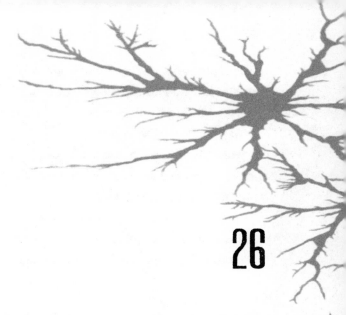

26

MY HEAD SNAPS OVER MY SHOULDER TO THE wagon. Emmett is peering into the cage, his fiddle abandoned at the fire.

Kane is stirring.

My breath gets fast. I throw a look to the little boys. Thanks be, they're still sleeping.

"Well, good morning." Julian appears out of nowhere. He climbs the riverbank like he's been out for a pleasure stroll. "He wakes."

My heart clenches as Julian saunters onto the flats. Kane rolls to his side and tries to push to his knees. His wrists give out, and he collapses face-first, back to the floor of the cage.

"Aw, c'mon, half blood, rise and shine," Emmett says with a laugh. He looks over to Julian, who grins back.

"Get a poker." Julian jerks his head at the fire. "We'll see if that gets him moving."

No.

Emmett steps to the fire and grabs the stick Julian was using to stir it. The end glows white-hot in the muted light of dawn. He hands Julian the stick, still grinning.

No.

"Hey!" I scream. The men stop dead. Julian turns incredulous eyes on me. My heart stutters. Think of something . . . "The girl—she needs water."

Julian exchanges a glance with Emmett. "Oh?" He tilts his head, an awful look on his face—like he's amused by me, and happy to kill me once he's done laughing.

"Y-y-yes," I say. I try to think fast. How can Charlie's tale buy us some time? "They won't . . . want her back like that."

The men glance at each other.

"Well, look who knows something all of a sudden," Emmett says. He and Julian leave the cage, their attention on me. My stomach plummets as they approach. Why did I say that? Got no idea how far I can stretch this lie. Don't know what Charlie told them.

Bleed it! Why didn't I learn more from him when I had the chance? Why'd I let my anger, my disgust with him, cloud my good sense?

Julian's before me now. He looks me over, a wolf eyeing a sickly lamb. "Tell me, just how will they want her?"

I swallow. "Healthy-like," I say.

Emmett steps closer. Squints. "You talk funny, you know that?"

The men glance at each other again. A strange look passes between them.

Behind them, Kane is on his haunches. He and Isi bend their heads together, talking low. Kane gestures to his moccasin. He's moving quick, alert. Was he playing at being hurt?

"You are not the half-wit you pretend," Julian says. He takes the poker from Emmett and steps close. "Where did you come from?"

When I don't answer, he juts the poker forward, stopping it shy of my face. The heat makes my eyelids flutter, my eyes water.

"Where did you come from?" he asks again.

My heart pounds in my ears. "Up north," I say.

His eyes narrow. "That's what the boy said, too. The thing is, we're quite interested in the north. So where, exactly?"

I swallow.

"Where?" he demands, lowering the stick to my neck.

"I—I . . ."

He presses the point of the poker into the hollow above my collarbone. Searing pain, a thousand bee stings at once, courses through my body. A cry tears from my mouth, but I remember the little boys and I swallow it back, choking.

Julian pulls the stick away. I gasp, expecting relief, but the sensation remains. Like an open cut, it pulses hot and raw.

"I think you had better tell—"

Emmett lets out a piercing yell. Julian spins. Emmett's eyes are wide and disbelieving. His hands are clenched around his thigh, around a bloody gash in his torn pant leg. He points to the ground. Kane's knife lies in the dirt.

Both men swivel and look at the cage, at Kane, who's crouched at the bars, his face contorted with despair. And I realize what happened.

Kane missed.

"You'll pay, boy!" Emmett hollers, holding his leg, his nostrils flaring, his face white.

Julian throws the poker to the earth. "Get him out of there," he growls, his voice low. Deadly. He grabs the key on his belt.

A hot wind blows through my head as they start toward the cart. Kane backs away from the bars, his eyes wide and scared. Isi cowers at the end closest to Matisa, his head turned away.

Julian grabs for the lock and twists the key in it as Emmett heads for the fire, where his rifle lies. Julian's hands shake with fury as he fumbles with the lock and pulls it from the bolt.

My heart is in my throat. The sun crests the riverbank over my shoulder, blinding me an instant. I blink, trying to find Kane in the gold glare. I close one eye, find the cage again, search for Kane and Isi—

But they are a blur.

They spring forward, throwing themselves at the door, knocking Julian backward. He falls as they barrel out of the cage and leap from the cart. Isi stumbles as he hits the earth and falls, unable to catch himself with his wrists bound. He lets out an awful scream, and somewhere in the back of my mind I picture those stitches I gave him tearing all the way open.

Emmett swings around from the fire with his rifle while Kane leaps onto Julian, fists flying. Julian's on his back, but he's big, strong. He bucks his body from under Kane, launching himself upward and grabbing at Kane's neck. They roll, the big man throwing his weight around like a bear, Kane fighting like a wildcat.

Isi swings an awkward double-fisted punch as Emmett rushes toward him, but he's off balance, and Emmett dances back. The movement must tear Isi's wound wide because he cries out and loses his balance, stumbling to the side.

Julian is on top of Kane now, his weight bearing down as Kane struggles, hands scrabbling, trying to keep them free of the big man's grasp.

Emmett steps forward and swings the butt end of the rifle against Isi's temple as Julian's fist connects, and Kane's head snaps back onto the earth.

There's a dead silence. It fills my head—somehow silent and deafening at once. I swallow air, trying to keep my thoughts from flying away, shattering.

Kane moves, anchoring me here. Still here.

The big man heaves himself up, breathing hard.

"Goddamn it," he spits. A gob of red lands in the dust. He looks at Emmett's gun. "Teach him," he barks, kicking Kane's body.

Emmett steps over Isi and levels the gun at Kane's head. He draws back the hammer.

Everything stops. The roar fills my head again. Can't speak. Can't think—

"*You shouldn't!*" It's Charlie's voice, echoing through the roar. "*They'll want him, too.*" He's speaking so far off, at the end of a tunnel or . . . or . . .

"*They will,*" Charlie's voice comes clear. "They'll want them all."

My eyes refocus. Emmett looks at Julian, gun still leveled at Kane.

Julian's eyes narrow. "Why?"

"They have claim. To this girl, too," Charlie says. "It's why they talk funny. Been living with them."

Them. *Them.* My mind works slow. Matisa's people, he means.

Julian tilts his head like he's considering. He spits red again. "Fine," he says.

A soft cry of relief escapes me. My knees are so weak I have trouble staying upright.

"But we'll make sure he can't try that again."

I watch, frozen, as Julian grabs Kane by the arms and rolls him over, facedown. Kane's body lolls in his grasp. Julian puts one knee on the center of Kane's back.

"Emmett, get the twine."

Emmett retrieves a leather strap from the back of the cart.

"You notice if he's left- or right-handed?"

Emmett looks at his thigh. "I'd say left."

Julian takes Kane's left hand and ties the binding around his wrist. He hops over to the cart and stretches Kane's arm long, tying the other end to the cart wheel.

What are they—

"Watch that red," Julian tells Emmett, nodding at Isi's lifeless form. Emmett walks over and presses the rifle into Isi's back. Julian fishes around in the back of the wagon. He finds what he's looking for and holds it high. It looks as long as the club but has a metal blade; some sort of long knife.

My throat closes off, heart pounds like it aims to bust right through my chest. Fear crowds into my mind like a rush of wind.

As Julian kneels again on his back, Kane begins to come

to, tries to pull his head up. His head snaps to the side, and I can see his wide eyes. This time, I can tell he's not playing at it.

He's terrified.

"Guess you'll have to learn with your right," Julian says, weighing the knife in his hand.

Kane's struggling now, pulling frantic at his tie. The big man's weight pins him to the earth—he can't move.

I find my tongue. "Don't!" But my throat is parched, and my voice is choked. I gather all of my strength and cry again, "Don't!" I fumble with my hand ties, rubbing my raw wrists against the leather, cutting the skin to shreds.

The little boys are stirring with the commotion, waking up—I can see them out of the corner of my eye. They're going to see—rage starts in the base of my gut, flooding my throat, burning into my brain. "No!" I scream.

Julian stops and looks back at me. He frowns.

"You need to still your tongue," he says. "Or you'll be short fingers, too." He looks at Emmett. "She could be kept for the men who like the freaks. Lame leg, fingerless hand . . ."

Emmett laughs but doesn't take his eyes, his rifle, off Isi.

Kane stops struggling and looks at me. He shakes his head. *Stop.* He closes his eyes. Breathes deep.

"I'll kill you!" I scream.

Julian smiles, turns away, and puts the tip of his knife to the knuckles on Kane's hand. "I'll just take two."

"I WILL KILL YOU!"

"Don't move now."

Julian raises the large knife high above his shoulder. He moves to pull his arm forward, bring the knife down—

Crack! The loudest sound, echoing through space, around my head.

The knife drops from Julian's hand. He swings around toward us, grabbing for his shoulder, his eyes wide and wild. A large spurt of blood springs from inside his armpit, a crimson puddle spreading around the shoulder of his shirt. He staggers, mouth open in confusion.

Emmett drops into a crouch. He raises the rifle's sight to his eye and swings around in a desperate circle, looking around wild.

Another shot rings out. Comes from behind us, in the trees. Emmett hollers and drops the gun like its a fire rock, clutching at his wrist.

It's one shooter. Can only be one shooter. One shooter with perfect aim.

And whoever it is approaches. Can't see from where I'm bound, but I can see it on the men's faces. Julian's glassy eyes focus on something behind us. Emmett freezes in place.

Julian puts his hands up as if in surrender. The blood is still flowing out like some nightmare spring—leaping out with each move he makes, staining his shirt shoulder to cuff, filling the hand clutching his shoulder.

A figure appears to the side of me, can see the gun barrel extending first. I hear the click of a hammer drawing back.

I crane my neck to see, and my heart stops.

He's standing there, gun raised to his eye, hands steady as anything. Wheat-blond hair glinting in the early morning sun.

It can't be. There's just no way—

"Let them go," Tom says.

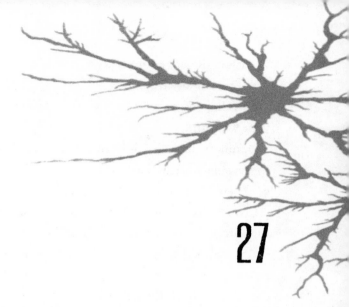

27

I'M DREAMING HIM; HE'S A VISION OF MY FEAR-addled mind.

No—he's here, standing so still, his blond head bent forward to the rifle. His name catches in my throat along with a sob of relief. Tom's face is calm, but he's watching careful, his body taut. We're still in danger. Julian is wounded, but he's upright. Emmett is standing there, gun at his feet, knife on his belt, looking to Julian for a signal.

Silence.

The air grows real still. Blood thrums in my ears.

Julian opens his mouth. "Friends," he repeats, as if in disbelief. "So many friends out here—" He wavers on his feet, stumbles one step to the side, and falls hard, face-first into the dirt. Like a broken bird he lies; one arm spread out, the other crumpled beneath him. A pool of blood stains the back of his shirt a dark red.

Tom takes a step forward, training his rifle on Emmett.

"Easy there," Emmett says, spreading his hands slow. "Don't want any trouble."

"Well, you got it." Tom's voice is a rasp. "Step away from your weapon."

Emmett does as Tom says, taking one foolish-large step to the side, his hands up in front of him. "What do you want, son?" He licks his lips. "Perhaps we can work out a deal."

Tom ignores him. "I'm going to give you a head start. You turn around now and get walking." He gestures with his gun.

Emmett's eyes widen. "But—there's nothing that way for miles." He tries to smile. Gestures at his leg. "I'm hurt. And I need food, water. My pack—"

"Those things are ours now. For our trouble."

Emmett's face darkens. "Look here, boy. You think for a minute you can—"

Lightning quick, Tom jerks the rifle to the fire and shoots. The neck of the violin shatters.

The rifle is back on Emmett's terrified face in a heartbeat. Tom loads a new bullet and pumps the bolt forward without taking his eyes off the man.

"Get walking," Tom says, real calm. "I ever see you again, I'll shoot you dead."

Emmett turns his scrawny frame in an about-face. And he runs.

Tom watches through the rifle sight. I blink, trying to make sense of what my eyes are showing me. Emmett's figure gets smaller as he scrambles up the low hill. When he disappears, Tom's shoulders relax. He drops the gun and turns to face us.

"Tom!" I choke out. My eyes well up, blurring his face.

And now, there's another sound, coming through the trees behind us. "Dottie!" Daniel cries.

Tom takes three giant strides toward the trees, reaching for me. At his touch, I burst into tears.

"Hey," he says. He smooths my hair away from my face.

"How?" I choke out through my tears.

"Came to see this crossing Henderson was speaking on. My pa healed up, and I—I needed to come. When I found that homestead, those mounds, and Nico's bow, I knew something'd gone wrong." He takes a knife from his belt and begins sawing at my ties. "Found Dottie yesterday and knew I was on your trail."

As the leather splits under the blade, tears stream down my dirt-streaked face. When I'm free, I realize I can't lift my arms. I step away from the tree, lose my balance, and stumble.

"Easy." Tom catches me, pulling me close. I suck into him, pressing my head into his shoulder, taking a shaky breath to quell my tears.

"Thank the Almighty for you," I say. I look over his shoulder to Kane, still facedown in the dirt, breathing shallow.

I start to cry again, and the blood from my cut mingles with tears in my mouth. "Free him," I say. "Free everyone but Charlie."

Matisa's face is ashen; her eyes are glassy. Can't climb to her feet. Can't talk. I bend toward her and press my hand to her brow. Like I figured, she's too hot. Her wrists are chafed raw where they were bound. Her hair is dull with dust and tangled into rope-like chunks that I pull away from her ghostly face. Looking at her close-up, my throat gets tight.

"Em?" Isi says, behind me. "What's wrong with her?"

I look over my shoulder. Isi is standing upright with effort, his hand pressed to his blood-soaked side.

"She was out in the sun too long behind that bleedin' cart," I say. "But she'll come around."

Isi's face is gray. I'll need to fix those stitches.

"We need to keep her cool and give her water in small doses." I nod in the direction of the grove. "We should move back into the trees," I say.

I look to Kane, who, like a miracle, sat up when I ran to him. He approaches, moving slow, but his eyes have cleared. There's a dark red mark under his left eye, and he's coated in dust, and he's the most beautiful thing I've ever looked on. The little boys crowd close to him, grasping at him with their dirty hands. They missed most of the horror, thanks be, but they're sticking right to him even so.

Isi picks Matisa up to move her. I look to the back of the men's wagon, where both the horse from the Keep and Dottie are now tied. Rebecca was riding Dottie when she bolted with Charlie. Tom found Dottie a day back, in the trees west of the river. Found her rider, too: a pale man, paler still with the bloat of death and riddled with streams of blood. No visible wounds; a desiccated corpse. Black tongue lolling from his slack mouth. The Bleed.

Tom coming out here without the remedy—could've been him. A wave of dizziness sweeps me, and I reach out a hand for Kane.

Kane draws me close, and the little boys crowd in against

our legs. He tilts my chin up and curses as he examines the burn mark.

"Killed me to have to miss," he mutters. He's talking about that moment he grazed Emmett with his knife. I can see in his eyes he wished he could've buried the knife in Julian's back instead.

"It was a good plan. It got you both out of that . . ." But I can't say it. The struggle floods back over me. Julian kneeling on Kane's back, taking out that long knife.

I grab his left hand and press a kiss into his palm, swallowing my sobs. If Tom didn't show when he did . . . If he wasn't sure with his aim . . .

"It's all right, Em," Kane says, grasping the back of my neck in one hand and pulling me close. "It's all right."

I press into him, let my tears soak his shirt. He's here. Right here. His chest beneath my ear, strong arms around me, chin tucked over my head.

"Shhh," he says.

We watch Isi lay Matisa down in the shade of the trees.

Long moments pass before Kane pulls back. "Should get the boys some water, something to eat." He takes them each by the hand and heads over to the supplies.

As I turn to join Isi and Matisa, Tom touches my arm.

"He'll bleed to death," he says, tilting his head at Julian.

He's still lying where Tom rolled him near the riverbank, faceup.

I walk over with Tom and study Julian. His entire right side is a mat of dark blood—so dark it looks black. His eyes are closed, his breathing shallow. He coughs. Blood spurts onto his neck and chin, trickles into his ear and streaks his blond hair.

I look back at Kane and the boys, rummaging in the cart. I press my kerchief to the burn mark on my neck.

Charlie watches us from where he is tied.

"I can . . . help him go quicker," Tom says. He hefts his rifle.

I look into his eyes. He's not telling me what to do; he's offering. And he's not the least bit scared to do it. Not the least bit afraid of what he's already done.

I think about Matisa tied to that cart. About the moment Julian's blade near came down . . .

"No," I say, pressing against the burn mark a tad harder than is comfortable. "Just roll him over." A pool of blood is gathering in my mouth again. I spit it into the dust at Julian's feet. "The others ask, tell them he's already gone."

In the shadows of the trees, Matisa's dark eyelashes match the circles beneath her eyes. Her face is too pale, her breathing still shallow.

Kane stands in the trees with the little boys, who are eating some sort of flat, dry bread. Tom circles our group, checking and rechecking his weapon.

"Are we safe here?" I ask Isi. I set my bag down beside Matisa and start rifling through my herbs and tinctures. "Do you think Leon's men will come looking for Julian and the rest?"

He shakes his head. "I do not know." He presses his hand to Matisa's forehead, and his brow knits with worry.

"I'll bring her round," I assure him, setting aside mint and dried rose hips for a cooling wash.

Tom stops his pacing. "How far is it to your home from here?" he asks Isi.

"A few days if our journey is untroubled." Isi looks at Tom appreciative-like. "We would be glad to have you with us. You are skilled with that gun now."

Tom's cheeks pink a mite, like the old Tom. "Been practicing." He pushes his blond hair off his forehead. "Course that was mostly with a bow and arrow, and just aiming with Andre's gun, but he let me shoot it a couple of times."

"What is that?" Kane nods at the gun. It's different from any of those we had at the settlement. The way he loaded it when he threatened Emmett—never seen anything like it.

"Don't rightly know," Tom admits. "Took it off that man I found with Matisa's horse. But it's more accurate than Andre's old gun and wasn't too hard to figure. I didn't have a gun, so it was real lucky."

Kane shakes his head like he can't believe how casual Tom's talking. "You left the settlement without a weapon?"

"Well, I had a bow and arrows," Tom says. "But with Andre gone I didn't have a way to get a rifle. People are right protective about them. Would've had to steal it, and I . . ." He shrugs. "Felt like they needed it more."

I study Tom. He's so different now. Last fall he was so scared to break his virtues he refused to help me uncover Stockham's secret until it was near too late. It took me being locked up, near put to death, for him to act. Mayhap he's making up for that now. Mayhap he's decided never to choose fear again.

"But I did have this," he says. He reaches into his pack and pulls out a scroll of soft paper. Kane and the boys crowd close as he kneels beside me.

"That a map?" I ask.

He nods. "A copy of Henderson's. Drew it up hasty so it's not complete." He unrolls it and spreads it before us. "Here"—he gestures to the right side—"are the plains to the east of the river." His finger traces the line winding north and south to a horizontal line. "There is the crossing, so we must be here." He points above it, to a cluster of circles. There is a word scrawled. I squint. "It says *cottonwood*," he tells me. "Henderson said they'd be losing their white seeds this time of year."

My snow-covered trees. "And this?" I point to a cluster of shapes—squares—to the right of the river.

"The closest Dominion outpost."

"The one Henderson talked about?"

He nods. "Probably ten days from the crossing, on foot."

I take a deep breath. It's so far.

He taps triangles on the left side of the map. "The mountains."

Isi peers at the map.

Matisa stirs. Her eyes flutter open and find mine.

"Isi?" she asks me.

"He's fine," I say, as he says, "I'm here."

"He stayed with you," she breathes. "I told him to."

I grip her hand. "He stayed."

"That was good." She smiles up at Isi. "Let's go home."

Isi gazes down at her, and the protective love in his eyes

near steals my breath. He nods and looks at me, including me in his answer. "Yes."

Her eyes close.

I can feel Kane's eyes on me, but I can't bring myself to look up. I'm too scared of what I'll see there. I know he's lost out here, drowning under the weight of all this.

And if I'm being honest with myself, I'm lost a mite, too. Attacking Ceril at the Keep, screaming at Emmett and Julian that I'd kill them. I meant it, deep down. In that moment I meant every word. And then leaving Julian there on the riverbank.

My world is changing. I'm changing with it.

But I can't bear for Kane not to be a part of it.

"Anyone know how to drive that cart?" Tom asks. "Seems a shame to leave it behind."

Isi nods. "Let us wait for dark to set out," he says. "It is better for Matisa to travel out of the glare of the sun. But we can be ready to go when she is." He looks at Kane. "Kane?"

Kane looks at the little boys beside him. At me. I won't ask him, not again. But the thought of leaving here without him . . .

Can't live, not knowing if he made it somewhere safe, if he's all right. His best chance for safety is with Matisa's people. Please, *please* let him see that.

"I can help ready the horses," he says, and my relief is so sharp I sit back on my heels, dizzy. I breathe deep.

"Let's see if those men had anything useful in their effects," Tom says, and pushes to his feet.

Isi nods. "Em will help Matisa." And the way he says it, like he has no doubt, makes me bold and pleased at once.

"Stay near Em," Kane tells Nico and Daniel. Daniel leaves him to come to me, but Nico shakes his head and grips Kane's hand. "It's all right," Kane says, soft. "I'll be right over there. And Em will keep you safe." That funny half smile pulls at his mouth. Like the Kane I remember.

I smile back, my heart full of so much pain and love I feel like it might burst. "Come help me mix this?" I ask Nico.

Out in the clearing, Tom and Isi manhandle the cage off the cart. It lands on the earth with a deep thud. Lucky stands nearby. She emerged from the trees a short time ago, a spindly colt close at her heels, searching for her milk. That horse has some Almighty-given good sense to have made herself scarce when the going was about to get rough like that. Either that, or Daniel named her perfect. She nuzzles her colt's rump while it drinks.

While Kane helps them organize, Nico helps me finish mixing my cooling wash. He sings to himself as we work, and as I catch the words, I feel a happy laugh build in my chest.

That rabbit song has a tune after all.

He and Daniel sit back and watch me dribble water into Matisa's mouth. I wash her face and neck and bathe her arms, taking care around her wrists. Her chest rises and falls. I wash her arms again. And again.

As dark falls, the trees around me shift, becoming tall peaks. The air is crisp, scented with something new—moist earth and evergreen. Tall rock walls reach high toward the stars, and I am home, so at home—

"Em." It's Tom, his hand on my shoulder. I start and look around. The grove is quiet and still. Kane is tucking our cloaks around two drowsy little boys.

I look at Tom's scarred hand, still on my shoulder, and I'm filled with joy. Wasn't sure I'd ever see those hands again.

I look back at Matisa. She's sitting up.

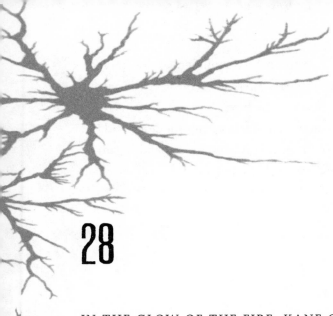

28

IN THE GLOW OF THE FIRE, KANE OFFERS MATISA a waterskin and some dried meat. Tom and I sit close as she takes small sips and nibbles at the jerky.

Isi fusses around her like some giant swallow flitting around its nest. She listens, quiet, as we tell her what happened when our group splintered. Her eyes go dark when I tell her about the First Peoples at the Keep, darker still when I describe the battle that helped us flee, but she says nothing. When I get to the part about Isi bringing us here, her face changes. She shakes her head and smiles up at him. "I am . . . surprised. And also not surprised."

His eyes go soft, a mite unsure—the way they get only when he looks on her. She tilts her head, and now she's looking on him a new way, kind of like she's seeing him for the first time.

"It was the right thing," he mutters.

"Don't worry," I say. "He's still as prickly as ever."

He shoots me a dark look, but he's playing at being angry.

"Em was more help than I imagined," he says. "But she was slow as an earthworm," he adds, and I scowl.

"Not so slow," Matisa says. "We still have time to catch the hunters before they leave." The hunters. I'd all but forgot. I count the nights quick in my head and realize she's right. Feels like we've been out here a lifetime, even though we parted with Nishwa only six days ago. As our eyes meet, I realize what she isn't saying: she's worried he ran into Leon's men. She's worried he didn't make it, didn't warn the hunters himself.

She pulls her gaze away and changes the subject. "You rescued us," she says to Tom. "How?"

Tom ducks his head at the compliment. "Left the settlement three days after you, aiming for that crossing. I had the map, so I could cut cross the land rather than following the river—Almighty, but it winds something awful. Would've taken me days."

I shake my head. I was so irritated at Henderson showing up the way he did. Turns out his bleedin' map is the reason Tom came upon us in time.

But I think back to him telling us about finding Matisa's horse and that man. It would've been enough to send the old Tom straight back to the settlement. He pressed on, somehow knowing he was on our trail. I study him. His prairie-sky eyes are clear and determined. This Tom doesn't look scared or resentful. Looks full of purpose. Like deciding to come out here has lifted his head high in a way life in the settlement never could.

"Matisa." Kane's voice calls my thoughts back to the present. "Why are your people looking for you?"

Matisa pulls her knees to her chest and takes a deep breath. "They aren't," she says. "When Charlie took me, he told me my people promised him protection in exchange for me." She shakes her head. "Something felt wrong with his tale. And when he told me they were wearing a red crest, I knew what."

My pulse races. The *sohkâtisiwak*.

Kane frowns his confusion.

"It was a group of abandoners from Matisa's people," I explain, quick. "They are dangerous." I lean toward her. "What did you do?"

"I knew that even if I could convince him they were enemies of my people, he wouldn't care," she says. "So I played along. I told him I knew where they were."

"But why this grove?" I ask.

"I dreamt you would be here," Matisa says. She looks over at the little boys, and her eyes brim with tears. I wonder if she knew it would be bad, wonder if she dreamt this, like she dreamt we would be separated.

"But we . . ." She swallows. "We were caught by four men the first night out. They were going to take us to this Keep you spoke of. But Charlie got the ear of the tall pale man— Julian. He told Julian I was special, that they could give me back to my people in exchange for something important. I could tell Charlie didn't know exactly what that was, but . . ." Matisa trails off.

"Julian knew," I finish.

She nods. "I overheard him saying something about 'safety from the Bleed.'"

I ignore Tom's and Kane's puzzled looks and urge her on. "What happened?"

She continues. "Julian pretended to strike an accord: Charlie's freedom for what he knew. Then he shackled Charlie once he got this location from him."

"And Rebecca?"

"Julian argued with the other men about coming to this place—there was a bunch of shouting about loyalty to Leon, that man you mentioned. They drew guns and split us up—the other men took Rebecca. Julian and that small man took us." She looks around the darkened woods. "I don't know how long we will be safe here; the abandoners—*sohkâtisiwak*—are looking for me."

"But why?" Tom asks. "What was Julian going to trade you for?"

Isi shifts behind her but doesn't speak.

I meet Matisa's gaze.

There's a flicker of indecision in her eyes. They harden. She takes a deep breath. "The sickness Henderson told your settlement about—the one that made this land dangerous for so long—it is out here still."

Kane frowns. "Out here?"

"It comes to small rivers and creeks. But it is impossible to determine which waters have it until it is too late."

"You mean you can't tell until after you get sick?" Tom asks.

She nods. "That is what makes it so dangerous. It is why so many of your kind died when they first arrived. They did not know what it was, or where it came from."

There is a silence as Tom and Kane take in Matisa's

words. Tom points to the waterskin in her hands and raises his eyebrows.

"I am safe from it," she says. "We all are."

"Safe how?" Kane asks. I risk another glance at him. His arms are crossed, and his eyes are fixed on her face.

"I am part of a small circle of healers who know a remedy for it. I have been sworn to secrecy, as it has long been our greatest asset." She swallows. "Julian and his men want the remedy so they can safely expand their territory. He planned to trade me for it."

Kane drops his arms. He breathes deep and rubs a hand over his head.

"The people Julian was going to trade you to, the abandoners," Tom says. "This is why they wanted you?"

"Yes. They may have stolen some of our stores of the remedy to forge an alliance with these newcomers, but they do not know how to create it. With the help of Leon's weapons, they could force us to reveal the method. But if they could get their hands on one of the healers—on me—they might be able to force me instead. Julian didn't know he was planning to trade the one person here who can create it. Fortunately, neither did Charlie."

"Matisa has been keeping us all protected from it as we journey," I say.

Kane's head snaps toward me. "You knew?"

I nod, avoiding his eyes. Choose my words careful. "I knew that we were safe with Matisa."

"But the settlement?" Tom asks. "How did we all survive—"

"The settlement has the remedy," I say. "We've always

used it, always been safe from the Bleed. Matisa assured me of this before we set out."

"You knew before we left?" Kane asks, and the disbelief in his voice forces me to meet his gaze. Hurt. Shock. Confusion. All of it swarms in his dark eyes, threatening to drown me.

"Em had little choice but to stay silent," Matisa says. "She knew I broke an oath when I told her, and she did not want me to do it twice."

But Kane speaks like he hasn't heard. "You didn't trust me," he states. And the broken tone of his voice . . .

I try to open my mouth to tell him he's got it wrong, but my throat closes off as I stare at his wounded face.

He shakes his head and turns away, his gaze going to where the little boys slumber.

Almighty. What have I done?

"If this group is looking for you," Tom's voice breaks in, "we should get moving."

"You and the little ones can ride in the cart," Isi says to Matisa. He moves to help her to her feet, but I'm frozen in place, watching Kane.

He stands in profile, his jaw working hard. The moonlight cuts a sharp bright line along his face.

Tom and Isi steady Matisa on either side and get her moving toward the horses.

I stand and take a step toward Kane. "I—" My voice is caught in my throat. I point at the little boys. "I can help you carry them."

He doesn't move.

I'll apologize. I'll explain. I'll tell him why I had no choice.

But he turns now and fixes his eyes on me, and my heart near drops from my chest. The look on his face—there's nothing I can say that's going to make this all right. Not now. Mayhap not ever.

Blood thrums in my ears. I force the words out. "You're . . . coming, right?"

Real slow, he nods. "Matisa's people have the remedy," he says. There is no anger in his voice. No love, neither. "It'd be foolish not to."

Kane waves off my offer of help and carries the little boys one by one, still asleep, to the cart. He settles them in the back among the supplies, beside Matisa, while Isi checks the harnesses.

I wrap my arms around myself as they pack, Kane's answer ringing around in my head. He's coming with us. It's what I've wanted all along.

But it's all wrong now.

He was supposed to choose our new life out here. We were supposed to head into the unknown together. We're heading into the unknown all right, but it's no longer a choice. He's doing it because there is no better option.

I clench my teeth in frustration, feeling the urge to hit something. Someone.

My eyes find Charlie. His thin, sad form is sagging against the tree, where he's been watching us. The flicker of anger blooms into a flame.

The moon is up over the far bank, but tonight I'm not comforted by its light. Tonight, I wish for dark.

"Em?" It's Tom. He tilts his head at Charlie.

"I'll deal with it," I say. I steel myself, feel the moon beating fierce on my head, and limp toward him. I stop two strides away.

Charlie's eyes widen as he realizes I'm not coming any closer. "You can't leave me here, Em," he breathes out. Coughs that wet cough. "Please. Give me a chance."

"You *had* a chance," I say. "Days back. When you told me you wanted to put the past in the past."

He licks his lips. "I meant it."

"No. You were planning to take Matisa all along," I say.

"But it wasn't anything against you. Don't blame you for what happened to my family, cast out like that. Never did." He nods his head at the group behind me. "Don't even blame Kane for my pa's death. I spoke up for him, saved his life." His blue eyes are wide, pleading.

I feel a pang through my anger. That last part is true. If he hadn't spoke when he did . . .

But I think about Matisa as that bundle of rags. Mayhap that was Julian's doing, but Charlie's actions put her there. He took her from us the first chance he got—and near took Isi's head off as he fled.

"If you'd just stuck with us in the first place, none of this would've happened." My voice gets hard. "You near killed us all."

He barks a laugh and shakes his head. "You're dead out here anyhow," he says. "And not just because Julian and his kind are everywhere."

My eyes narrow. "What are you speaking on?"

Charlie looks at me a mite smug. "There's a bad sickness out here. The Bleed, Julian called it."

So he does know.

"It's just luck you all aren't corpses already." He coughs and then glares at me. "That ain't my fault—it's yours."

"How's that?"

"You brought that girl into the settlement thinking she was our salvation," Charlie says. "And then the whole world turned to hell. And for what?"

"You would never understand," I say.

"I'm willing to bet you don't understand, neither."

"You know nothing!" I spit out. "You're just like everyone at the settlement—protected without even knowing it and fearful of all the wrong things!" My temper's rising bright and hot.

"If *you'd* been more fearful of Matisa—"

"She kept you alive out here!" I shout, and the scorn in my voice could split bark. "*You're* lucky you aren't a corpse; *we* were never in danger!" I've said too much now. I snap my mouth shut.

His eyes lose their mean shine. "What are you speaking on?"

I look away, my anger running hot under my skin.

There's a silence.

"You're speaking on that place," Charlie says and coughs. "Ain't you?"

I turn back. "What place?"

"Julian said Matisa's people know a special place that cures the Bleed," he says. "Said that's what they were offering me; its location."

I frown. A special place that cures the Bleed?

"When Julian caught us, he was headed north to find it."

North. My thoughts fly back to Elizabeth and Ulysses Sharapay, threatened by Leon so they'd map the way north. That's why Leon wanted the map? Because he believes in a place that cures the Bleed? All at once I want to laugh. This means Leon and his men don't understand the remedy—or the Bleed—at all. But the thought of Leon's men finding my fortification sobers me. I remember how surprised Henderson was at finding our settlement; Leon's men might think they'd found that special place. My settlement outnumbers them, but Leon's weapons are far more powerful.

"How many were going with Julian?" I ask.

"Why?"

"How many?" I demand.

"Just Emmett and him," Charlie says, his brow creased. "Said he wanted to be the one to find it first." He shakes his head. "Swore me to secrecy, told me he'd share it, but I know now he was just using me to get there. He wasn't planning to keep me alive."

My thoughts fly back to Julian with that poker, asking me where I was from.

We're quite interested in the north.

The worry in my chest eases. Julian is lying in a bloody heap on the bank of the river. And Emmett is heading into lands he'll be hard-pressed to survive. I raise my chin. "Julian knew nothing," I say. "And you betrayed the people who could've helped you."

"C'mon, Em," he whines. "What was I supposed to do?"

"You were supposed to do the right thing."

He straightens up and looks me in the eye. "And what *is* that, out here? Mayhap the 'right thing' was clear in the settlement, but out here it's different. And you know it. You leaving Julian there, choking on his own damn blood, proves it."

A sickness rolls in my gut. The moon feels too warm on the back of my neck.

"I ain't judging you for that," Charlie says, soft. "You and me both know he deserved it."

I swallow. Slashing that man's face at the Keep. Staring at Julian's sickly form, listening to him drown in his own blood. Is this what I am now?

"Got nothing no more. Got no one. Ain't that penance enough?" His eyes are wide. Pleading.

Something in my heart twists. I press into my bad foot, focus on the wash of pain for a moment.

Him speaking up for Kane doesn't change what he did.

Doesn't change what he is.

Does it?

Grinding my teeth, I press my fingers to my brow.

Nothing's the way it's supposed to be; is that all his fault? I showed him mercy before, and look where it ended us. If Tom hadn't found us when he did . . .

I take my knife from my belt, weigh it, one hand to the next. An image swims before me: Brother Stockham's eyes before he pulled that trigger. What they held. Relief. *Relief.*

I look into Charlie's eyes now, so full of despair—and I know.

I know why I gave Charlie a chance. It wasn't about letting him wash the stain clean like I did. It was about Brother Stockham pulling that trigger. It was about all that happened after that.

Deep down, I've been wondering, if I'd somehow been able to make Brother Stockham see, if I'd shown him he could turn from his pa's teachings, mayhap those scars on his back wouldn't have found their way inside his mind like that. And then—then my pa wouldn't have died to protect me.

I gave Charlie a chance because I thought it would pay for my sins of not giving the same to Brother Stockham. Thought it might pay for the death of my pa. But . . .

This is a new world. It brings things we cannot help. Isi's words drift over me, flood my heart with resolve.

Charlie made his choice. There was nothing I could've done to change that.

All I can do is make my own choice. Right here, right now.

"I can't give you another chance," I say. "Can't do that to my people. Not again."

I wrap my right hand firm around the knife handle and steel myself. Raise it slow.

Charlie drops his head to his arms, as if that might protect him.

I take a deep breath.

And hammer the knife forward.

It splits the bark, drives deep into the flesh of the tree. When I drop my hand, a small glint of the blade and the bone handle jut out from the trunk above Charlie's leather ties. Close enough to reach or just out of his grasp; I'm not sure.

"But mayhap the Almighty will."

I turn and head for the horses.

I don't look back.

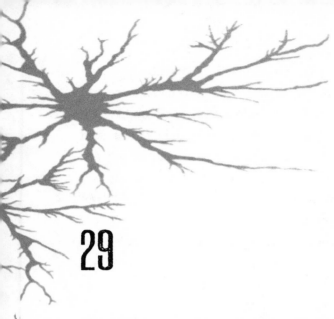

29

WE SKIRT THE FOREST AND RIDE THROUGH THE sweeping hills, the moon lighting our way, stars bright above us.

Our pace is quick. We found valuable gear in Julian's cart: a rifle like the one Tom has, bullets, three knives, including Julian's long blade, food stores, and also gear for the horses, real bridles and blankets.

Isi drives the cart with Matisa and the two little boys in the back. The boys are wrapped up against the chill and fast asleep.

I double with Tom on Dottie behind the cart. Kane rides beside us on Blue, but he doesn't seem inclined to talk. Or look at me.

Charlie surfaces in my mind. I lost my tongue to anger, dealing with him, but some of it was anger at myself. Just glad I figured that out before it was too late. Before I did something I couldn't take back.

Like keeping Matisa's secret from Kane.

Bleed it! How can I fix this?

I risk a glance at him, but his eyes are elsewhere—like he's thinking hard, considering something, but mayhap he's just playing at looking occupied so he doesn't have to look at me.

We ride an hour or more in silence. When Isi pulls the cart to a stop atop a large rolling hill, giving the pull-horses a moment to rest, I look back at the giant ribbon of river glinting silver in the moonlight. The *mâyimitos* forest is now a small patch of black to the east. To the south, shadows.

Matisa pulls herself up and stands in the back of the cart, waving off the hand Isi offers for balance. "I am fine," she says, and peers out at the darkened land. "The quickest way is due west, but we will need to go north from here," she says.

"Why?" I ask.

"The drylands are over this next rise," she answers. "They are dangerous this time of year, when thundershowers can show up with little warning. With rain, they become a lake of mud."

I recall Henderson's words about seeing these drylands in the rain. Said they could drown a man.

"Rain like that?" Tom asks from his perch behind me. He points. Over the mountain shadows in the far west, a dark bank of cloud is stirring.

Matisa lifts her face to the air. "The wind does not blow this direction," she says. "But we should not take the chance. We will skirt them to the north."

Like she understands, Dottie swings her neck in that direction, ears pricked forward. The harnesses on the pull-horses jangle as they turn their heads the same. They hear something.

"What is it?" Isi asks, tilting his chin at the hills to the north.

Kane puts the spyglass to his eye. He scans the hills and curses. "Riders," he says.

My throat gets tight.

I look to Matisa. Her face is grave. "How many?" she asks.

Kane counts. "At least ten."

"Can you tell who—"

Kane shakes his head, lowers the glass, and pulls his horse close to the cart. He hands the spyglass to Matisa for a look.

"*Sohkâtisiwak?*" I ask Matisa.

"Maybe," she says, scanning.

"Do we take a chance that they're friendly?" Tom asks.

We look around. There is no shelter in these hills—no place to hide. We have two rifles now, but only a slingshot and knives beyond that. If they aren't friendly, taking a stand here would be courting our own death.

"Can we outrun them?" Tom asks. He points to the dark hills in the south.

"Not that way," Matisa says. "Beyond those hills the drylands stretch south for miles. I do not think we should risk it."

"How far do they stretch to the west?" I ask.

Matisa looks torn. "A night's ride—no longer."

"But couldn't they skirt to the north and catch us on the other side?"

"It would take them far longer," Matisa says. "We could be long gone before they reach it. If it doesn't rain."

"And if it does rain?" Tom asks.

"Then it will be very dangerous," Matisa says. "But if it looks like it will rain—"

"They are less likely to follow," Isi finishes her thought.

We look to the clouds gathering in the west, dark and heavy, creeping slow, blotting out the stars.

Kane looks at the rise that hides the drylands, and then at the little boys. "Any other ideas?" he asks.

No one offers anything.

We look back to the north.

The clouds scud across the moon and reveal the riders streaming down a small hill. Ten dark shapes on horseback— full silent from this distance, riding hard. A ways off still, but close enough for our horses to hear. And closing fast.

"Down into the drylands," Isi decides. "It is our best chance."

Matisa hops down from the back of the cart. "The earth will be rough and our horses might stumble. I will ride with Tom," she says. "Em, you ride with Kane."

I slide from Dottie and Kane puts a hand out to help me in front of him.

Matisa settles herself in front of Tom and takes the reins. "Come on," she says, kicking her horse forward.

We go.

I crane my neck and glance back as we crest the last rise. The riders are closer still—about half the distance they were before. They know we're here. If they see us head into the drylands, will they follow?

As if in answer, the dark sky before us flashes an angry bright light. The night is calm, but the air is getting heavy, like it does when rain is coming.

Below us, the drylands stretch out, dusty and cracked. I see now why they are dangerous: they are a series of steep coulees made from precarious, sandy soil. Our only route is down into the canyon, where we will be surrounded by high, crumbling walls.

Walls that will run like waterfalls in the rain.

We move down into the canyon as quick as we can, but the rough terrain makes it tricky for the horses to find their footing. The night is cool, but I don't press backward to steal Kane's warmth. His chest grazes my back, his arms encircling me to hold the reins, but it feels unfamiliar. Like I can't remember the feel of his body against mine.

Down in the canyon, the cliffs are like dark creatures with cracked faces, eyeing us silent as we traverse the crumbling earth. Matisa clucks her tongue, urging her horse to pick up the pace.

The leather of the riding gear creaks as we join her, moving at a fast walk. Kane handles Blue like he's done it a hundred times before.

Hours creep by as we traverse the canyon at this pace. Everyone watches the sky, reluctant to speak—as though our noise alone might call the rain. The air is thicker still, bringing a scent that usually makes my heart swell but now makes it tight.

Isi gets the pull-horses to pick up the pace. The jostling wakes the little boys. They sit up, rubbing the crusts of sleep from their eyes. Kane tells them, firm, to stay seated.

"Lucky!" Daniel calls. The mare and her colt have been wandering at their own pace and now stand ahead of us.

Lucky raises her head from a small patch of rock daisies and watches us go past. "Come on, girl!"

The high walls of the coulees around us are so different from the plains, the rolling hills, I feel like they're closing in on us. Can't see the sky, can't see what's coming. I feel my heart speed, my breath coming short and fast.

"Easy, Em," Kane mutters. It's the first thing he's spoken to me in hours.

There's a low rumble over the ridge. It echoes through the valley, off the canyon walls.

Matisa speaks to Isi in their language, and he slaps the reins on the horses' necks, urging them faster. Our horse keeps pace beside the cart.

"How much farther?" I ask Matisa.

She shakes her head, her mouth pressed in a worried line.

The cart gains speed. A cold wind snakes into the valley, whipping my hair into my face. I pull it free with one hand and watch as the little boys clutch the sides of the cart. The pull-horses falter as they run, stumbling now and again in the loose shale.

"Hurry!" Matisa shouts.

We urge our horses faster still. Kane tightens his arms around me and I steel myself, waiting for those first raindrops to fall. They'll feel like fire, I know, like a peppering of hot coals, because they'll signal death. There's no shelter. *And the rains will turn the drylands into a lake of mud.*

The wind blows strong against us, and the wagon wheels screech as we rush through the blackening valley.

The pull-horses stretch out their necks as the ground becomes more even and they can lengthen their strides. And our horse, sensing the sure ground, puts its head down and gallops faster still. We are flying along, the wind rushing around us, the hoofbeats clattering loud, echoing through the valley.

I hear a shout and look back. Isi is pointing at something ahead. I squint. In the distance I can make out two large, dark shapes, standing like sentinels in the dark. And beyond and above that, a soft glow—like the light of a hundred torches. Our horse strains with effort as the ground gets steeper.

We're climbing out of the valley. There's a wide path here, wide enough for two wagons to traverse side by side, and the earth is packed, as though by many travellers.

We're nearly there. Even if the heavens opened right now, we'd make it in time. At the thought, relief courses through me and, with it, exhilaration. I turn my face to the wind as our horse gallops, feeling my heart racing along with the beast's strides.

A laugh escapes me. I feel light as air. Lightning flashes again—the storm is moving to the northwest. I almost wish the rains would come now and drench our dusty skin.

Up we go, our horses straining, the cliff walls flying past. Up to solid ground.

We get to the top of the rise, out of the valley. Kane pulls our beast to a halt.

I feel a joy so deep I want to shout. I look behind to share the moment with Kane.

But his face is not joyful. He shakes his head. "Almighty," he swears and swings down from the horse.

Matisa and Tom join us. She nods at Kane. "You rode well," she says.

Kane doesn't reply. The cart pulls alongside us with the little boys, their tear-streaked faces staring out. Kane goes to them, making soothing sounds.

"Look." Isi's staring into the dark hills before us, pointing to the glow I remember seeing from down in the valley.

My heart's still racing from the ride. "What is it?" I ask.

"Perhaps a settlement," Matisa says.

"Should we avoid it?" Tom asks.

Kane straightens up. "Why?"

"It might be Leon's men," I say.

"So *now* we're tired of risking our lives?" He crosses his arms, his voice cutting and bitter.

My excitement is snuffed out.

"Kane—"

"Shhh!" Matisa hisses and holds up her hand for quiet, peering into the dark before us. She draws in her breath as two shadows emerge from the dark hills.

A light appears, blinding us a moment, freezing us in place.

My eyes adjust, and the two figures before us come clear.

Their faces are pale and round, their clothes are rough and plain. One older man and one young. Their light-colored eyes watch us, curious-like. The older man holds a lantern. They have no weapons.

"Who are you?" Isi demands.

The older man gestures to the drylands valley and asks us something in a tongue I've never heard. The boy points to the hills and speaks the same.

They don't speak English.

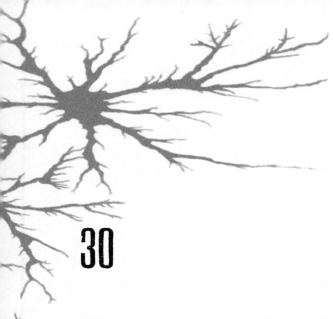

30

THE VILLAGE IS CLUSTERED IN THE FOOTHILLS, nestled like pinecones in the boughs of some low-growing spruce. It's quiet, no signs of life, but as we approach, I notice there are eyes everywhere. Lanterns dot the shadowed hillsides, and as we approach and the sun comes up behind us, they wink out. I can't see the faces of the figures holding those lanterns, but I feel their gazes.

When the man and boy beckoned us to follow, we'd hesitated. But then Blue stumbled and took a knee, righting himself with effort. Looking at our bone-tired horses, realizing Matisa still needed rest—that we all did—we decided to take the chance these two are as friendly as they seem.

There is a fence encircling this side of the settlement, one made of sheared poles sharpened to wicked-looking points at the tips and tilted forward like spears. A warning.

A sliver of fear springs to my chest, but I force myself to remember Elizabeth Sharapay and her husband. Not everyone out here is looking to harm us.

The young boy pulls aside a gate in a jangle of poles and metal, and as we pass through, the sun breaks over the hills behind us and washes the village in a rose light.

The worry in my chest eases. This place doesn't feel dangerous.

The buildings, though, are right curious. They're built into the sides of the hills and constructed with poles similar to those of the fence. Laid side by side, the poles end in steep peaks and the cracks between them are sealed with mud. The rooftops are alive—covered in earth that sprouts new grasses. Atop each of the triangular dwellings, a thin line of smoke wisps out from a metal chimney. The backs of the houses disappear into the earth like the hills are embracing them, keeping them safe from the winds.

Never seen anything like it. I look to Matisa and Isi, but it's clear from the expressions on their faces that they haven't, neither.

The old man leading us waves his hands at a cluster of speckled chickens in our path. They're nothing like our brown hens; their soft feathers are dotted white and black and they have crests of bright red on their heads. They cluck and stretch their yellow legs as they scatter.

A little girl is out in front of one of the houses, beating a rug with some sort of woven stick. She wears a colorful scarf of intricate yellow and red flowers on her head. It covers her blond hair, frames her pink cheeks. Her blue eyes widen as she sees us, but the man holds up a hand and says something, his voice gruff but reassuring. She nods, puts down her stick, and offers us a small smile before hurrying off.

"They don't seem too surprised to see us," I remark.

I think about when Matisa and the boys came to our settlement. How some people crowded near, wanted to touch them, wanted to ask them everything under the sun. How others avoided them, hid away.

"No," Matisa says. "And they do not seem surprised to see us together."

She means First Peoples and . . . whatever we are. I exchange a glance with Kane.

The man beckons us forward, leading us toward a large building that stands in the center of the village, free from the hills. Thick mud walls end in a thatched roof—similar to our roofs at the settlement—and there are two small windows on the side. The man pushes open a thick wooden door. Warmth and the smell of brine rushes out to welcome us.

We are ushered into a large room. A long wooden table lines the far side, and the man gestures for us to sit. He disappears.

A woman enters through the doorway. She is clothed in a rough wool dress that is covered by a dark apron. Her head is covered by a scarf. She carries a tray with a large pot and bowls and starts laying it out before us. She gives us a mild-curious look but says nothing as she ladles out portions.

Her silence is catching. Either that, or we're all still too shocked to find our tongues. We look at one another, silent. When the woman leaves, Daniel tugs at Kane's arms and gestures at his bowl. He's hungry. Kane nods.

The little boys burn their mouths in their haste, and Kane

hurries to take their spoons away so he can blow the soup cool.

The door creaks open again. A girl our age enters, followed by the little one who was banging out the rug. The little one looks real pleased with herself, like she's finished an important task. The older girl has dark hair and bright blue eyes, with the same pink cheeks and turned-up nose. Her head scarf is bright, like the little girl's. The sleeves of her pale yellow dress are rolled to the elbows, and the hem grazes the tops of brown leather boots. She looks like the rest: strong. Healthy.

Her mouth twists as she takes us in, and I realize at once how we must look. Muddy and bedraggled, bruised and scarred. The little boys wolfing their soup like they haven't ever seen food.

Her eyes linger a moment on Kane. The little girl pushes her elbow. She snatches her arm away and shoots the girl a look before turning back to us. She smiles.

"I am Genya," she says, her words clipped. "Welcome."

We stare, surprised.

Tom clears his throat. "Obliged," he says, throwing us a look.

"Y-y-yes," I stammer.

"You speak English," Matisa says.

Genya's smile gets a mite shy. "My mother teach me." Her brow creases. "My uncle tell me you are come through"—she searches for the word—"valley."

We nod.

"Is dangerous. Why you were there?"

We look at one another.

"Some men were following us," I offer. "We went into the valley to escape."

"Escape?" she asks. "These are bad men?"

"Yes."

She nods, her eyes dropping to the floor like she's thinking hard. She raises them. "I know," she says.

"You know the men?" Matisa asks.

"There are bad men. Out there." She gestures with her hand. "But here is safe."

I think about that nasty-looking fence. And all the guards, like Watchers, in the hills. "What is this place?" I ask. She frowns, like she doesn't understand the question. "Are you—did you come from the east?"

"Ah." She nods. "Yes."

"From the Dominion?" Kane asks.

She turns her eyes on him, and her cheeks go more pink. She nods. "They allow us to come."

"These bad men," Matisa says. "Have they come to your settlement?"

Genya shakes her head no. "We don't see them; only hear about them before we arrive. But we make our village safe."

The woman from before bustles in with a tray heaped with braided bread and boiled eggs and something in a covered dish. She places it before us, then turns and speaks to Genya before she leaves.

Genya smiles at us. "You are hungry," she states. "Eat." She gestures at the food. "After, you will rest. You are safe here."

When we have eaten, Genya tells us we can bathe and change.

Matisa and I are led to a different building in the center of the village.

We follow two women, winding our way past the curious houses and a row of barns. This village is a quarter the size of our fortification, but the goings-on feel familiar. People bustle about feeding chickens, digging gardens, hauling wood. They turn curious eyes on us as they work, but their gazes don't linger. They're friendly but busy.

Inside the building are two rooms—one a kitchen, the other a sizable room with rows and rows of spring wildflowers hanging from the rafters, drying in the warmth of the cottage. There is a table with other herbs laid out, drying.

With a pang, I remember Soeur Manon's hut. Everything is so different here, yet it feels so familiar. The bustle of this little settlement, people going to chores, laughing and shouting.

A small part of me yearns for those ordinary things—the things I used to think were a bother. Collecting eggs, hauling water . . .

I wonder what Kane is thinking right now.

He and the boys followed Genya to her family's dwelling to wash and find new clothes. I felt a mite uneasy being separated, but it wasn't because I'm worried about what these people have planned for us. There's nothing sinister here; just hardworking people making a life. It's clear they don't want trouble from outsiders, but they're willing to help people in need.

Two blond women fuss around, chattering to each other. One helps us with our muddy clothes as the other struggles a large tub to the center of the room. My face flames hot as I am stripped bare in front of these strangers. The women take no notice, though they cluck their tongues and speak low to each other when they see the burn mark on my neck. At the sight of hot water being poured into the tub, I forget to be shy.

Matisa and I stand in the tub and scrub the mud from our skin with heavy cloths. The women help us wash our hair with a kind of hard soap that smells like spice and earth. When we are clean, they leave us to dress ourselves.

"We'll have to do something about this," I remark when my hair is near dry. I stand, wrapped in my towel, holding up the clothes they left us on the table. There are two light blouses—thinner than I'm used to but practical enough, with long sleeves and collars that can be closed against the sun—and two strips of cloth that stretch and hook one end to the next. Can't figure those, but the real problem is the two long skirts that are so wide there's no way on Almighty's green earth they'll stay up on our hips. I pull one on over my towel and show Matisa.

"Even if we cinched them, they're . . . ," Matisa says.

"Not practical?" I say.

Matisa nods. "Not great for riding." She looks around the room as if she might find a solution.

One of the women reappears in the doorway and offers us a hairbrush. Matisa points to the skirts, then she gestures to the tiny window at the end of the house. The woman steps close, peering out. "There," Matisa says. "That." She gestures to her bare legs.

I raise my eyebrows.

"I am showing her what the men wear," she explains.

The woman stares at us like we're plain addled. She shrugs and heads for the door.

There's a mirror in this room. I step close to examine myself—for the first time in days. The face that stares back at me is not one I recognize: all shadowed eyes and gaunt cheeks. Under my chin is a soft pink scar, and the corner of my mouth is a flowering purple bruise. An angry red line cuts through its bloom.

I step away quick-like and turn to find Matisa's warm brown eyes on me.

"Let me braid your hair," she offers.

She's brushing it in long, soothing strokes when the woman returns. We are still wrapped in the towels, and the blouses are a mite big, but Matisa figured out the stretchy cloths were for under the blouses, across our breasts.

The woman hands us two pairs of pants, an amused look in her round blue eyes.

"Thank you," Matisa says.

She shakes her head and leaves us.

The pants aren't soft like my leggings, and they billow a bit, but they're tight at the ankle and with my *ceinture* tied over the untucked blouse, they're heaps better than the skirts.

Matisa is quiet as she braids my hair.

"You all right?" I ask over my shoulder.

She draws a deep breath. "Yes." She ties the end of my plait with a strip of cloth. "I am thinking." She hands me the brush and turns her back to me so I can brush her hair.

"Did you know?" I ask. "About what would happen at the grove? Did you know it would be bad?"

She dips her head. "For weeks my dreams have been showing me terrible things. One dream showed you being taken from me, another showed us being reunited. Both were very painful. With bloodshed."

"But you bringing those men to the grove—you didn't have a choice," I say.

"Perhaps not," she answers. "But even when your choice seems clear—"

"It doesn't always feel right," I finish.

She nods. "I am grateful to your friend, Tom."

"Me too," I say. I look around the cheery room, so warm, so familiar with its scent of drying herbs. Sounds of the village life outside reach our ears, muffled through the thick walls. "Do you think your people know about this village? It wasn't on Henderson's map."

"My home is only few days from here by horseback. Our scouts would have found them easily."

"These people seem good," I venture, tying her hair.

"They do," she says.

"How do you think they're surviving?" I ask her. "Do they have the remedy without knowing it— like we did?"

"I do not know." She turns to face me. "It doesn't seem they've had a visit from *sohkâtisiwak*."

"But that's something I don't understand. There are *sohkâtisiwak* working for Leon at the Keep, but there is also a group out looking for you. And they can't be the same, or Julian wouldn't have needed Charlie to learn their whereabouts." A memory niggles at the edge of my mind.

She squints at me. "Perhaps they were once the same group and they split over differences."

"And the prisoners at the Keep?"

"Those who refused to do Leon's bidding?" she suggests.

The memory floats, not quite in reach. "But that could mean that the group looking for you refused Leon, too, but escaped. They might not be willing to help him at all. Mayhap they weren't even trading the remedy."

"But then what were they offering Charlie?" she asks.

It rushes in at once, those last moments with Charlie. "Julian thought there was a place that could cure the Bleed," I tell her. "He didn't plan to trade you for the remedy; he planned to trade you to find out its location."

Matisa frowns.

"He said it was in the north."

Her eyes widen.

"What is it?" I ask.

She looks down. "*Sohkâtisiwak* talked often about"—she looks up—"the forbidden woods."

"The ones around my settlement?" Years ago, Matisa's people sent scouts to those forests to look for the Lost People they had been dreaming—us. When they never returned— when Brother Stockham's grandpa killed them—the woods became a forbidden place, like they were to us. No one dared venture into them. No one until Matisa.

"As they became more suspicious of our lore and my circle, they often mentioned the forbidden woods." She chews her bottom lip, thinking. "They believed the woods were forbidden because there was something powerful there—something to do with the remedy."

"Did they believe the Bleed could be cured?"

She shakes her head. "I do not know. It's possible."

But if Leon and *sohkâtisiwak* believe in this place . . . "Do you think *sohkâtisiwak* are planning to go there? The woods?"

She shakes her head. "Everyone feared the woods, even if they did not know why they were forbidden."

"But you didn't," I point out. "You came to find me."

"Because I was guided by my dreams, not by suspicions."

I hope she's right about them fearing that area. And, for the first time, I'm a mite glad my people are still fearful, that our settlement is well fortified. I may not have loved ones in that settlement anymore, but it doesn't mean I wish them strife. My dream comes back to me: the fortification walls, the voices from the river, my pa, calling to me. *Make peace with it.*

"I dream about the settlement," I say. "I keep dreaming about the Watch flats."

She tilts her head. "What do you think it means?"

I rub at my brow. What *does* it mean? At first I thought my dreams were urging us to leave the settlement. Then I thought mayhap they were talking about the past, telling me to let go of what happened, let go of my guilt. But the last dream I had was like the first, and I was . . . burying Matisa.

I look at her fresh-scrubbed skin, long dark hair. The image of her lying in the dirt, and me heaping soil upon her.

I take a deep breath and tell her all of it. I tell her that in my first and last dreams she is sick with the Bleed. I tell her about the war starting up around us, about the Watch flats, about the voices of the dead under the river singing out. I describe how I am burying her.

She listens careful, her eyes thoughtful. When I am done, there is a long silence. Finally she speaks. "Perhaps your dreams show you what is yet to come." She says it real calm. "Like they have done so far."

A sliver of fear races through me. No. That would mean they're asking me to accept that Matisa will die. Like I had to accept my pa's death, and all the rest.

"Don't want that to be true," I say.

Again she is quiet, her eyes tracing the floor. She shakes her head. "'Make peace with it,'" she murmurs. She looks up and meets my eyes. "Perhaps we still can. The secret of the remedy is still safe."

I frown, trying to figure her words. *Make peace with it*. My eyes widen. I heard those words as a command, telling me to accept something I've been feeling guilt over. She hears them differently: *create* peace with it. It: the remedy.

I think on this. It's true that in my dreams she holds the remedy in her hand.

"Perhaps if we can protect the remedy long enough, the sickness will decide this war, and we will have a chance to negotiate peace with the survivors, as we always planned."

I nod. This makes sense. But then why does she discard the remedy in my dream? And why are we at the settlement? I scrub my hands over my face. "Mayhap my dreams are just addled thoughts," I mumble. "Been having enough of those of late."

"The fact that you dreamt the grove and found me proves that is not true," she says.

"But if I hadn't insisted on bringing Charlie along, I would've never *needed* to dream you. I created that mess—"

"That is not how it works, Em," Matisa says. "And you are not responsible for others' choices." She holds my gaze until I feel tears well up.

I blink, blowing out a long breath. The choices I've made since leaving the settlement filter through my head, filling me with a strange mix of emotions.

Matisa waits for me to speak.

"Back last fall I was determined to prove my Discovery virtue a new way," I say. "And I did that. You helped me do that. And ever since then, the virtues haven't held the same meaning." I swallow. "I've been thinking on my Honesty virtue. It's not one I'm real good at."

Her face softens. "I should not have asked you to keep the truth of the sickness from Kane," she says. "I am sorry."

"No, that's not what I mean," I say. "I always thought that Honesty was about being truthful with others; but mayhap that's not right. Mayhap Honesty is more about being truthful with yourself." I press on. "You didn't ask me to keep a secret from Kane. You told me it was safer, and I made my own decision. Coming to terms with why I did it, that's the Honesty part."

And coming to terms with why washes me in relief. Haven't been honest with myself about much these past days, but if I search deep down, I know keeping the truth from Kane was about making the choice I thought was right, the one I thought would keep him safe.

296

Trouble is, he might never understand that.

Matisa's face is warm, but her eyes are a mite sorrowful. "Our choices have been difficult out here," she says. I know she's thinking on Nishwa, on sending him on alone . . .

"We'll leave straightaway," I tell her. "The rains are not yet done; we will reach your hunters in time."

She shakes her head. "We will leave tomorrow. We have not slept, and our horses need rest." She pats my knee. "Let's make some tincture for your foot." She draws herself up. "And let's find out where this village is getting its water."

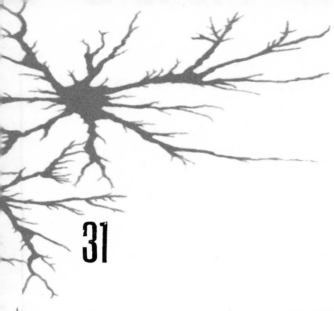

31

MATISA FROWNS DOWN INTO THE DANK ABYSS. We stand at the south side of the village, peering into a stone well that looks much like the one we had at the settlement. Only—

"There is no river nearby," she remarks, pulling her head up and frowning in confusion at Genya.

"River, no," Genya says. "But come"—she beckons to us—"I will show." She starts off past the barns. We follow her around the corner of the nearest building, but I am stopped in my tracks. Before me is the most bizarre cart I have ever seen. It is made from metal, with large wheels and a chimney stack stretching tall to the sky.

"What is that?" I ask.

Genya searches around for the word.

"Tractor," Matisa says.

I look at Matisa, confused.

"It tills the land," she says. "Helps to plant crops." She looks at Genya. "How does it run?"

Genya frowns.

"How does it . . ." Matisa churns her hands about to indicate movement.

"Ah." Genya twists her mouth, her blue eyes lost in thought. "The water in the air. What is the word?"

"Steam?" Matisa answers.

"Yes!" Genya says. "Steam."

Matisa notices my lost gaze. "We have them at home," she explains, following Genya up the hill before us.

I put this tractor in the mysteries-of-Matisa's-world basket and follow. Over this rise I can see the fence again, with its death poles poised at the ready. Genya waves to a figure who stands atop a hill outside the barrier. Another Watcher. Before us, tucked between the hills inside the fence, is a grove of dark green trees, all out of place in this sweeping, grassy landscape.

She leads us into the foliage, and as I drag my foot through the deadfall, I notice the ground is getting softer. Moister. When we reach a rise in the pocket of trees, she stops and points. Before us is sheer rock, like the hillside has been shaved off to reveal a small wall. And it's weeping. Water trickles out from tiny cracks and fissures along its surface. It runs down the face and disappears into the earth at our feet.

"Of course," Matisa says. "A spring."

I look at her, puzzled.

"This water passes through layers of silt and clay; the sickness is only in water that runs open to the air," she explains. "Their water source is safe."

‡

That evening we eat with Genya's family. It is another meal I can't quite believe: a whole roasted chicken, root vegetables, brined cabbage, and rolls of dark bread with butter.

The little boys are beside themselves—they ask for two helpings before they are dished.

Kane scolds their manners, but I understand their delight: it's more food than I've ever seen all at once. Surely the villagers are making an effort on our behalf: no way they'd have the stores to eat like this all the time.

But as Genya's ma, Dorotea, speaks to us in halting English, we learn that there is plenty of food, for everyone in the village. She says they brought many things with them from the east—livestock, seeds, supplies. She says her ancestors knew how to work this soil—that her family came from across the sea—from a country with similar, unforgiving land. They tell us about settling here at the end of last summer: digging ditches at first, and sleeping in those as they built their homes into the hills.

They chose this spot because it is protected by the drylands to the east and south, and the low hills here give them shelter. They don't seem to know anything about the Bleed reappearing. No one in the village has been sick.

As we talk, Genya translates for her pa—a serious man but friendly—and young brother and sister, who look just like her with their turned-up noses and bright blue eyes. They ask questions and tug at her arms, their voices happy and lighthearted.

This is a dinner table I don't recall. Pa and me often sat silent, him thinking on Ma, me thinking on my Stain. Thinking on how to stop failing my virtues. No happy chatter. Just the sound of scraping bowls.

This . . . this must be what Kane's table was like. The food itself would've been meager, but the feeling—it would've been like this. And looking at Kane now, seeing that worry off his brow for the first time in I don't know how long, I know I'm right.

I dart a quick glance at Genya, at her pink cheeks and shiny hair. She's so healthy looking and strong. This village—it's our settlement. Just better. It's what ours could have been if we hadn't been living in fear all those long years.

I look at Genya again—she's smiling at Kane—and fight down the panic in my heart.

The chatter continues.

I listen, distracted, as they describe seeing people who look like Matisa back last fall. Saw them from a distance only, passing by on horses. They didn't speak with them.

Dorotea wants to know where we are headed and who we have seen.

Matisa and I take turns recounting the journey—leaving the settlement, finding people from our own who had been banished, having to send Nishwa on ahead. Genya translates for her pa. They listen, eyes knitted like they're a mite confused, but when we get to the part about the burning homestead, Dorotea holds up a hand to stop us.

"The children." She gestures toward Daniel and Nico. "They see this?"

I start to answer but notice her face—it's white: she's plain horrified. Genya's eyes fly to Kane, wide and alarmed.

Shame shoots through me, hot and bright. I haven't even told the worst of it. I look around at our group. Our thin, bedraggled group.

A silence descends on the table.

Genya's pa clears his throat and speaks up.

"He says—" Genya stops. "We hear this story later."

Dorotea shakes her head, clucking her tongue. She looks at the little boys.

When dinner is over, we are left in the kitchen as the family prepares for bed.

No one seems inclined to speak. Isi paces the small room until Matisa's narrowed eyes stop him in his tracks. Tom sits where Nico has fallen asleep in a trundle bed near the stove. He busies his hands, checking his rifle.

Kane is slumped in a chair with Daniel asleep on his lap. Daniel's cheek is pressed against Kane's chest and two of his fingers are twined in Kane's leather shirt laces. Their clean skin shines in the firelight. Kane's dark eyes trace the floor.

Dorotea's shocked eyes surface in my mind. It took me a moment to understand her alarm. So much has happened since we left the settlement, I've all but forgotten how awful it is. When did horror become normal to me? When did I decide it should be normal for Daniel and Nico? For Kane?

How would I feel if I were him right now?

These villagers have to protect themselves from outsiders, sure, but the youngsters, at least, are sheltered from that. For me, the fence around this village would always feel like a cage. But for others . . .

There is warmth here. Food. Safety. Love.

My heart is pierced through with that last thought.

"We leave in the morning, then?" Tom's voice breaks the silence.

Kane's eyes snap up and find mine. I glance away, pretending to look to Matisa for an answer.

She answers, a mite halting. "Those who are rested."

I have to go with Matisa. But Kane . . .

Kane has a different responsibility. His little brothers would be welcomed here—I saw it plain on Dorotea's face. They would be safe. They'd never go hungry.

"We should not delay further," says Isi. "The way was longer to the north, and the storm would have slowed them, but the *sohkâtisiwak* will be close."

Matisa nods.

I look over at Tom, at Nico's slumbering form. I look at Daniel breathing so peaceful. I look at Kane. His dark eyes haven't left my face.

A torrent of emotion washes me—guilt, anger, sorrow— and bursting through it all, a love so strong and fierce for Kane, and for his brothers, I feel like I might shatter.

And what steals my breath in this moment is not the realization that I can't ask him to come with me, it's the realization I don't want to.

I don't want him to leave his brothers.

Not even to be with me.

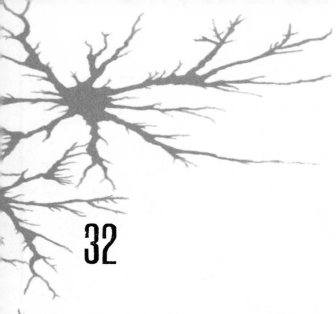

32

I PUSH OPEN THE SOLID WOODEN DOOR OF GEN-
ya's home and step outside. The sun has disappeared, but
the last glow of its light remains, painting the air a dull violet. The village sounds are soft and muffled as people retire
for the night. A chill descends on my skin. I wrap the shawl
Dorotea gave me tighter around my shoulders and step to
the side of the door, gazing about at the little houses. Their
chimneys puff, and the small windows in their fronts glow
with light.

The door creaks as it opens again.

Tom's blond head appears. "You all right?" he asks.

"Just needed some air," I say.

He steps out and closes the door, and I see he's dressed in
his cloak and carrying that strange rifle.

"You heading somewhere?" I ask.

"Just to look around," he says.

"With your weapon?"

He looks down at it. Shrugs. "Better in my hand than in

one of the little boys'. That Daniel's a precocious sort. He's just like Edith."

I smile soft, thinking about Tom's little sister, her mischievous little smile. Always chasing after cabbage moths and asking me about my day.

Tom scans the courtyard and houses. "Such a strange place," he says. "These homes, built into the hill like this."

"Nothing like our settlement," I say. "But somehow . . ."

"Feels like our settlement?" he asks, finishing my sentence and turning to me.

I nod. The way he stands, with his head lifted like that. "You weren't . . . scared to leave?" I ask. "Alone?"

"A mite." Tom shrugs. His eyes get shy. "It was foolish, but I brought some of that tea you left for Pa. It helped heal him, so I brought it. Felt like you were nearby."

I smile, thinking about Tom sitting round his own campfire with my tea.

He continues. "And then everything was so fresh, so new, I kind of . . . forgot to be afraid."

I think back to our first night out in the woods. The wild song, the starlight. I was so content. "The stars out here," I think aloud. "Never seen anything like it."

Tom nods. "The river at night was real peaceful." He smiles. "And in the morning, with the mist coming off the water before the sun burned through? Was like some fairy-tale land from those books of Soeur Manon's."

I swallow against a sudden lump in my throat. That beauty he's speaking on—it's all around us, still.

Isn't it?

"This settlement's a good place," I say.

His prairie-sky eyes measure me.

"It's safe here." My voice catches.

Tom wraps an arm around me and pulls me close. Rests his chin atop my head.

I press the heels of my hands to my eyes and take a deep, shaky breath. "Nothing's happened like it was supposed to."

Tom answers by squeezing my shoulders.

"If I had known . . ." I trail off because what I was going to speak next isn't the truth. The real truth in my secret heart is that even with the danger, even with these unknowns, I would be out here. I know I would.

Tom speaks, his voice ringing out clear in the cooling night. "Andre taught me to look far beyond the Watch flats. Taught me to look careful at what's around us." He draws back and looks down at me, holding my gaze meaningful. "But being able to see doesn't change what's coming."

It is full dark, and the boys and I are all drowsing beside the fire in Genya's kitchen when Matisa appears. I start, unable to remember when she left us. She touches Tom's shoulder and looks at Kane and me.

"Come," she says, her voice low and her eyes sparkling. "I want to show you something." She speaks to Isi. "*Kânîmihitocik.*"

Kane looks to the little boys, tucked together in the trundle bed, and back at Matisa, unsure.

"I will stay with them," Isi assures Kane. There's a mysterious smile on his face. Tom and Kane and I look at each other, puzzled. But we wrap up against the cold night and follow Matisa from the warmth of the kitchen.

She leads us from the center of the village, away from the torches and fires. We head southwest, to the hills Genya brought us to earlier, near the spring. But instead of heading into the grove of trees, we climb until we are at the top of the hill. Matisa turns to the north and points to the sky.

Tom is the first to turn, and his eyes go wide.

Kane and I do the same, looking up into the black of night.

My heart stutters.

The sky to the north is exploding in all shades of color, like the brightest wildflowers in spring: purple, pink, blue, and green. The air shimmers and dances, bending to brush the tops of the hill, stretching to reach the farthest star. The light blends and glows and disappears, reappears. The entire starry sky is bathed in magic light.

"*Kânîmihitocik.*" Matisa's voice comes from behind us. "The old people tell us they are ghosts, dancing in the sky."

The sky shimmers. All shades of heartbreaking color burst and flow.

Ghosts. "Why would they say that?" I ask. I think about the dead—sent to the Cleansing Waters for peace. The Crossroads ensured the spirits of the Waywards never returned to get revenge. The notion that the dead would come back like this . . .

"I believe it is a way of reminding us that we are a part of the land, and air, and water," Matisa says.

I think about my dreams. About the dead under the river, calling to me. They're here, regardless. The things we bury—they have a way of resurfacing.

Tom frowns. "But the dead appearing in that sky . . . doesn't seem right."

"Why?"

"Because it's so beautiful."

"So are the people we have lost," Matisa says.

Tom's face fills with wonder. I look to Kane.

He's standing, head tilted up to the stars, cloak drawn back, his shirt laces open careless-like, the moon glowing on his skin.

My chest hitches. I think about Sister Violet being one of those soft lights, reaching so tall into the starry night. Andre, too. And my pa.

I tilt my head skyward, and we watch for long moments, until the dancing lights dwindle to a soft yellow.

When I look back down, Matisa is giving me a knowing look. She touches Tom's arm. "Let's go," she says. "We should sleep before our journey."

Kane and I watch Matisa and Tom climb down the hill and disappear into the house.

And we are alone. A silence stretches between us.

I risk a glance at him and see he's no longer looking at the sky. His arms are crossed and his eyes are fixed on the soft glow of the village. My heart is so heavy I can barely speak. But I have to. We can't part, having this between us.

"I—" I swallow. "I thought I was keeping you safe," I say.

He looks over at me.

"I should've told you." I choke on the words. "I'm so, so sorry." Tears well in my eyes, but I brush them away and press on, determined not to cry.

He sighs deep and turns to me. Uncrosses his arms.

"And I understand if you want to stay here. I truly do.

But I can't bear leaving you, knowing you think I don't trust you." My voice is closing off with tears.

His eyes go soft. "Em—"

"Because I do."

He reaches for me, takes my hand in his, and just his touch, his gentle touch, starts the tears anew.

"I know," he says. "Hey—" He cups the side of my face in one hand and brushes at the tears with his thumb. "I'm not angry."

I search his face.

"I was," he admits. "But I'm not anymore."

"Truly?"

"Truly," he says. "Thing is, I have no right to be." He takes a deep breath. "I kept something from you, too."

I draw back, my heart skipping a beat. What could he have kept from me?

"I knew my ma was angling for that crossing all along, even before we set out," he says. "She knew we were headed west, but she truly wanted to head to the Dominion to look for kin."

I stare at him, taking in his words.

"I think she was hoping to change my mind," he says, "either before we reached Matisa's people or after."

I remember feeling surprised she was so agreeable about the Jamesons. But mayhap it was more about that crossing. I think aloud, "When Nishwa got hurt . . ."

"It was an excuse to head where she wanted all along," he says. "And by then, there was no talking her out of it. But I should've told her no from the start. Should've told her if she wanted to come, it wasn't possible. I didn't." He sighs. "I was hoping she'd give up on the idea."

I stare at him, unsure if I'm hurt or relieved. "Why didn't you tell me?"

"You were so happy leaving the settlement. So sure of yourself, of helping Matisa. I . . ." He searches for the words. "I didn't want to ruin it. Didn't want you worrying about what my ma might decide." He shakes his head. "But it wasn't fair to either of you."

"Do you think she would've still come if you'd told her to forget going east?"

Pain flashes in his eyes. I realize this is something Kane's been battling with since the homestead. Wondering if telling her no would've dissuaded her from coming out here. Wondering if it would've saved her life.

I grab both his hands and hold tight. "It's not your fault," I say, fierce. "We all make our choices."

His eyes search my face.

"And we have to make peace with what they mean." I grip his hands. "But my idea of my life out here? It always included you, Kane. Always."

"I know," he says, and I can tell by the heat in his voice that he means it. "I should never have said it didn't." He takes one of my hands in both of his and pulls it to his chest. I can feel his heart beating beneath his shirt. "We belong together."

I grasp his shirt with my fingers and pull him toward me, and he takes my face and pulls my chin to him. Presses his mouth to mine, soft. Careful. Searching, like he might find his way out of all of this in our kiss, but . . .

There is no way out.

He breaks away, and we stand, the dark air whispering velvet on our faces. The night sky is so vast above us it feels like it could swallow us whole. I tilt my face and let the starlight bathe it, take deep breaths, trying to drink this moment in. Trying to keep it in my heart forever.

Because tomorrow . . .

Tears well up in my vision, and I blink them aside as I turn to look at him. The stars shine bright on his dark head, his eyelashes. I hug my arms around myself, try to memorize his every feature. His large dark eyes, the new dark hair on his head. His shirt, open at the neck, showing collarbone and the curve of his chest. And those arms, the bare forearms I daydreamed on, hanging at his sides. Standing there so full of sadness but still so strong.

"I'll come back for you," I say. My voice breaks, and I look to the stars again, blinking tears away. There's no sense in crying. No sense in doing anything but reassuring him it's all right.

"Em—"

"Soon as I can," I say, firm. But he reaches for me, and I pitch into his arms, wrapping them around me, burrowing into his shirt. Breathing in his scent. Drinking him all in, trying to keep him with me, the memory of him on my body forever. A peace settles over me.

He pulls back. His eyes are grave. "Don't," he says.

"Don't what?"

"Come back for me."

The peace shatters. "What do you mean?"

"Promise me. Promise me when you reach Matisa's people, you will stay with them. Stay where you are safe."

"I'm not promising that!" I cry.

"*Please*," he says, his voice taking on a note of panic.

"But why?"

"Because I can't bear the thought of you coming back through this mess for me."

"You said we belong together!"

"We *do*," he says. "But you risking your life so it can happen is foolish."

"I need you."

"Em," he says, his voice soft and sad. "Needing and wanting are not the same thing."

I stare into his dark eyes. My gaze shifts to the bullet scar on his temple, to the reminder of the first time I thought I lost him. Sorrow washes me—so deep it near stops my heart. That same sadness stares back at me, reaching right into my soul.

I stumble forward, reaching for him, reaching . . .

And his arms are around me, and his mouth is on mine, and my despair shatters as desire surges through me, so hot and sure I no longer have the strength to stand. He pulls me to him, down with him, down into the soft prairie grass. And his hands are everywhere, his mouth is on mine, and my fevered skin is bursting into flame. I clutch at him, pulling his body against mine, desperate for his breath, his scent, his warmth.

But a hollowness sweeps me. And something breaks inside.

I bury my head in his chest, and he holds me tight while I cry a river of tears.

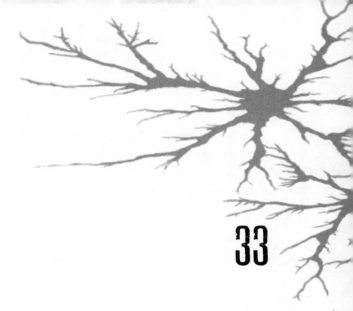

33

THE THAW COMES LIKE A FEVER. ONE MOMENT the frozen winds of *La Prise* are shrieking in your head like they won't ever stop. The next: silence. A dead calm.

And the Thaw comes, bursting into existence, rushing light and water everywhere. Through the land. Through your blood.

Like an answer to your prayers.

You wake from your icy nightmare and you know. You know that life isn't forgotten. You know the things you dream of are still in reach. You know they're possible.

You know, because you've waited so long for this.

With the Thaw comes promise.

The drip of ice melting from the boughs, the small green shoots that have been waiting, patient, for their day in the sun—all signs that life begins anew. That *your* life begins anew. And finally, finally, you can choose that new life. You can choose the unknown. The path is clear.

But it's not that simple.

In the Thaw's haste to bring life, to free what was buried, some things are swept aside and pulled apart. As the land explodes with new purpose, rushing out to greet the sun, some things perish.

Some things are left behind.

The Thaw has unearthed many things. Thoughts I have kept frozen below about what I have brought upon the people I love, fears long buried. The notion my pa might have died for my dreams that were wrong, that his sacrifice was for nothing.

Choosing a new life is not simple.

I lift my eyes beyond the hills to the horizon. The mountains in the distance gaze back with stony faces, dark clouds hang over their snowcapped brows. The hills roll gentle and soft around us. A great herd sifts along the grasslands to the southwest.

The sky is brightening from dusty pink to gold, dusting the tops of the hills before us—sunrise, but somehow just like the very first sunset I ever saw. I was standing on the fortification wall with Andre and I thought my heart might burst from its beauty. From the mystery of it all.

The last time I saw Kane, he was alone, watching us leave from the top of the west-most hill.

A lone poplar against the prairie sky.

I promised him I wouldn't be back. Told him I wouldn't risk my life to return. And I turned away.

But I didn't turn because I don't want his hands in mine. I didn't turn because I think my path lies elsewhere. I turned because a fire has started in my heart I didn't want him to see. It burns away my doubt and fear, lights me up with purpose. And its flame reveals one thing that's certain: I've never been good at telling the truth.

The Thaw bursts into existence with promise. But in her rush to bring hope she also brings despair. She is a spring flood, nourishing the trees but destroying new nests and plants along the river. She is not all that you dreamt.

But her promise remains. And if you are patient, if you remember this, you can weather her storms. The long days will arrive, shimmering in shades of green and light, and, with them, new life.

And I will return to start that life.

With Kane.

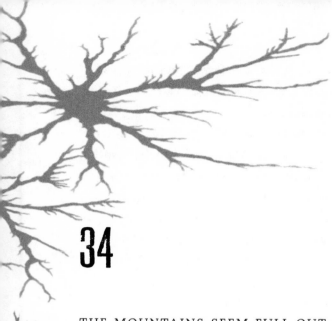

34

THE MOUNTAINS SEEM FULL OUT OF REACH. WE climb grassy hills that become dotted with rocks as we press west, our eyes on the mountain-scarred horizon. So far away. A lifetime. Matisa and Tom speak together in hushed tones. Isi is focused and silent.

There is no sign of *sohkâtisiwak*.

We travel all day before arriving at a dark forest. The mountains disappear behind rows and rows of black spruce. Our horses bend to the task of traversing the impossible land. Pressing through swamp, they pull their hooves clear of muck and grasses. We climb over deadfall, make a miserable campfire beneath the tall and scraggly spruce.

My nights are dreamless, and the hours blend one into the next: row upon row of spruce, pressing forward, the horse's stumbling steps beneath me, the darkness of the forest echoing a darkness creeping into my mind.

When I am sure we have lost our way, sure the forest is all there is, all there has ever been, we arrive.

The forest thins, emptying us out into their midst: the mountains.

Large and looming, stretching tall to the skies, covered in spruce and not—sheer cliffs ending in bright white snow. The air here is different: fresh and heavy, with a bite beneath. The ground under our feet becomes both rocky and soft. Carpets of juniper stretch out low and fragrant, and the trees here look hardy—as though they made the decision, years ago, to survive no matter the odds.

Matisa points ahead, to a valley deep in the mountains. "Our home," she says.

But I know. I know because I have dreamt this place. I know this smell, this air, this ground beneath my feet. We press west into the shadows, and a river that appears beside us urges us on. It appears and disappears, winding fierce behind walls of rock, its white water singing like it's calling our arrival.

We reach my dream lake.

It lies in the valley, calm and shining like a polished stone—a color I have seen only in my dreams. Not blue like the prairies skies, not green like the new spring buds. Something in between, and so beautiful my heart might break.

"Matisa," Isi says.

I tear my gaze away to see where he gestures.

There is someone coming along the shore. A rider on a white horse. The horse gallops fast—a white flame—and the rider's long dark hair streams out behind like smoke.

I look to Matisa. She smiles.

The rider crosses the distance in moments, pulling up in front of us, his horse's hooves clattering on the rocky shore. Now I see the horse is not white but smoke-gray, and its rider is a young man. He, too, is beautiful—his hair is glossy, his cheekbones are high, and his lips are curved. He wears the same blue-colored clothing that Isi and Matisa wear, but his chest is covered with a leather plate, and his wrists and hands are wrapped with leather, too, his fingers free and gripping the reins.

He stares at us, his eyes wide and incredulous, looking from Matisa and Isi to me and Tom. As Matisa steps forward, he leaps from his horse. He lunges and pulls her into an embrace. I look to Isi. He's smiling wider than I ever imagined he could. Matisa laughs as the boy pulls back and embraces Isi the same.

This boy launches into their language, a string of talk. He seems to be asking questions without waiting for the answers. Isi finally halts him with a word, but he is laughing. Matisa looks to us, her face open. Happy.

"This is my cousin Eisu," she says.

I raise my eyebrows. "Cousin like Isi?" I ask. "Or cousin?"

She laughs. "Cousin." She gestures to me. "Em," she says, "and Tom."

Eisu gestures toward us and asks Matisa something in their tongue.

"Yes," she says, and smiles. "These are the Lost People."

Eisu looks at us. This time his gaze lingers, his dark eyes searching over us—over our strange clothes, no doubt, mayhap our strange skin, too. It's a strong gaze, like Isi's, a gaze I've come to expect.

"Welcome," he says.

"Hi," I say, and nudge Tom, who is silent. I turn my head.

Tom is staring at Eisu with a look I've never seen on his

face but know well in my heart. His eyes are wide, his mouth is open a breath. I nudge him again, and his eyes snap to mine, his cheeks going pink.

Eisu doesn't seem to notice. He remarks something, and Matisa bursts out laughing.

"What is it?" I ask.

"He says I am in big trouble for leaving the way I did and he hopes you were worth it."

Now it's my turn to laugh. Tom joins, but it's a tad forced—like he's actually nervous about being worth it. I shoot him a look.

Eisu turns his head and speaks to Matisa.

Her shoulders heave with a relieved sigh. "Nishwa," she tells us. "He made it." She asks a question that Eisu answers in earnest. "And he caught the hunters before they left."

My heart soars. I watch as Matisa and Eisu continue to talk. I catch Isi's eye, and he returns my look with his usual fierce gaze, but in it, now, is acceptance. I look to Tom beside me. He's regained his composure, somewhat.

And all at once I'm so happy I feel light, like air.

Eisu speaks, spreading his hands. Now he's not asking questions. He's saying something important, I can tell, because both Matisa and Isi lean in like it might hurry him along.

Matisa cuts him off with a question.

He hesitates.

"*Eisu,*" she says, a warning in her voice.

He answers with a nod.

Matisa and Isi share a look. She looks to the west, gazes toward that valley.

"What is it?"

Matisa's eyes meet mine, and they are clouded. "Some of my people say the remedy has lost its power, that it no longer protects us."

Tom and I exchange a look. "Why do they say that?" I ask.

"Six people have died from the sickness."

I frown. "But . . ." If the remedy no longer works, then they have protected a secret for decades for nothing. And our plan to negotiate peace . . .

"Can he be sure they are taking it?" I ask.

"He says they are," she says, soft. And in this moment I see her not as the fierce and mysterious dream figure who freed my people and brought the promise of a better life. I see her as she has always been: a girl. A girl who has finally reached her home but is still somehow lost.

I swallow, looking out across the dream lake, toward that valley I've never seen but somehow know deep down in my bones. Is it no longer the safe haven I dreamt?

I see Matisa caked in the dream soil of the Watch flats, sick with the Bleed. Me digging desperate-like, my hands heaping dirt upon her—burying her . . .

A rush of despair fills me. And then, anger. I close my eyes and clench my jaw. We have risked too much, given up too much, for my dreams to foretell her death. She has always believed that finding me will prevent disaster for those we love. I have to believe that, too. I press my palms to my brow and think hard. I think about burying her in that soil, with the river voices singing out . . .

My thoughts pause there. Something feels wrong. In the

dream, I'm desperate but not sad. Surely I'd be broken with grief if I were saying goodbye to Matisa?

And now I realize the image itself is strange: we don't say goodbye to our dead by burying them under the soil. We have always cast them to the Cleansing Waters to send them to their peace.

But if I'm not burying her, what am I doing?

Make peace with it.

A flicker of hope starts in my heart. Mayhap there is more to all of this than either of us can see right now. Our dreams have not yet shown us the path, but that path feels in reach—like the long days of summer that stretch out just beyond the Thaw. If only we are patient, if only we weather the storm.

And I vow we will make it to those long days of sun.

"Let's go home." I hold out my hand to Matisa. She looks up at me. "We'll see what needs to be done. Together."

Our hands clasp and Matisa draws herself up, bringing her head high. I look to the valley of craggy rocks and snow-capped peaks, the wind whispering through the trees. My hair whips into my face as the breeze picks up, churning the waters of the lake into white waves that flash in the sun. And as I gaze out over the choppy, glittering lake, that fire inside me starts anew.

We set off west to the valley, my skin washed with soft air and the scent of evergreen. My bones sing out to this place I have never seen.

And my heart burns bright with promise.

ACKNOWLEDGMENTS

Thank you to my agent, Michael Bourret, for champion-ing this series from the start and for being responsive and generous and kind. I hope you are walking me through pub-lishing for many years to come.

Thank you to my editors, Erica Finkel at Abrams and Rebecca Lee and Alice Swan at Faber & Faber, for helping me to re-see this book, for encouraging me, for pushing me to work hard. I am thrilled to have your enthusiasm and exper-tise.

My team at Abrams deserves enormous thanks for all of the support and kind attention to my work. Thank you to Susan Van Metre, Michael Jacobs, Jim Armstrong, Nicole Russo, Jason Wells, Mary Wowk, Jess Brigman, Elisa Garcia, Maria T. Middleton, Shane Rebenschied, Nancy Elgin, and Rob Sternitzky.

My team at Faber has my immense gratitude for believing in my work and for giving it the very best chance at success.

Very special thanks to Leah Thaxton, Grace Gleave, Emma Eldridge, Susan Holmes, and Hannah Love.

Thank you to my foreign rights agent, the supremely fancy Lauren Abramo. We will use those umbrellas some day! Thank you to my UK agent, Kate McLennan, for taking care of everything across the pond.

More thanks than can fit on this page are due my first reader Dana Alison Levy, who cheers me on even when my writing is awful and celebrates hard when it is not. Thank you for weathering my (often) ill-timed and (occasionally) panicked emails about *every little thing*.

Thank you to Bethany Griffin, Angela Sparks, and Rachael Allen for reading early drafts. Thanks to all of the litbitches for being my sooper sekrit writing batcave, and for making my very first signing (!) so memorable.

Merci beaucoup á Marc Piquette et á Thérèse Romanick, et merci á Louise Caron. Je suis trés reconnaissant pour l'assistance avec le francais. J'espère que un jour bientôt je n'aurais pas besoin.

Thank you to Carl and Reuben for taking my calls with kindness and humor. Thank you to Jennifer St. Arnault, nitotem, for sharing your knowledge so graciously.

Thank you, as always, to my Rimbey girls (Cake! Champagne! Drag queen ensemble!) and my Edmonton girlfriends (Childcare! Katecare!).

Thank you to my family for loving me and being proud of me.

Finally, thank you to my readers. I'm so grateful for you.

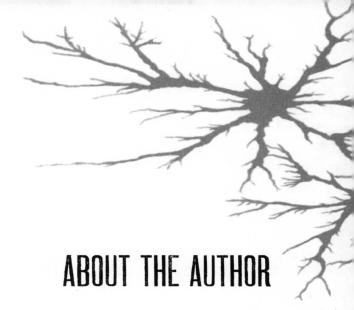

ABOUT THE AUTHOR

KATE BOORMAN is a writer from the Canadian prairies. She was born in Nepal and grew up in the small town of Rimbey, Alberta, where the winters are long and the spring thaw is a highly anticipated event. She lives in Edmonton, Alberta, with her family, and spends her free time sitting under starry skies with her friends and scheming up travel to faraway lands. *Darkthaw* is the sequel to her young-adult debut novel, *Winterkill*.